Neil Gevisser was born in Durban, South Africa and responded to the atrocities of Apartheid through poetry and music. At 21, he rose to fame on the South African University campus after releasing an anti-government poetry book, *Picking up the Pieces of Yourself*. Six months later, he was given eight hours to leave South Africa to avoid facing jail. It wasn't until 2005 that his South African passport was returned to him. He now lives in Britain.

To Rodney
Enjoy the
read!

THE TYRANNY
OF TRUST

Neil Gevisser

Book Guild Publishing
Sussex, England

First published in Great Britain in 2014 by
The Book Guild Ltd
The Werks
45 Church Road
Hove, BN3 2BE

Typesetting in Sabon by
Ellipsis Digital Ltd, Glasgow

Printed and bound in Great Britain by
CPI Group (UK) Ltd, Croydon, CR0 4YY

A catalogue record for this book is available from
The British Library.

ISBN 978 1 90971 620 9

Dedicated to the two women in my life,
Zena Zulman and Emma Elliott,
and my late friends Ken Moldenhauer
and Gorden Spaeth of The Fleshtones.

Special thanks are due to the following people who have encouraged and assisted me enormously with this novel over the past forty years: Phil Saunders, Ben Dunk, Cathy Duval, Christine Prefontaine, Jackie Jackson, Allyson Christy, Jill Berntsson, Alan Potash, Hilary Farrell and Emma Elliott.

Background

District Six is a washing machine where the colours have run.

Eric Tile (1971)

In South Africa, the Nationalist Government under the racial policy of Apartheid, dating from 1948 and known simply as a separation among the races, enacted such laws as to define and enforce racial segregation. Whites included primarily two groups: Dutch/German/French-Huguenots, as branded Afrikaners or Boers (farmers), who speak Afrikaans, and finally, English-speaking Europeans.

Under Apartheid, Black populations lived in separate homelands located in areas where various tribes were traditionally found, but were later restricted to greatly reduced areas. The living conditions in these homelands were cramped, while the 10% minority of white South Africans annexed 85% of the richest farmland.

Opportunities for employment or gainful farming for Blacks in the homeland areas were poor to non-existent, which suited Whites, needing them instead for manual labour. It would have been deemed self-defeating for Whites to improve the situation in the Black areas, as their need for a large, cheap and available Black work force was of paramount importance.

Laws forced Blacks to carry the dreaded 'Dompas' identity book in order to work in White areas. Those without residential permits were allowed no more than seventy-two hours in the White urban areas, where there were frequent, brutal police sweeps. The conditions for these urban Blacks were deliberately unaccommodating, lest they should want to remain.

Apartheid demanded segregated living areas for distinct races within cities and towns, including separate travel for non-Whites. There was also separate and unequal education for all races at every level, and dissimilar employment reserved for Blacks and Whites.

The Coloured, of mixed blood, were also categorised as non-White or non-European, and their segregation was similarly regulated and enforced. The classification 'Coloured' included members of the same family assigned indiscriminately to one group or another. Black parents could have children classified Coloured or vice versa. Coloureds were even broken down further into 'Cape Coloured', 'Griqua', 'Indian', 'Chinese', 'Cape Malay', 'Other Coloured' and 'Other Asiatic'.

To further confuse, the Coloureds, who are considered the 'bastard' cousins of the Afrikaner, as they are the offspring of those White Afrikaners who procreated with their non-White servants or slaves, share not only the Afrikaner's blood, but language as well and to some extent, their Dutch Reform religion, while their skin colour runs the entire pigmentation gamut from dark brown to pink, with every kind of hue in-between.

Using their own scientifically slanted evidence, the Apartheid regime instilled an ideology that the mixing of the races would lead to racial decline and attributed such an interpretation of the Bible to arguing that racial integration was not only genetically a reckless practise, but against the Word of God.

The setting of this story is the central area of Cape Town, known as District Six, which for over a hundred years was predominantly a Coloured or a Mixed-Race area, but was later declared White in 1965, with thousands of families forced to relocate to a new township many miles away. Those Coloureds who could pass for White and other poor peoples from other ethnicities, who were also living there, remained for a while in the area.

The story opens in Cape Town, as a White man is about to move into what was only a few years ago a predominately Coloured District Six, but what is today a renovated, 'white-washed' area.

Appearance

To see, or not to see, that is the answer!
Irreverent Reverend Tom Groans (1972)
(Graffiti artist and anti-Apartheid poet)

The structure of features and the differing colouring of skins tended to blur in racist, Apartheid South Africa, particularly for sociological, economic or fashionable reasons. When it suited the Regime, certain people even lost their specific profiles. A few lucky Coloured people who were light-skinned enough and had both parents appearing to look like White Europeans could be reclassified White.

The narrator, raised and immersed in this feverish environment dedicated to one's appearance, recorded what he saw, always faithful in his fidelity to his detail-orientated, penetrating eye.

This writing is what occurred on the outskirts of what remained of Cape Town's District Six during the year 1972.

Aaron's story is filled with an inexhaustible fund of observational knowledge which percolated in his mind, as he tried to make sense of the people dancing around him in that dangerous visual game of 'Label me if you can!'

1

There are corpses wandering about this country of illusion and having never eaten of empathy, have already died of starvation.

Irreverent Reverend Tom Groans
(Graffiti artist and anti-Apartheid poet)

When I first saw Angela, I fell under the spell of her serene gracefulness. Her agreeably relaxed posture indicated to me a sex drive both full-blooded as well as earthy. I felt regenerated in her company. Her body shape implicitly represented sensual comfort and yet Angela was also a killer.

I could diagnose contradictory forces at play within Angela, as her gentle, disarming smile often veered off to become a mischievous off-centre smirk. Her refined nose terminated in a marginally bulbous tip and her eyebrows were shaped like 'ticks' from the centre outwards, the way cartoonists portray villains. She was a person who knew her faults and was prepared to rectify them by backtracking, or reversing her opinions if she thought she had something to gain from such a reversal. And reverse she often did, as she also had the unfortunate capacity of seeing falsehood and deception at every turn. This repulsion prevented her from ever being radicalised towards any political extreme and allowed her to abandon herself to only those things that were of crucial self-interest to her. She could U-turn on a pinhead.

Angela was unpredictable, yet her decisions were driven by a strong logic and an even stronger irritability when in the presence of hypocrisy.

She was beautiful and was often underestimated.

Angela in Wonderland's persona, just like Alice's, was influenced by whatever corridor in life she, Angela, found herself in. The huge disruption of scale between these differing personas marked her as the patron saint of anything goes. This girl was uncorrupted by romanticism. In fact, she was unaffected by anything other than that which could literally knock her off her feet, or take her considerable breath away.

Angela embarked on all her missions knowing that her abilities were honed. She was aware of her strengths and weaknesses and was cautiously appreciative of her adversary's attributes, never underestimating anything.

There was no official order for the particular action that happened, it was purely personal. The target was a government agent and professional killer: the leader of a Death Squad, a certain Captain J.B., a man indirectly responsible for the death of one of her friends a little more than a year earlier.

Angela's target, the foe she was to kill, a thin man of medium height, in his early thirties and wearing a blue suit, did not even know of her existence, or of the enthusiasm that through her surged. Experience and stealth, that element of surprise was mounted on her side.

Captain J.B. had come out of the police station entrance punctually at half past noon, just as he had done the previous two weeks. He rotated his head, checked both sides of the street before he turned left and headed up into the business district towards the park. There, every day previously, on a secluded 'Whites Only' park bench, he had routinely eaten his two cheese and tomato sandwiches that his wife always packed for him in tin foil.

On that day of reckoning as the Captain made his way uptown, a great reddish sun that hung over the coast had warmed the bald patch on the top of his head. There was a cooling breeze, 'The Cape Doctor', that sanitary wind blown in from the sea, which had stirred itself into town, helping sweep the inhabitants along their different ways. Cloud-topped Table Mountain had stood sedately and watched the city beneath it.

In the city, the different-coloured heads had jostled one another, diving away from each other. Black, White and Mixed-Race; Coloured faces spun along the pavements. Shoes pounded, turned and scattered in different directions like fragments of a shuffled puzzle. The people themselves were fragmented into privileged Whites and those that were not quite White enough.

Meanwhile, everyday life with its concerns of work and play, hatred and love, ran its regular course, independent of political alliances.

Angela chose to tail her target using a scooter, as scooters were abundant in the city and it allowed her to tear through traffic at high speed, or proceed at almost snail pace, depending on her spontaneous need. If she needed to make a quick break, being on a scooter made it much more difficult to be identified or caught in the midst of all the other vehicles whipping about.

She chose a plain, worn and yellow helmet that inconspicuously matched her blonde hair. She then sprinted across the street to where the scooter was conveniently parked, jumped on it and followed the man from about 20 yards.

Angela was not the only one tracking her prey. She had noticed that across the street and walking parallel to her man, was a diminutive, plain-clothed policeman, someone she had seen many times over the past year coming and going from the station. She had not seen him before on this watch. In fact, over the last fourteen days the target had no surveillance whatsoever as far as she could tell, but in spite of all her professionalism, she had not checked to see whether he had had anyone shadowing him while he ate his picnic in the park on previous days. This could have been a grave faux pas on her part.

On any earlier day other than that one, had she actually entered the park towards which she was now heading, she would have noticed this short, awkward-looking bodyguard, sitting there alone on his high-chair, opposite an empty bench, eagerly awaiting his charge's arrival.

Angela had erred on the side of caution by not entering the park the previous two weeks, because she was afraid that she might have been noticed in the park's enclosed environment. In fact, she might well have been observed by her target's minder, as the pint-sized man was not only exceptionally observant, with the eyes of an eagle, but also had a highly developed sixth sense.

Angela knew that as she was a fugitive from Apartheid justice, for past terrorist infractions, there was a hazy, out-of-focus photograph of her being circulated around the country's police stations. She thought that it was possible that a diligent observer within the confines of the park might recognise her. It was a chance she could not take.

On that day of reckoning, the Lilliputian minder was late for duty and therefore he was forced to follow the officer, Captain J.B., instead of preceding him to the park as he had done on every previous day. This was the reason Angela had not seen the detective before on that watch. The new situation she then found herself in threw a fly into her ointment, as that specific day was the day she had put aside to eliminate her target. The next day he was set to head back to Pretoria and Head Office. She had ascertained this nugget of information from a spy who worked as a janitor assistant in the precinct police station, which the intended victim reported to every morning while in Cape Town.

*

Captain J.B. kept turning his head about him, his eyes riveting left and right as if he were checking two rear-view mirrors. On previous days when Angela had followed him he had not done that. That day he also did something else; he changed his routine by circling the park twice, as if in an effort to flush out anyone tailing him.

Angela parked her scooter, lit a cigarette then checked a map of the area that she had withdrawn from her inside jacket pocket and studied it, as the man went around the park for his second circumnavigation. The tiny plain-clothed police-man had also done the circuit twice on the outside pavement, passing Angela once, but ignoring the innocent blonde on a scooter as being nothing more than a young hippy on a motorcycle. Arcane then made eye contact with Captain J.B., gave a polite acknowledgement of recognition with a quick raise of his stubby, little, right hand, with its spatula-shaped 'murderer's thumb' and then abruptly turned back towards downtown and the police station, much to Angela's relief.

The designated spot in the park that Captain J.B. chose to take his lunch was at the crescent of a slight rise on a small gravel track, somewhat off the main tarred path. He was surrounded on three sides by bushes. The road beyond the outer-railed circumference of the park was almost deserted. Every so often a car drove past. There were no pedestrians about. Angela would have liked it busier, but on the other hand there were fewer onlookers to identify and hinder her purpose.

The man was seated at his usual bench with his back to the near road, while directly behind him, imperceptible to all, except perhaps a professional killer, was a sliver of a corridor that was clear for a bullet to penetrate unimpeded towards its 'sitting-duck'.

Angela circumnavigated the park on her scooter, stopped at the exact spot and sat facing straight ahead, down the road. She extracted a Smith and Wesson 39 from a large inside pocket of her jacket, rotated her body 90 degrees to the left, checked her target and noticed that a few seagulls were circling just above the man's head in anticipation of crumbs. They were birds of ill omen. She stiffened, held her breath and told herself,

'Wait! Wait! Don't shoot too soon! Count to two slowly.'

She aimed through the clearing and on the count of three, fired twice. There was a very brief fusillade of two very dull thuds around her ears, as the silencer muffled the sound and the gun jumped twice. The quiet was palpable. The target's head dropped forward. The impact of his chin hitting his chest immediately bounced his head back up to its original straight position. Calmly, Angela aimed and fired again. Again, this third thud echoed only around her head. The man's body, 20 yards away, gave a last jump and slumped listlessly to his left without any fuss or commotion, having enjoyed his last sandwich.

A couple of seagulls hopped onto the reclining figure and continued to pick at the cheese and tomato sandwiches, unperturbed by what had occurred.

The proper thing to do is to expire on cue.

2

She deceived and I believed, because I lied.
Irreverent Reverend Tom Groans

Crossing the line to kill has always been easy for Angela. In fairness to herself she hastened to think, there were no nasty motives involved in the murder of the captain. No jealousy, hatred or any other disgusting passion. She did it for revenge and to eliminate a possible future threat to herself or to any other enemy of the State. There has been no betrayal of self-interest that could cloud the mind with second guesses and doubts. Happiness had entered her life that even if undeserved, felt comfortable and correct. Being born with the right pastel colour but wrong genealogy, as a mixed-race person, had given her a cause to pursue.

Meanwhile, right at this moment with sexual intimacy in plain sight as she disrobes before me, I know nothing about her violent past. An air of quiet serenity permeates her nakedness as her sleek, ivory-skinned body on firm coltish legs, barefooted and steady, glides forward towards me. I am seated in the steaming, effervescent bathwater. She is withdrawn in contemplation to the point of ineloquence, but who needs to be erudite with words when one is nakedly exposed?

Before me, this tall, muscular yet sinewy girl has shown

her breasts that are no longer constrained with a bra as she steps into the hot bathwater which is almost waist high above my seated body. My buttocks hold down the plug at the tap end.

Our lives had collided only an hour before in this rundown hotel bar, one of seeming melancholic ambience. The bar room in which a fire smouldered in the centre had smoke lingering around the rafters before curling back down into the span. The dozen or so patrons seated about the evenly dispersed tables, except for this girl, had appeared old and in various states of decrepitude. Long hair, blonde and blue-eyed, with sun-touched skin shaded a light-almond hue; she appeared sexy with a wide, partly-opened and plump-lipped smile of magnetic intensity. Conversely, her teeth were even, with a barely discernible over-bite.

This captivating girl's eyes smiled tenderly, their large, dilated pupils signalling arousal. They were also lowered in a compulsive gaze in the customary come-hither position. She was the only person seated at the counter, on a tall, well-worn, oak swivel-stool. I took my post at the near end of the bar counter on the first tall stool. The other chairs at the mahogany bar besides hers were unoccupied and stood like obedient, docile and dumb waiters. I ordered a glass of bottled water on the rocks with a twist of lime.

The red, yellow and green fluorescent feathers that hung around her long neck were practically blinding, even in the dimly lit smoke-filled room. I was watching her intensely.

The bartender, whose worn, troubled face peered through thick lenses, looked hollow-cheeked and solemn. He shuffled, half-crouched like an ogre, and watched impassively as the beautiful girl swivelled slowly towards me and said, 'Hey, man, come and talk and if we're going to get intimate this late at night, we might as well do it drunk.' She winked, smiled and after a moment's hesitation asked, 'I'm not bothering you, am I?'

'Yes you are, finally. Thank God!'

'You're so accommodating,' she exclaimed.

'You're not from Sex Anonymous, are you?' I enquired, moving to the chair alongside her.

'What's that?'

'When I get the urge for sex, the organisation sends someone like you over to have a drink until the desire passes.'

She laughed deeply.

'You're a doll!' I joked.

'That's because my eyes close when I lie down.' She giggled, leaned forward and in a soft voice said, 'You do know that dolls are only put on pedestals so that they can't join in the conversation underneath?'

I raised an eyebrow.

'I'm being serious!' she insisted then after a long inhale of her cigarette, with the smoke coming out of her nose and mouth, added, 'There are a band of Western Women Lib dolls that I despise, whose personal agenda is for them to be seen as being victimised by exclusion, by being put out on a pedestal and away from the action. They need to define themselves as courageous victims, so as to get the sympathy and the attention they so desperately crave.'

'Yeah?'

'Yes! The proof is in the punitive pudding!' She scrunched up her brow as she formulated the thoughts that would underpin her argument and said, 'Most of these Western feminists show solidarity with many Middle Eastern male-orientated regimes, whose barbaric punitive measures are unforgivable and are totally silent about the horrendous fate of the women persecuted over there. If they were to make a noise about the dire circumstance of their "sisters" in the Middle East, their Western predicament by comparison would have to be reconsidered. They're hypocrites because if they highlighted the horror stories in those Muslim countries, the Western Patriarchy might have to go and battle for their cause, which would make them have to additionally admit that there is also justification for some wars. On the subject of dolls, young women can be as pretty as dolls, if they're born white. Here, every resident is dunked like a doughnut into either dark coffee or white milk and it is the colour with which one emerges that determines rights or lack thereof.' She smiled as the cloud around her dissipated. She would make a great sailor I thought, as she certainly could change tack in a hurry.

She lit and took a deep drag from the cigarette and continued, 'I see you don't like your drinks neat. You aren't planning on having a long relationship with that glass of ice water, are you?' She eased closer. While making an exploratory search of my body with her eyes, she added, 'Now don't give me that hippie bullshit of alcohol is poison, but grass is cool, man. Bartender!' she called out. 'Two triple vodkas for my friend and me.'

We studied each other as the drinks were poured. There was something intelligent about her gaze that denuded and exposed me, but I was comfortable with that, very comfortable.

The room had felt claustrophobic and shrouded in smoke. Now the soft light bathed her. A faint hint of jasmine and sandalwood drifting over from her direction engulfed me. Fragments of her reflection were caught in the back mirrors and brass lamps of the bar. Karma was teasing, stirring me. A portal of sexual opportunity had reared up and I could hear my heart.

Her skin-tight jeans outlined her slim but muscular thighs and small waist. The high ridges of her cheekbones flared up like a wolf's, but she resembled a jaguar. Her savannah rawness, which bespoke some kind of subtle risk, was tied together by refinery with an expensive, antique Patek Philippe wristwatch that was wrapped around her lean, left forearm. Ascendancy was in the air.

I considered her facial features as refined and elegant, so her language seemed incongruous with her appearance. This unilateral conversation projected outwards in three directions, aimed primarily at me, but nominally addressed to the bartender and loud enough to reach an immodest distance towards anyone else in the room.

'What are you doing in Cape Town?' I asked.

'I'm a head hunter,' she answered and took a drag from the butt of the cigarette. She blew a smoke ring over my head and smiled.

'You kill people?' I enquired.

'No, I hire people for specialised jobs.'

I didn't know if she was kidding, for she kept a straight face and shook her hair off her forehead. She lit another cigarette, taking a sip of the vodka and continued, 'What do you do?'

'I'm a contractor,' I said with a half-smile as I took a gulp of the strong drink.

'You kill people?' She raised her left eyebrow and scrunched up her eyes, cocking them in my direction, squinting to check if I was fibbing or not.

'No, but I do blow people away.'

She sat up straight and raised both eyebrows in surprise. 'Yes? In what way do you blow people away?' She leant forward again with a marked stare, blowing the cigarette smoke out of the way, through the corner of her mouth.

'I play the blues harp.'

'Cool!'

I sensed a genuine relief in her response to my answer. She lightly gripped my arm for a second then let go.

'I'm Aaron. What's your name?'

She lifted her drink. 'Cheers to you, Aaron.'

We shook hands, her hand lingering a little longer than usual and I could feel her temperature. She scouted the room to make sure no one was watching and whispered in my face as she learned forward, 'I'm Angela and I haven't been laid in a while and you're the only eligible candidate I've seen in months.'

She had a clear, well-educated, upper-class English accent

that was quite deep, but at the same time feminine. I was intrigued.

'It sounds good to me, Angela.'

'It's about time we undid our Manichean heritage and embrace this dirty body's rapture.'

She said this, pulling a strand of hair past her right ear thoughtfully while with her other arm she reached back, stretching like a contortionist over her head to scratch between her shoulder blades.

'Cheers to your agility,' I toasted.

By 'agility' I had meant physical flexibility, but Angela, needing to have the last word, had thought I meant mental agility and responded, 'To be well spoken is to be agile, but...' She took a quick sip of her drink and continued, 'Even being well spoken can repel intimacy by silver-tongued, left and right jabs. To be quiet is I think the best way, especially when in the pink. I am not boring you, am I?'

'I wasn't listening,' I said with a straight face then enquired, 'Pink as in "birthday suit"?'

'Yes!' She quieted, touching her glass against mine. I smelt her vodka and cigarette breath as she leaned closer. She continued, 'I try to tap into my instinctive faculty while also using good judgement.'

'Instinctive faculty?'

'All human brains, from idiots to intellectuals, have a visual faculty allied to music. This balanced order is innate. For example, it is balanced facial features that have the power over our sensibilities and is what we consider beautiful. The power of numbers always tyrannises and holds sway over us.'

'But, Angela, can we trust that what we see or believe is correct, or are we subject to the tyranny of appearances? Can our choices be guided by something other than the information brought to us by our senses?'

'You mean, can we learn from experience and thus create

some defences against our natural impressionableness, so that tyrants will find it harder to exploit us?'

'Yes, trust is the issue. Every tyrant asks for our trust in him. Trust is faith, but can we trust that what we see or believe is correct and if we put our trust in a person who vanquishes others to hell, is that not tyranny at its finest?'

'Aaron, I believe that our intellect can protect us if we just take the time to use it.'

'The problem is that most people will never have the patience to take time to reflect. For the masses what looks good will always win because it comes like an arrow, straight from the bi-polar heart and not the head.'

'Yes, I like your idea of the bi-polar heart. Emotions do have a tendency to be like on/off switches. For example, when someone does something which affronts us, we either decide to get angry or laugh it off, but we don't seem able to have an option for adopting something in-between.'

'Angela, it's the animal in us; either fight or flight as anything else would take precious time.'

'And if we get angry, but later choose to forgive them, that seems to take a binary format too, one moment we're still holding the grudge and the next all is forgiven. Another interesting case is the whole concept of trust. If we decide to trust someone, we somehow believe that they won't let us down at all and then get shocked when they eventually turn out to be less than completely a hundred per cent trustworthy. Our brains should know that they are fallible and so we shouldn't expect anything beyond best efforts. A simple infidelity really shouldn't have to be seen as the end of a relationship if good intent remains intact.'

'That reminded me about a friend of mine whose wife once had an afternoon fling with a baseball player who was on her PR firm roster. The evening after her affair, at the end of having sex with her husband, as she was climaxing, she screamed,

"Fuck me, big boy, with your big black cock!" She orgasmed and his mediocre-at-best erection simultaneously subsided, as he was neither big nor was he Black. The husband didn't mention anything at the time to his wife, but it ate at his ego, especially as he was aware that his wife worked with Black sportsmen and one particular Black baseball superstar who was known to emerge from the shadow of his ever-ready, gargantuan, indefatigable, eleven-inch organ. The next day at dinner, the husband, on a hunch, blurted out that he knew that she had fucked so-and-so. She immediately admitted to it and said it was a mistake and that it wouldn't happen again. But the fact remains that ever since that one-off penetration, the baseball player's perpetual hard-on is constantly in the wife's mind yearning to be someplace else and unfortunately the enormous "impolite façade" is also in her husband's head. The marriage is still holding though.'

'Yes it's sad, but that is the way we are, Aaron; we fantasise that fidelity will be absolute and cannot handle it when the illusion gets battered. The truth is that we have other fantasies too and may occasionally succumb to temptations, if an opportunity to realise them comes our way.'

That ended our conversation at the bar, before she took my hand.

Meanwhile, here we both are, Angela and me, two congregants awaiting a communion of sorts in the hotel's marbled, cloistered bathroom, beneath a large glass skylight. I am ruminating over Angela and conclude that her mind, matched by that body and face, is a formidable combination, an unholy trinity.

Anticipation swims across my mind. What a wonderful thing is a beautiful female body, unhitched from complicated buckles, belts, pleats and fabric. The two of us today are surrounded by silence, because we are up earlier than even the handsomely burnished, gold-feathered cock. It is too early in the morning and too late in the night for it to render unto the darkness its shrill, cockerel aria, the sound of which is louder than a soprano organ blowing.

Everything's a consequence.

3

When action isn't married to blurbs, then diseased in deed, indeed are words.

Irreverent Reverend Tom Groans

Unbeknown to me, this naked girl who is now lowering herself into the bathwater, after slipping a 10-gram slice of the hallucinogen peyote onto my tongue, has a modified Smith and Wesson Model 39, complete with silencer and side-lock that is set to safety after being recently fired, lying alongside her hairbrush and lipstick in her handbag, which is set upon a nearby chair. The Model 39 is 7 inches long and has an aluminium frame, curved back-strap and a blue, carbon steel slide that carries the manual safety. The handgrip is constructed with three pieces: two walnut wood panels, joined by a metal back-strap that has a magazine release located at the rear of the trigger guard. It was originally designed to eliminate guard dogs on sentry duty without disturbing the rest of the 'household'.

I know none of this, nor can I imagine that she had intentionally sought me out to seduce and win me over. She knows that I am about to become the new tenant at the house on Napier Street and she is in need of a mole on the inside to access this house. Neither can I imagine just yet, the effect that the tiny, dried peyote cactus bud is about to throw on my perception of light, colour, formation and sound. Liberated from any form of anxiety, I feel like I am now at the very heart of affluence, where I am free to indulge in this perceptive constellation which those in abject poverty, those concerned with basic survival, could never break into.

At this moment in the bathtub, a profound abandonment of purpose has endowed me with an even more profound relaxation. I am not just having these sensations; I have in fact become the sensations. I am an island in the middle of an ocean facing her, another island. We are both isolated from the world. I have no point of contact with the rest of civilisation. The width and depth of my perspective is her body. Angela's view, on the other hand, embraces the entire room, this hotel, the street, neighbourhood, city and Table Mountain. For the moment, though, I have the majority of her attention.

I am watching her in rapt tranquillity. Her body is languidly purged of any sort of tension, as if she has stepped off a trampoline onto solid ground and does not need to push off and fight gravity. My pulse is lowered even though I know I will be entering her soon. Quiet is obviously her way when nude. 'Doing one's thing' has replaced formal convention with a type of boudoir anarchy.

Her sensual style is more Spartan than Baroque, the opposite of what I think is her rhetorical manner. Intellect is usually polished, while genitals need to be readied for unabashed, changeable dexterity. Indecent transparency has reared its seductive little head in this bit of a bathtub backwater.

I feel like I am a dog paddling in St Peter's in front of the Madonna. Somehow I feel privileged, as if I am the first to hold this post, or bedpost, or bath soap of hers, since the Reformation of her puberty. Of course I am not, but such is her undivided attention to this occasion. It is possible to detach the mind from the maintenance of equilibrium when one has such an agreeable disrobed symmetry that having ambled posture-perfect towards you, now awaits your touch in the warm, Epsom-salted bathwater. Beneath her illuminated veneer of puritanical, naked smoothness and inside that angelic artifice as she drifts in my direction, stands a premeditated killer.

Here in the bathtub there is no hurry, nor any rush of blood. Angela bends her knees, lowers her midriff into the bathwater and now seems suctioned into the vacuum of liquid, as though pulled into softened bed sheets. Her white breasts and belly rise above the surface, appearing truncated in her repose, as long limbs disappear in a delicate dissolve into the soapy fluid. She dunks her head backwards and downwards towards the surface of the water and says softly, 'This is my regular ritual of immersion which is life affirming. Water is the symbol of life, since the percentage of water in anything living is highest in the embryo and declines with age.'

Now, her torso and face, both soft and buoyant with the moisture of youth, disappear beneath the bubbles that camouflage her marvellous upper half, in this wonderfully-close-for-comfort, ritual bath of ours. Only her two legs facing me that are bent at the knees, shins forward, protrude above the surface on either side of my hips. I rest my forearms on them as if on the arms of a warm, wet, fleshy sofa.

She now bobs back out from the depths of the bath to a sitting position. Her large eyes sparkle radiantly and her lips are parted with a hint of a smile lifting the corners.

There is a suspension of that bridge that links reality from the visceral, internal bodily world of sensations. This emotion I feel is a leftover relic that has emerged from a pre-natal memory. A liquid pre-birth consciousness revisited of living in the flood. This flood will recede again later. This I know and our two separate, solid islands will emerge once more.

*

Angela is sitting now, almost waist-high in the water facing me and closes her eyes. 'Aaaaaah!' she exclaims as she takes in a full, belly-deep breath of air, facilitating a meditative state. Raising arms outwards, her palms upwards and as if giving thanks, she whispers, 'Khecari.' She remains very still and in a closed-eye, prayerful position continues to slowly draw in her breath, inflating her capacious lungs. This hypnotic state is aided by her simultaneously sealing all her bodily orifices, beginning with contracting her rectal muscles and additionally aiding this contraction by pressurising her anal-perineum area, by sitting on her left lower leg which is curved under her buttocks and using her left heel to seal the opening. Her stomach is protruding now and what was a clearly defined six-pack only five minutes ago now appears to be replaced by the configuration of a nine-month pregnancy as her breath circulates deeper into her lungs, while expanding her ribcage considerably. Her stomach is bulging dangerously close to bursting, while behind closed lids there is focus. It has been almost six minutes and she lets out the air via her mouth very slowly, saying, 'I'd love a big horn section right now!'

'What?' I am startled by the remark, it being somehow antithetic to the business at hand. I notice by her sideways glance at the radio on the dresser that she is referring to the rock music being broadcast. I am somewhat relieved that her comment has nothing to do with any shortcomings on my part and I am further assured by her smile and her quick, furtive glance at my resting privates that she has made a joke.

She has a completely convivial way of putting one at ease. As I am snugly sited between her breasts that are both velvety and beautifully ample, there is a real danger that just through relaxation I could fall asleep during the 'trailer' and miss the main event.

'I'd also love to pull a cork!' she exclaims with another of her innuendos, referring to a bottle of wine in the bedroom. She stands up abruptly from the sitting position and with the vacuum in the tub left by her sudden upward-motion that agitates the water about my still-seated body, I feel like Huckleberry in the middle of the Mississippi, or a docile dummy recently fallen off the ventriloquist's knee.

Angela climbs out of the tub. She walks slowly and regally from the room towards the bedroom to retrieve the bottle of wine. She tiptoes with all the excitement of someone about to indulge in something bootlegged and clandestine. I am left alone in the virtually empty bathtub except for a small, rubber duck, which she had initially thrown into the bathwater for fun and has now beached itself alongside my genitals on the dry dock that is my thighs.

Two minutes have passed since she stepped out of the room to do the uncorking. She returns, handing me the bottle. I acquaint it with my lips and proceed to sip and appreciate it via the viaduct of my tongue. The aged wine is delicious and dry, with a fermented, grape-full expression.

She explains casually, 'After a few years of efforts to achieve enlightenment when I lived in Nepal, I learnt to open my body by deep-breathing, while exercising the colon muscles independently from each other, which felt so exhilarating that I kept repeating the habit and lost interest in the enlightenment.'

Having taken note of her lung capacity and having witnessed what her tongue can do when we had kissed, I stare at this girl, dumbfounded, simply thinking, 'Holy shit!'

This eccentric free spirit sits in the full lotus position upon my hips, meditating above me in the nearly empty bath. She rocks backwards and forwards with a quiet vivacity of self-confidence, wearing her large, upright breasts with an air of sophistication. I know that above those breasts is a lucid mind with ideas that cover much ground and that she also, just as importantly, understands the fine detail of what is at hand.

She has jettisoned language for the moment and is gargling

the sound 'ah' and other vowels as she enjoys herself. After some initial, first-wind passion is spent, she nonchalantly adds some consonants to her repertoire of sounds, breaking the silence.

'Buddhism is impersonal, but I've taken its discipline to learn to be open and have married it with a bit of Kabbalah.' She explains this in situ, as she continues to sit and ride slowly.

'Kabbalah?' I ask.

'Yes, it encourages pragmatism mixed with curiosity. It's my carrot and stick approach!'

'What do you mean?'

'You're my carrot and I stick it in!' She laughs and continues, 'This is the only social climbing I do.' She climbs a fraction closer to my torso and laughs a little louder.

'How did you get steered towards the Kabbalah?' I enquire.

'My mother's a lapsed gentile with mystical leanings, while my father's a non-practising Muslim. He's also a great jazz pianist,' she responds as a matter of fact. Jokingly, she adds, 'My parents call themselves Lapsed-Landers.'

'Your father's a Muslim?'

This could churn up any number of biting questions for anyone here in Apartheid South Africa, as virtually all the Muslims in the Cape are of non-White Malay descent.

'Yes, Aaron. He's half-European, a quarter Malay and a quarter Khoikhoi or Hottentot. My father's well known around these parts as the pianist, Pound Currant. He changed his name initially from Gregory Abraham to Gregory Ways to Pound Currant when he rejected Islam thirty years ago.' She stretches her slim arms above and behind her head, yawns and cracks her neck, pauses and continues. 'He wanted to distance himself from any fundamentalism. Anything to do with male dominance and cultural bullying is anathema to him.' She says all this while watching me intently and then abruptly changes tack, referring back to her earlier statements about her heredity. 'You are in fact being sexually intimate, to put it darkly, with a Coloured!'

I swallow, feeling my Adam's apple bob up and down quickly, whilst giving a faint glimmer of a half-smile, acknowledging my predicament.

She nods and with a shrug continues. 'Yes, I'm certainly an advantaged Coloured person, for even though I went to a Coloured high school, I was fortunate to have been home-schooled as well, so that I received distinctions in all my A Level subjects. I'm doubly advantaged because I can also pass for White, even though my father can't. I'm a "red herring" swimming through the system!'

'And I'm a red-neck trying to keep the sun off my face!' I feebly joke.

She adjusts her neck with left-right chiropractic clicks. 'Yes, we both suffer red-necks badly, no doubt. In fact I'm proud to precociously say that I'm an unabashed, White "red herring". Despite an unpromising, un-moneyed and unsophisticated beginning, except for my looks and uncommon sense, I've done some extraordinary things.'

She is not being facetious either.

'Red herring?' I ask.

'Yes, it is the tactic of diverting attention away from something of significance. For example, here, I'm identified as a Coloured and having slept with you, a White man, I could garner myself the label "criminal". Nature has wonderfully cast me in a light-skinned light through the employment of this false skin covering. My education and enunciation using loaded Oxbridge English is another deceptive trick. The authorities' suspicions are misdirected, allowing me to go undetected. I'm the false protagonist in this story you and I are living in.'

'And there are many reasons why you've done extraordinary things,' I mention, having got the gist of her point about red herrings.

'My looks and my uncommon sense being two of the reasons I've succeeded, no?'

'Yes, so the other reasons don't matter!' I try to be smart.

She is still moving above me and I am somehow maintaining an erection while knowing at the same time that I have broken the Immorality Law of 1950 by sleeping with a non-White. If it were found out that I have been sexual with Angela, I would quite naturally have to plead my case that she looks whiter than I, so how was I to know? Depending on which official got wind of this, my case would either be thrown out, or I would be found guilty, as ignorance is no excuse in racist South Africa. It is like playing 'Russian roulette'.

Angela continues in the same vein. 'Dad used to say his scepticism gave him a sprinkling of spiritual discomfort that drove him towards the blues, women and drink. He always says that there is no consensus that holds any society together anymore.'

I nod in agreement and say, 'There's no consensus anymore, because all morality today is relative morality. The primary cause is a fear of showing prejudice. This prevents criticism. Everyone now can express themselves in their shapeless non-arts and formless non-books and their tuneless non-music that can all be explained in their esoteric all-non-sense terms. A terrorist attacking you and one's retaliation for that attack are now regarded as morally equivalent. That's unconscionable and insane!'

Her thoughts now, though imperceptible to me, have reacted to my use of the word 'terrorist' and so she changes tack, subtly attacking my bull-headed position and says,

'I have always thought that if you have what you want too long and too completely, you become miserly. One should give up fixed notions in order to grow.'

I shake my head in disagreement and repel with, 'This "don't reflect on the past" mind-set lacks discrimination and so exposes nothing, especially the truth. The "everything is cool" ethos is superficial. This personal morality and the anarchy of words go hand in hand!'

Angela nods, adding, 'Ah ha! The privatising of language is a good case in point, like the word "Coloured", under whose banner our huge motley group have been described. Challenging the established morality, though, is not necessarily a bad thing if the dominant morality is immoral, as it is here. In terms of language, I agree with you. Poor words equal poor clarity. People speak badly because they are ambiguous and elementary and they mumble their words with inarticulate, low-class accents, because if we can't tell what they're slurring, we won't be able to judge them and they don't want to be judged, because they don't know what the hell they're talking about!'

'Yes, that's exactly my point. The relative meaning of words begets a relative mind-set where "every man is for himself" and that mind-set unravels the blanket the community used to bond under.'

'Yes, Mr Bond. And as an aside, "every woman is also for herself" and my "biological clock" is quickly ticking, so until I get my next period in three weeks, if I should get pregnant by this delicious union, only I would be able to decide whether you, young Aaron, will become the proud father of a bouncing baby Coloured child!'

My erection subsides immediately. I move off her body and sit alongside her. She smiles, but I am certain that there has been a veiled threat implied. I must be good to her.

She reaches out and touches my ear. There is lightness, yet certainty in her trace. I feel that I am in deep water, but that keeping afloat requires relaxation, a certain flexibility of giving myself to the element I am in. I breathe deeply and relax into the moment, enjoying her fingers on my face and her naked existence, as a strongly pacifist mood engulfs me.

Angela continues in her vein of thought. 'We Coloureds here

are overwhelmed and there is no real resistance to the big brute, just yet, but it will come I assure you.' She changes tack again and with a sense of the ridiculous, exclaims, 'A great power, whether it be an empire or a penis, when surrounded by a vacuum, will expand into that vacuum, until it feels the growing pressure of resistance.' She gives herself a congratulatory belly laugh at her expansion of this political idea into the sexual arena. Sitting on my midriff, she reaches out and lightly ruffles my hair, saying, 'Sexual, as well as governmental, politics enflame every nerve in me. It's what turns me on, a man's astuteness in these matters.'

She is astute and there is no doubt about it, that her mental athleticism is a big turn-on. Her extreme beauty alone, even if it were to encase a brain the size of a peanut, could keep me riveted to her for at least four seasons.

Coincidences are major features in my life at the moment, such that Pound Currant, whom Angela mentioned is her father, came to the club where I was playing my harmonica a few days earlier. He, the revered pianist and renowned rake because of his numerous romantic dalliances, had come to Smuggler's Inn to listen to my blues band, A Bass of Time, perform. With the harmonica at my lips, engrossed in a musical riff, I saw at the club's entrance, in silhouette, what I thought was a statuesque woman who had been vigilantly observing me. I could not be absolutely sure because the person in question was ensconced in deep shadow, listening.

After finishing the set, I left the stage and walked across the club's floor, manoeuvring between crowded, loud and boozed-up tables of patrons. As I approached the silhouette, the form suddenly stepped out of the darkness. With a hand extended in my direction, the stranger said in a highly pitched feminine voice, even though the figure was now clearly a middle-aged male, 'Good chops Aaron! Very cool playing, man! You sound like Paul Butterfield, but with more vibratos.'

His height, long hair and the bone structure of his cheeks and jaw line were, in retrospect, almost identical to Angela's, but his nose was different and broader at the tip. His eyes were almost almond-shaped and he was obviously a Coloured man, because his pallor was a darker shade of brown with a yellowish tinge. He looked like a very handsome man of indeterminate age, anywhere between thirty-five and forty-five, with photogenic, film star quality appeal. He was in fact fifty-five.

'I'm Pound Currant. Let's jam sometime.' He said this confidently, as if he had expected me to know him, which I did not at the time. With a twinkle in his eyes he repeated that I was 'Very cool man! You let your music possess you. Brilliant! One has to give totally of one's sensitivity. I try to get that over to young kids in music today, but in these more affluent times, young musicians live mainly in their heads and everything is a cerebral exercise, rather than it having a releasing, cathartic effect. I once knew a really talented young musician who always used to say that she was embalmed and immersed in sound and I used to reply that maybe she was immersed in sound, but she was never capable of unbridled sensuality in her playing, that her tempestuous passions were always reigned in and resisted the carnal elements. She had wonderful hand dexterity and ravishing technique, but she was so separated from relating to other people that her music talked to no one. It was too clean, too sterile and lacked that dirtiness that brings a signature style with it'.

'I'm sure you dirtied her up a bit, no doubt? I sure bet you put some dirty old blues into her clean sheets? Music sheets of course!' I jested.

'So you know her?' he joked back.

'That's why I lean towards the blues,' I said, adding, '...and rock and roll, where the music is more earthy, where the sounds are blown up to, or bent down to pitch, with over and under tones and where the wind blown through the wood and steel blurs and broadens the sound, adding that dirt you just talked about. Just like the human voice; it's real. Yes and add to that, the Black man's histrionic, lascivious behaviour on stage and you have a spit at White decorum.'

'Yes, Aaron. I often say to my young girlfriends, "Don't be caught between a cock and your hard face!" Loosen up and take it easy.' He laughed.

Pound Current and I connected, with both of us speaking the same musical language. Flashing a quick glance around the club, on whose stage his music could be played, even though, ironically, as a Coloured man, he would be barred from eating, he did an easy about-turn and sauntered out the entrance.

The coincidence of the Pound Currant and Angela connection now has me staggered. Angela is a construct in which demonology and sex, free of convention, feed off each other. She being the taboo demon, yet a figure perfectly poised is also her essential beauty. She has the composure of a bird in flight, though relaxed in that movement of lyricism. Her special value is complete directness. She does not seem to lack an emotive quality either and there is none of that generic bluntness that one would generally expect with such frankness.

I am a watching-listener without any outside claims made upon me and my passion is brought to complete quiescence by this girl. Angela is not simply a Mulatto. She is an exegesis, an interpretation of the Coloured person's text and the result of an unadulterated strategy of assimilation.

I am not just seducing any woman whilst I penetrate Angela, I am fucking South African history.

We had entered the bathtub gratefully to a Grateful Dead overture and morning broke two hours ago after we had simultaneously reached gratification to the last movement of

Beethoven's Ninth, when her vagina, seized by the tiny spasms of her orgasm's pulsating response, gripped me. I am now settled down into a wonderfully clichéd Seventh Heaven.

We glove to glove each other in abstract handshakes, snug in our solitary confinements.

4

Though delicacy is the prize of breeding, with every thrust, there's lust self-seeding!

Irreverent Reverend Tom Groans

Sex with someone I had met only last night was the novelty that had added spice to my first and only evening in that cheap hotel in Cape Town. I did not know her, so what I saw initially was totally my creation. We did have an in depth conversation prior to coming up to my room. That *tête-à-tête* revealed that we shared a similar sense of humour, as we both understood what was implicit and unspoken in what had made the conversation funny. We had also both agreed that a pronounced sense of ironic humour is often the characteristic of a loser who laughs at everything and that even jokes that are self-effacing are usually conceit dressed up as humility as if to say, 'Look, I'm so worthy, I can even afford all of this self-deprecation.' Angela had mentioned in that same vein that a sense of humour shows a sense of proportion, but she had emphasised that anything that is overwhelmingly important is not usually emotionally proportional. I had mentioned that totalitarian states also abhor irony because they don't believe in anything proportional. Her response was, 'Touché!'

Stripped of fashion's pretensions, butt-naked Angela had given me a certain psychological tonic: a mood replete with all the exhilarations that occur when one senses within oneself a stark carnality. We both recognised the euphoria and mutual pace of the other, but it is the setting that can never be known by its tempo in the way people are described by their gait. Unalike people, with their contrasting paces, define similar positions differently.

'People,' she said, 'are often not what they look like.'

'Yes,' I concurred.

'And witty remarks are usually useless.'

'I've nothing witty to add.'

'And style is a caricature, just shorthand,' she interjected and then continued, 'The moment we introduce ourselves, we conceal ourselves.'

'Ah! That's why we have post-concealment sex,' I responded.

'Sex is so much better without thinking too much, without thought's deceptions,' she parried.

'Sex is better because passion is allergic to analysis,' I backhanded.

'And passion allows one to fly by the seat of one's pants and be in the zone.'

Thus concluded our first round of verbal foreplay, with our converging energies connecting with synchronicity and comfort.

Cities have thousands of converging sounds, intertwined at varying settings and speeds with everyone's noise defined by their own peculiar nature and circumstance. A city can set an ambience. Johannesburg, with its goldmines, tries to explain why we live; Durban, with its busy port, tells us we are alive and Cape Town, with its great mountain, tells us how we should live. A depression lingering over one's personal realm can be understood as a calm that similarly permeates the individual dominion of yet another person.

Graffiti written in red spray-paint on a partially dismantled old wall, surrounding a recently renovated, single-storied, old Cape Dutch-style house in District Six, reads:

One small step for man, one giant weep for mankind.

This place fulfils each person's particular function, just as the smell of seaweed misting over from the breakers picked up by one individual, is unrecognised by another.

Empathy is hard to find.

5

Don't mock a sin of mine, until you've walked a mile in my moccasins.

Irreverent Reverend Tom Groans

Angela is an assimilated Coloured woman of twenty-six years and it is only the severity of race separation in South Africa which has made her all the more aware of her Mixed-Race position. This moniker she assumes with courage. To be sure, her Nordic blood, blonde and blue-eyed appearance, would so permit it, but she has not completely dissolved into her 'Whiteness.'

Though she has not deliberately tried to overlook her legally racial status, she does hide inside her White appearance when convenient. Angela belongs to a world so acquainted with violent death that the element of sudden fatality does not deter or shock her. She, in fact, has certain expectations about how a conflict should be resolved, especially a personal grudge where honour is the root cause of the aggressive response.

Angela is the recipient of a 300-year-old legacy subtly inherited down one strain of her musician father's mixed genetic and cultural ancestry: the Scottish clan, not his Malay or his Khoikhoi forbears. This aggressive conditioning she interred through vibrations of a social milieu that have long rippled patterns from the past into the present.

Her focus on the morning before we first met was an honour killing to avenge a wrong done to a friend some time ago. She murdered her target, a man she had been shadowing for a fortnight, and she dispatched him in broad, South African daylight, in a public place, on a day when no one could save him.

Walking in the light at night.

6

There is a tyranny of appearance in South Africa.
Irreverent Reverend Tom Groans

When is something so inconspicuous that it is conspicuous? The answer: when it is a dwarf who is an undercover police officer.

Angela, with her substantial observational skills certainly had taken note of the diminutive undercover policeman, Officer Arcane, as he had followed the soon-to-be late Captain J.B.

Arcane had been moving uptown at midday and his trek in the sun ran parallel with and in the same direction as Angela, but he chose the opposite side of the street to make his excursion. He had been tracking, and for a different purpose than Angela's, the now-dead Captain J.B., because the Bureau of State Security's office in Cape Town had heard from a double agent working in the precinct police station that an attempt on the Death Squad leader's life would soon take place.

Because of her innate lack of bias, she had not placed too much weight on Officer Arcane's very apparent lack of weight and dwarfism, or of the peculiar choice of some department to choose a man as a tag-along who would need three steps to every normal person's one stride.

The undercover man, a 4-foot, 9-inch proportional dwarf, did take note of the blonde girl with the yellow helmet and over-sized sunglasses, reading a map while seated on a scooter and smoking a cigarette.

Coincidentally, Officer Peter Arcane, the petite undercover cop with a PhD in clinical psychology, had also graduated from Oxford University, the same university where Angela is at present enrolled.

What Officer Arcane did not do that day was make a special note of Angela's timely appearance, which happened to be at exactly the same time and locale as Captain J.B.'s regular midday sojourn in the park. He merely noted her in passing and not in detail.

On any other day, Officer Arcane would have been pedantic and taken into account the entire minutia about him, as he usually does, but on this day Officer Arcane was abnormally distracted by the entire shenanigans of the past week, surrounding his private family life.

During his two weeks in Cape Town, the late Captain J.B. had insisted that he needed protection. He had requested this demand for security from Officer Stratagem in Cape Town, without mentioning this request to his head office in Pretoria, as he had pretty much carte blanche to do whatever he wanted, wherever he was.

Officer Peter Arcane was appointed as his shadow. Every lunch hour Arcane would shuffle on ahead of Captain J.B. on the journey uptown, in order to arrive at the park earlier than the captain. Arcane would then seat himself on the park bench opposite the one on which Captain J.B. eventually would choose to eat his cheese and tomato sandwiches. Arcane would sit there for the duration of the picnic, watching the behaviour of the seagulls hopping about after scraps of food.

Angela, although she had been thorough in following Captain J.B.'s entire route to the park every day these past two weeks, had not ventured into the park herself. So, she was unaware that the miniature officer was there all along, seated opposite her victim every lunch hour.

The reason for Officer Arcane's utter distraction on the last day of Captain J.B.'s life was due to the shocking revelation after a special stake-out of his home village, by Officer Skanky, that revealed that his fourteen-year-old son, Mark, had, over the past week, been up to monkey business in their neighbourhood. As a consequence he was late getting to the park ahead of Captain J.B. that fateful day, because he needed to collect his thoughts. The reason he U-turned on reaching the park and had not remained with Captain J.B., but returned to police headquarters, was that it was vital that he convince Officer Skanky to drop charges against Mark and that he would sort him out himself.

A conversation took place between Officer Skanky and Officer Arcane, on Arcane's premature return to Headquarters that day. Unbeknownst to both these officers, at this exact moment, Captain J.B. was being shot at and killed in the park, so Arcane's lack of focus and negligence was as yet not an issue.

Officer Arcane had explained that his son has a warm and gentle nature and is totally focused on his academic school work. Officer Skanky replied that generally, Mark may have a gentle aspect to his personality, but that over the past week whenever Arcane's son passed one of their five neighbour's houses and the front veranda was unguarded, his son would shoot out the front porch lights with his BB gun. Officer Arcane explained that the boy was standing up for his father, as the kids on their street were mocking his height. Arcane in fact was proud of Mark! Officer Skanky then agreed that anyone who has that kind of dedication speaks for something.

Officer Stratagem, Skanky's boss, suggested that the whole episode be swept under the table and placed under wraps. None of the neighbours were told the truth and of course the occurrences stopped as suddenly as they had begun.

That conversation happened in the early afternoon and prior to the department being informed of Captain J.B.'s murder. Immediately after the killing, Officer Stratagem, who had made Officer Arcane responsible for Captain J.B.'s healthy survival, knew that any wrongdoing or lapse of judgement on Arcane's part in not protecting Captain J.B. would reflect badly on himself, as the buck always stops at the superior's front desk. Just as those in senior positions invariably take credit for the successes of their subordinates, so the reverse is also true. So, Stratagem and Arcane closed ranks and denied that there had been any break in Arcane's protocol or rules of conduct that day.

Stratagem and Arcane were like Siamese twins, joined at the head and therefore they were not ever likely to blow their own brains out in an act of professional suicide. Everyone in Stratagem's department also kept their heads down and their mouths shut, lest they should get caught in any potential crossfire. Fortunately for Officer Stratagem, it was he who got the tip-off about a possible attempt on Captain J.B.'s life and it was fortuitous for him that he had acted independently of his bosses in Pretoria, who had no idea about what had been going on in Cape Town, or the rumour that had abounded about an attempted assassination of their 'main man'.

Nothing Stratagem or Arcane did *vis-à-vis* Captain J.B. was official as far as Pretoria was concerned, so the unspoken principle of 'plausible deniability' of any misconduct on their parts was set forth between the two of them.

Skeletons in glass closets shouldn't throw bones.

7

Having only faith and restraint against the tyrant, damns the saint!

Irreverent Reverend Tom Groans

Peter Arcane's previous life, the six years immediately prior to joining the South African Police Force, were spent in England at Oxford University, where he earned a double first in Psychology and Russian and became a senior tutor in both subjects. He was conversant in Russian, where he painstakingly studied Tsarist censorship and the St Petersburg Censorship Committee and how the intellectual writers of the day tried to circumvent the committee's censorship taboos. Years spent understanding how the Russians tried to usurp the law honed his psychology skills.

Arcane is a right-wing bohemian and a man of contradictions. Even as a tiny man he became an avid church bell ringer, yet he abandoned the church virtually the day he started pulling those ropes at Oxford. Initially, when learning bell-ringing, on a few uncomfortable occasions, he would fly through the air with the greatest of unease when forgetting to let go of his grip, thereby learning that timing is everything. Arcane also disdains pomp, yet ironically enjoys musical ceremony.

Another of Arcane's incongruities is that one of his keen

interests is articulacy and rhetorical flexibility: the marshalling of language to make one's point. Interrogation using words and mustering them to undermine an adversary's position fills him with happiness. He sees the popular glib talk of the 'back to native' generation as counterfeit currency. He sees the love of anything obscure as a smokescreen that hides a shallow emotional, as well as intellectual landscape. Arcane has a fondness for the bluntness of the Russian people and their way of living in the moment, yet Communism's control over individualism is detestable to him.

Most of Arcane's ideas about language, Communism and psychology he shares with his nemesis, Angela, whose existence he is unaware of at this moment.

Angela also earned a double first, but in German and Psychology, after which she went on to do her Master's Degree. She is now on a year's sabbatical and will return to her doctorate in clinical psychology next year.

Arcane and Angela are both very much on opposite sides of the political fence, with Arcane feeling that Apartheid is a buffer against inter-tribal conflict, with the Whites being just another African tribe. Angela, a left-wing elitist and being of Mixed-Race, thinks Apartheid and its definition of race is ruled by arbitrariness and hypocrisy.

Angela and Arcane are also familiar with the unproven assertion that a leading South African mining conglomerate acted duplicitously by supplying both the Allies, whose side they were meant to be on, as well as the Nazis, with vital industrial diamonds during the Second World War, thus prolonging and sabotaging the war effort. It was heard that they provided the US with much less than the States requested out of fear that if the war ended quickly, the stockpile of diamonds in the United States would affect the South African's monopoly of those gems. The company's defence was that the diamonds that were sent to Hitler were surreptitiously smuggled out from beneath the company's unsuspecting noses in the

Belgian Congo. This argument of the conglomerate being ignorant of the goings-on in Belgian during the war rings hollow to both Angela and Arcane. Treachery, treachery everywhere and playing both sides against the middle is how they see big business dealings, both in the past as well as in the present.

For both these Oxford graduates, Russian history is a preoccupation; he leaning towards the Bolsheviks' perspective and she nodding slightly in favour of the Tsar.

Ironically, Arcane and Angela swapped political positions from their respective political stances on Russia when it came to South African politics, with Arcane supporting the right-wing, Apartheid incumbents in South Africa, while Angela, who leaned towards the dictatorship of the Tsar in Russia, gravitates today towards the majority, Communist leaning, African National Congress. Angela's choice of siding with the Communist ANC is also doubly ironic because she supports majority rule and 'one man, one vote', which is her attachment to that organisation, but she is strongly and virulently anti-Communist in theory and practice as she sees Communism as just another form of totalitarianism and group control. Angela knows however that Capitalism taps into our human acquisitiveness to accumulate and that Capitalism's great flaw is that public debt, if not forgiven, will eventually overburden the majority, disenfranchised public and kill economic growth for all.

Angela, with a background of advanced karate that she perfected in Nepal, her fluency in Arabic that she learnt from her paternal grandparents and her abhorrence of Communism, attracted the American CIA while she was at Oxford. They had been watching her at the inter-university debates where she was a pre-eminent and celebrated debater, but what sealed it for them and what convinced them that she had the bona fides for the job, was her spontaneous response to three questions put to her. The first question was for her to name five things she would *not* do in public, and the recruitment officer wanted an immediate answer, without hesitation. Her five answers to the first question were short, sharp and to the point; they were that she would not defecate, fornicate, masturbate, urinate or procrastinate in public. She answered that in rapid-fire time. The second question was for her to name five things about herself that make her feel proud; the five positive behaviours she attributed to herself were the regularity of her defecations and urinations, the way she fornicates, masturbates and the fact that she never procrastinates. The third demand put to her by the recruitment officer and again with him wanting an immediate response from her, was for her to tell any lie or untruth. Her answer was that she and a pregnant girlfriend were caught in the middle of a riot downtown, where dozens of dangerous teenagers belonging to various gangs were destroying shops and raiding all the contents of a supermarket where they had gone shopping. The two girls were caught at the wrong place, at the wrong time. Not only had the gangs emptied the shelves completely, they had even stolen Angela's pregnant girlfriend's breast milk before she had even had a chance to express it. They considered Angela's sense of the ridiculous as a huge bonus.

Since 1955, the CIA, under the direction of the National Security Council, was assembled into a Cold War machine to 'create and exploit troublesome problems for international Communism', to 'develop underground resistance and facilitate covert and guerrilla operations'. The anti-Communist Angela was perfectly poised to infiltrate the Communist-inclined ANC, as she was a non-White and therefore genuinely and fundamentally supported undermining the Apartheid regime. At the same time, however, she could become a double agent, helping to undermine the very organisation that she in many ways also supported.

The contradiction between the United States' covert operations and the US overt policies shaped Angela's comfort with ambiguous behaviour. The principle of 'plausible deniability' if the covert operations go wrong, is 'so planned and executed that any US Government responsibility for them is NOT evident to UNAUTHORISED persons and if uncovered, the US Government can plausibly disclaim any responsibility for them' in a case of plausible deniability.

The 'authorised persons' responsible, who were unimpeachable and unnamed, did not include Congress or the US Government, who the CIA director should have reported to. He reported to no one. The 'authorised persons' applied to just a few CIA, inner group of operatives, 'freelancing' as it were without and within the system. This band of freewheeling agents, were a law unto themselves just as Angela was to become, *vis-à-vis* South Africa.

Again, Angela and Officer Arcane are united while sitting on opposite sides of the proverbial fence. Both have an understanding and use of the concept of 'plausible deniability'.

In the past, Angela, as a beautiful blonde Caucasian woman, had enjoyed extended holidays for a number of years with various Arab boyfriends in the Middle East, reporting to and acting covertly on behalf of the CIA, both as an observer, as well as a deep undercover operative. Angela now acts on behalf of both the CIA and ANC, as well as on her own behalf. She is a triple-agent.

Arcane and Angela, one could almost say are a match made in heaven, except for their twenty-year-age and two-foot-height differences and that of their political leanings.

There is another area politically that they both agree upon, and that is Mandela's moral compass. They both abhor the fact that Mandela, the founder of the A.N.C.'s terrorist arm, has never condemned his own organisation's indiscriminate terrorism against civilians, collaborators and those that did not toe the party line. All this brutality Mandela and the A.N.C. learnt from Yasir Arafat, according to both Arcane and Angela.

Arcane's life has been one of evolution with one emotional building block from the present placed on top of another from his past, whilst Angela's previous life, the one she has crossed over from, she has camouflaged out of sight to everyone but herself. She can never return to her roots as there would be no self-recognition. The bureaucratic glare from the racial stamps of status on the white paper hurt the eyes of those sensitive souls of the wrong hue. Angela never tried to avoid that glare. She could never understand those poor specimens who could not stand that spotlight in their eyes. They must be too sensitive, too fragile. Yes, that must be it, she reasoned. She had lost her innocence and more than that, she had lost some sensitivity along the way.

With time, one loses either one's mind or one's body. Angela has so far, kept her body and mind intact, but some element of femininity's maternal empathy has dissipated along the way, especially when it concerns subjugating her enemies. Can she ever give up control to someone else and relax? Yes she can, in her boudoir.

It was in her bed that first night in the cheap hotel that Angela's warmth was exposed. Her touch felt focused and confident. She appeared to be one of the least emotionally hypocritical people I had ever met. From her non-White position in the South African experience, as she lived it as a child, what could she do? If you live alongside a monster there are all sorts of alternative frustrations to choose from, but when you live in the teeth of a giant, you just settle into the jaw as comfortably as possible and do not worry about a thing. She withdrew into her holistic body and infused it with education, inhabited it with sensuality and permeated it with sexuality. In an untenable, 'check-mated' world, she became a pro-activist in looking after herself first and foremost.

This was the last conversation we had in the hotel at three in the morning, before dropping off to sleep in each other's arms:

'Aaron, most say that being good means considering others

before oneself; well then, from that standpoint very few smart people are innocent. I consider it righteous to consider myself first and despicable to feel otherwise.'

'Life is certainly not fair then, with all these despicable people being admired.'

'No, it is this way, in order to keep us humble, because there are so many despicable fiends not incarcerated in jails. It gives thought to the fact that just because you don't have the label 'criminal' attached to you, it doesn't preclude you from being one! It makes you constantly question yourself. There's a lesson in the paradox.'

'Is it not narcissistic?'

'No, it's not narcissistic at all. I do everything initially out of self-interest and then later I'll garner a conviction out of it in order to follow that self-interest through, which might even help others if they're on my radar. But, a beautiful man, no matter how superficial he is, anywhere along that track, has been known to distract me off the path of my conviction.'

'So, I don't distract?'

'No, your penis does.'

'That's your congenital wishful thinking.'

'No, your penis is tangible! Congenital wishful thinking is anything out of the imagination, like God. Wishful thinking ideas should be open to debate. For example, a religion is only as strong as its sense of humour, that it could be wrong.' Angela, stripped of emblems, denuded of ornamentation and bare of inessentials, had lain quite prostrate, facedown upon the bed. I grooved a line of sperm straight down her back, with finger used as pen; a signature, quick-dried and faded desert-white, like ancient bushman art.

Looking out of the hotel's gabled window, Table Mountain had been an awesome sight. A sense of savage isolation had crept over me under the shadow of its peak, yet I also had sensed an air of calm and subtle security prevailing over the city. It is, The Eminence, huge and relatively unchanging that imbues my head with these thoughts. Pain can come and go, the city can rise and fall, people will live, die, centuries will pass, but the mountain will always watch.

Not one bone of contention between us.

8

Let us take the back path, the light load, the least travelled, the dirt road.

Irreverent Reverend Tom Groans

Watch as I, a twenty-year-old White man, leave my parked car and cross the road in this formally Coloured neighbourhood. Now, as I stand on the white, broken line in the middle of that road waiting for a truck to pass, I feel the connection between the warm, tarred road and the tepid soles of my boots. The heat gathering within me pushes the excess sweat out of my pores and into my dampening clothing, particularly under the armpits and the small of my back. Glittering beads of sweat perch on my exposed skin, waiting to run off or evaporate into the dry, hot air. I yield to the drought-coaxed wind and stand with a resigned stillness.

Now watch the stray dog standing alongside me on the white, broken line in the middle of the road. I am oblivious of the animal's presence. Consider, as I stride onto the kerb and into the café. The café is called 'The Flame'. The outside of the double-storied, steep-roofed, turreted and gothic-influenced building is painted with swirling kaleidoscopic, Van Gogh-like brush strokes. This flamboyant façade seems to be attacking the very blandness of claustrophobic, suburban life. This particular urban life is both the breeding ground for mahatmas as well as monsters.

This building with the savage, artistic grace of its frontage is the visionary outcast's hallucinated crossroad, their exit out of philistine, middle-class 'main-street'. Beyond its portal and on stepping over the threshold into the room's interior-delinquency, drugs and sex mingle with beatniks, politics, bebop, and rock and roll. The whole room embraces and subverts the embodiment of the Victorian way, where its visual lavishness is leavened by a decadent, Pagan downslide. Hard materials and strong colours give a sense of immoral purpose. There is a collision of two worlds – good God and bad God. Meanwhile, you can just lose yourself in its eccentric bombast, merely for its own sake.

Teen angst fractures culture.

9

When the worms come out of the woodwork, they're nasty and they strut your stuff and no matter how much they've eaten of you, they can never get enough.
Irreverent Reverend Tom Groans

There is a high-pressure system over the ocean, nearly a mile away. Its cool, high winds draw me languidly into the café. The sound of anti-establishment, cult hero Sixto Rodrigues singing 'I wonder', a song about casual sex, is heard emanating from the boisterous room. Rodrigues's voice and the sounds of the revellers inside seem to collide into each other with crude discord. The noise has a cutting edge that ricochets around in tangled form. The room is a pressure-cooker at the point of over-bubbling. Suddenly there is movement before me. Someone has been spun in my direction. A tall, blonde female staggers sideways towards me. Her head has snapped back as a result of a blow. I shake my head. The blonde-haired woman looks almost identical to Angela. The resemblance is startling. Her eyes search in my direction. Her refined, straight nose is cut and bleeding. Her blouse is ripped down the centre and blood has dripped onto her exposed breasts. I run forward with slow reflexes but her legs buckle and she collapses out of my reach which breaks my stride as I trip, tumbling over her. I was too slow to arrive. I feel suspended in space and time.

I hear a loudly, slurred, distorted female voice somewhere above us.

'Don't you fucking act White to me!'

The rough feminine voice spits in our direction as we lie on the wooden floor. Her message is intended for the girl intertwined between my legs. I turn over, trying to rise, and peer towards the direction of the voice only to catch the back of a skirt as it vanishes out the door of the café and into the daylight. Gone!

Within an increasingly alienating framework, I feel removed from the scene, like an onlooker viewing a macabre painting. We help each other to our feet and I look into her eyes. The uncanny resemblance to Angela is truly amazing.

'Do you know someone called Angela?' I ask.

'No.' Her answer is a little too quick and too adamant. 'The Mixed-Race whore that hit me was drunk! The Coloureds keep coming back to this area, to sell and buy drugs,' she says with a shrug and a weary smile. She offers me no name and abruptly leaves the café, dissolving into the encroaching darkness outside.

A patron dressed in naval uniform approaches me, explaining, 'The whore was annoyed that the District has been declared a White area with dozens of Whites moving in.'

The expulsion in District Six is profound and immediate. The severance is as complete as an amputation. The incision is severe. Nerves are exposed. Purging with a pen's stroke is like a bureau dealing with livestock. In reality, South Africa is a country where one's colour is carefully weighed and measured.

Dreams beget reality and nightmares do as well.

10

Magic is a comfortable bird, soaring in its own space above the herd.

Irreverent Reverend Tom Groans

I had entered this locale in order to enquire about the address of my new home on the outskirts of District Six. I ask the café's owner about Napier Street and he tells me that I am where I should be. I return to my car. There are no lights in the entire quiet neighbourhood as I drive up the empty street in silence. In the moonlight, cobblestones stare back at me like prying beast's eyes.

After travelling for less than thirty seconds, my flickering headlights strike a T-junction at the top of the hill; its bright beams rivet like jail spotlights on the embankment ahead. I am lost in the middle of what was slum-land. There are no visible numbers on the dirty, brown shacks and renovated, white-washed houses. There is a hallowed beauty in the decay.

Turning the car around, I park it alongside a well-worn kerb. What the hell? I will get out and look, I say to myself. The cool darkness envelops me with its mist.

There is a silence and it speaks.

11

The proof of the puddle is in the stepping.
Irreverent Reverend Tom Groans

I have left my car and having verified that I am at the correct address. I have ascended a few steps from street level and approach the front door of a house. I knock. Knocking! Knocking! There is fever for life in my knocking as the area has a reputation for being dangerous, especially at night. The door does not budge. I knock again and again. There is only silence. Then the post-box lid attached to the door shivers as a draught runs through the house. At last, footsteps are heard approaching from inside. Excessive knocking has paid off. Thumping footsteps are heard on the floorboards. They are slow with a heavy tread like those of a drunk without shoes. The footsteps are gliding, sounding off the stone corridor and away from the muted colours of the wall, flowing into my ears. It must be a long passageway. I bend down and peek through the post-box slit by lifting its lid. What do we have here? Left! Right! Left! Right! The motion that keeps time with the church bell that has started to chime the hour. Bong! Left! Bong! Right! Bong! Left! Right!

I take a closer look through the post-box. My field of vision through the gap is of two hairy legs and a barely flaccid penis flanked on either side by two enormous testicles. They are bearing down on me from my vantage point. I clinch my eyes and quickly stand upright, dropping the post-box lid. I become aware of a key turning. The knob rotates and the door is unlocked to the final stroke of the church bell. Bong!

Abruptly I am exposed, blocking the passageway to the outside, moonless night. There is a soft mist with no light to illuminate my face. The mute darkness behind me has allotted me cover to avoid whatever dangers the area might render. In front of me the scenery has subsided. The door has been withdrawn and is now replaced by a long, narrow stone corridor at the end of which stands yet another door, but smack in the middle of this setting stands the owner of the penis.

'Aaron?' The voice is a foot above me and his features come into focus. Above me is a rectangular face with a high crown of long, dark hair on top of a tall, thin, angular body. The lines running down on either side of his nose and around his wide mouth are deep for a man only in his mid-thirties. There is nothing frivolous about him and there is something sombre about his appearance. He has a twinkle in his wide-set eyes. There is a dirty yellow tinge to his white skin that could be an indication of irritability, or the exaggerated colouring of cartoon criminality. It could also be the light seeping from a dusty, faded light bulb. His long, thinly muscled arms dangle loosely at his sides, hanging slightly beyond where his penis rests. There is a slight stoop to his bony shoulders as one would get from many hours piano-ing over a typewriter.

'Hello.' My voice crackles.

'Welcome. I'm Fredrik. Folks call me F. I live downstairs. Please come in. Let me take your suitcase.' He smiles in a melancholy way. His voice is sonorously deep and almost lazy. He is an Afrikaner, a white man of Dutch heritage and has only a slight guttural thickness to his English. 'Follow me. Your rooms are down the corridor, through the end door and into the courtyard. You then walk up the flight of stairs, which leads up to a balcony that overlooks the city. On either side of the balcony are your two rooms.'

Following F through his house into the courtyard, I am aware of the starless film of night.

In my room I scribble into my diary the events of the day. I hunker down upon my mattress that lies on the wooden floor and contemplate the details of what has happened so far. One's present focus may in many circumstances have a tunnel-vision effect, blowing things out of all proportion, which at other times would only procure a minor place in the circumstance. For example, here in South Africa, skin colour, which is mere pigmentation, has an immense influence in procuring one's end. In this reality, though, culture is just as significant as this colouration in terms of the attitudes and behaviour of both the viewer and those viewed. F's testicles and penis, which were bearing down on me when I first peered through the post-box, are not disproportional to the bigger story, because they are right now in my consciousness of living in the moment, the only big story and the only picture show in town.

Everyone is to the manor born; the question is, knight or pawn?

12

Today's tears will distort tomorrow's features.
Irreverent Reverend Tom Groans

I am standing in the bathroom facing the mirror; my past bundled into this framework. I stare back and try to recall how I got here. I try to accost my memory and turn it, according a new perspective, a retrospective on how I got here, from there and who I really am. Should I be here in this house belonging to someone who was forcefully dislocated from it? How do I correlate the level of my wrongdoing in this stolen place?

I think there are levels of comparatives on a gradient, from horrendous and bad, to the acme of good, philanthropic. Where do I stand in this hierarchy? Well, I am only a little altruistic. I justify my being here by impressing upon myself that I will write a book about the transformation going on and show its dehumanising effects on the few remaining Coloureds before they leave. So what? In order to write a paper, I participate in fucking up a person's life by joining in the stampede to chase them out of here? Maybe, if I tear at chains, something will be rendered? This is my rationale. The question is, am I a link, or a chink in this chain of armour? This paradox is not easy, but I am far from being a martyr or hero, for with all my convictions, it is remarkable how rapidly this stolen place has risen to a position of home in my head. I have not raised an objection, only an eyebrow.

I request further instructions from the consensus within me. Malefactor, benefactor, transgressor, villain, paragon of honesty, scoundrel and rogue could be any of my titles, or possibly an amalgamation. One has also to be of two minds: microscope and telescope. How do I see the forest and the tree?

The conservative Whites I meet do not trust the Blacks, suspecting they will, in turn, act undemocratically towards the Whites were they to ever gain control. My response is that this paranoia must be based on history attributed to an issue over 125 years ago when White leader, Piet Retief and his men, including his son, were murdered by the Zulu king, Dingane. In 1838, despite warnings, Retief thought he could negotiate with the Zulu king, to secure permanent boundaries for the County Natal Settlement, in a prior agreed exchange for returning cattle that had earlier been stolen from Dingane by a rival Bantu Black tribe. A deed of cession was indeed signed and witnessed between Retief and Dingane. The Zulu king then invited Retief and his party for a feast, whereupon they were hoodwinked into leaving their weapons aside. Dingane's soldiers were ordered to capture Retief and his men who, caught unawares, were butchered. The undamaged deed of agreement from Retief's leather purse was later found.

These diehard traditionalists would conclude that I am an apologist for the Black wrongs done in 1838, which I am not. I sense there is a defensive alliance taking place with these threatened Whites, as I switch position, at least in their minds, from fellow White to Kaffir-Black-lover. I sense their King Dingane projection onto me as a turncoat has unconscious reverberations going back over 100 years.

I scan quickly, now that you have unravelled.

13

The Devil also loves the person, no matter what the crime.

Irreverent Reverend Tom Groans

It is a bright, but cool day and at the bottom of the hill I have bought a newspaper. I have it placed under my arm. I lower my head into the gusting wind that originates from the crest of Table Mountain as I walk up to my house. At the first cross-street, 50 yards ahead of me, a few Coloured youths are involved in the start of a fight. Not all the Coloureds have been moved out yet. These boys have been drinking heavily, having come out of an illegal brew-house, a 'shebeen', situated down a long, narrow passageway between the houses near the corner of this particular street. What is it with this area and fighting?

Two groups of boys are involved in the conflict, edging closer to each other for first strikes, for dominance, circling like scavengers, cursing and spitting venom, gnashing their teeth, curling their upper lips and swearing.

Before the battle commences, a police siren is heard. In an instant everyone is out of sight. The strong survive and the weak perish, exactly as within one's own family. It is tough to be good-hearted when life offers little hope. These unruly kids are definitely not an endangered species.

I notice that one of the kids, known as Deadmouse – a dark-skinned, seventeen year old who lives somewhere up the street from me – has separated from the others, making it appear as if he and I are together. Doing so, he has distanced himself from the earlier conflict. I have engaged in quick, polite exchanges with him a number of times before at the corner store.

'Dis is no treasure island, brotha!' he jokes in broken English that resonates with a gravely Afrikaans twang.

'What's happening?' I ask.

We both continue sauntering up the road alongside each other.

'Oh, just gang shit! Usual kak, but we all frustrate here, what the fok wit you whiteys movin' in and all that! Not poes cool.'

'Yeah,' I say and mean it and I do feel a smidgen guilty.

'Check wot I'm takin' bout. Wot's happening is not level, man. It's a big mind-fok. It's just that deep. We're been fokken murdered in dis country by motherfokken shadowy serpents, who jus movin' us outa here. Jus like dat!'

'Yeah,' I repeat. I am guilty as charged.

'John Lennon was no walrus, an David Bowie was no spaceman, but this government says dey is right, and dey is, because dey have right of way. It vewwy real. Fok da haters. We rad as fok!'

Good point made is what I think and I just nod.

Deadmouse is on an assertive roll and takes a hand-rolled marijuana joint from behind his ear, lowers it to his lips, lights up and presses on. 'Shit is dope to escape, man! Not poes-cool. We need to put handbrake on di fokken rollacoaster, an spank da faggots. Afrikaans is language dat should be banned, excep' it's my language.' He gives a belly laugh, having noticed the irony of his statement. We both laugh. He is inhaling deeply on the spliff, walking and talking and looks like a steam engine with smoke from his lungs exiting through his nose and mouth with every word he speaks.

As we near his street, he spits out, 'Who give a shit bout skin pigment? There gonna be hectic futuristic bloody scene soon! You ma se poesfok!'

A friend of his from one of the houses we are passing puts his head out of the window and addresses me, but I do not understand what he is saying in Afrikaans.

Deadmouse answers his friend with, 'Hey, Spastacase, shut da trap, faggit!' then continues to address me, ignoring his friend's response. 'Ders some hoodrat ghetto-shit right here. Der be good, straight neighbours alongside old perverts who will buy drugs fo yo hot underage chicks, an yu can buy weed fwom every fourth house in da neighbourhood. Whatta household is dis, but tis my hold. Dis is fokken farm for seizures. Pleaseeeee have a lookkkkk I tryin' to make sense of dis. My swag is still fly. I try make sense of dis bow-wow shit. Jus' bunch of lunatics suckin' da life force out of da oneness. Black, white, yellow, red, stupiiid, yu come from da same planet, fool, same shelf. Jys all het a monster kak gevang! I mus' go, man. Ciao!' With that goodbye, Deadmouse turns down into a narrow alley and disappears.

I am practically at the apex of the hill, astonished at how a distraction like an affray can enable time to sprint ahead. Maybe it is within the human constitution to be at loggerheads with those outside one's own milieu, so as to assess one's psychological and territorial edges by testing those boundaries. Possibly this friction comes from something more pathological, like according those outside our group the myth of being all bad, instead of attributing to them the positive myth that the archetype must surely possess. Maybe the myth of reconciliation is an incorrect myth? Maybe some 'things' cannot be reconciled?

Completing the circle of my thoughts, I return to the tenet of a scapegoat, that maybe we do hanker for scapegoats. With a common threat we affiliate with others who are similarly threatened by a mutual enemy, a sort of 'love through hate' occurrence.

With all things said, it is a delicate balancing act to see things in a healthy perspective.

Like a mutually shared salt, rubbed into our own wounds.

14

What dangerous, idiosyncratic people you have skirted with, oscillating on their whims.

Irreverent Reverend Tom Groans

The system can decide to change an area previously designated 'Coloured' to one designated 'White' the same way number plates are changed. Let me give an example: we are now in the process of changing our number plates yet again. Originally, ironically enough, we had the old white-on-black plates. Later came black-on-yellow, then different colours for different provinces and now it is a plate with a background picture for each province. When the traffic department complains that the picture of the elephant obscures the numbers on the Eastern Cape, we will most probably be forced to change them again.

Life here shifts rapidly.

Here is another example of South African logic: a church in a town called Bethel, which was not a member of the ruling Dutch Reform Church, was re-allocated the number 666 by the government.

Labels are nearly always attached to packaging.

15

Life is a test to find areas of earnestness.
Irreverent Reverend Tom Groans

The mountain stands mute and imposing in front of me as I discard my army boots over the side of the balcony and into the alley, which runs alongside the property. These boots I have been carrying around as excess luggage since I was discharged from the army over a year ago. It is the same alleyway that leads to the Shebeen, the illegal brew-house. Someone will find the sturdy boots useful. My specific aversion to army boots lies not merely in their heavy and uncomfortable weight, but it is a masked expression of some deeper memory conjured up from the past. The aversion is a symptom brought forward from my stint in the South African military. That time period is memorialised as a collage of anxiety and physical pain. When I consider my military experience as I do now while discarding these boots, the collage is visible in my mind's eye as an agitation. One would have to live here in the Police State to comprehend that the military is itself an autonomy: a Police State within a Police State. If you are singled out for punishment for whatever reason, no court of law will come to your aid. You can be detained indefinitely without trial. To be White and anti-government is treason.

The South African Government's success in the subjugation of its population is achieved through a carefully constructed demonising of those outside the ruling party's common interest. Its success at implementing this subjugation is through its fetish for secrecy. Everyone must keep their particular nose to their own particular grindstone and concentrate their minds on their own particular business. It is dangerous for anyone who does not adhere to this code of silence. The imagined, but seldom seen, ever-hearing ear of silence and secrecy listens, always watching, always telling who is included, what is to be excluded and what is to be prohibited. We are in a two-way mirror where we are looking at ourselves and they are looking at us. We sit in silence, wrapped in our passivity or at best, we huddle down in our ineffective and passive resistance.

Now I look down at the two boots that have landed perfectly upright, left boot on the left, right boot on the right, as though carefully placed. In the army they certainly seemed out of place on my feet, as I should not have been there in the first place. As a teenage conscript, the military's intense reality, with its physical punishment and verbal abuse, hit an existential chord. It was not the physicality of it, per se, but rather that question I had never asked myself: what am I fighting for?

It was there in the military that the boy in me morphed into a man overnight. I could not abandon this reality, like switching radio channels into flights of escape. It demanded maturity of spirit to deal with where and what I would become. The reservoir of openness was now, in the military, suddenly frozen by anxiety and by some inner mettle on my part. For the first time, I questioned the orders I was to obey. I basically refused to follow those orders by marching incorrectly at first and then by just refusing to do anything after a period of time. I had already put up with three months of harsh basic training. Two weeks before the end, after the initial mastering of weaponry and self-defence, something happened that sent my life spiralling downwards.

*

We were eating in the soldier's mess when a very loud commotion, screams and cursing, bellowed from the kitchen. I abandoned my table and sprinted down the aisle through the swing doors and into the kitchen, up to the bain-marie: a 3-foot high, metal, hot food container that separated the kitchen from the serving line. On the kitchen side of the bain-marie, in an area where the eating utensils were stacked and in front of the giant dishwasher, Head Chef, Flight Sergeant Libber, was assaulting a cowering Black man with his notoriously large pocket-watch chain, striking the cornered man's head and arms. Streaks of blood were oozing from the man's exposed flesh. Libber's grey eyes were hard, menacing and measured. Libber's eyes were glinting crosswise, as if focused on the tip of his nose. He continued to brain the man, unburdening himself of his frustrations on Amos, the Zulu dishwasher, his rage striking terror for all to see. He was a perfect sadist, devoid of any talent and coupled with an indifference to life in general. Authority allowed him to impose his percolating aggression against subordinates. Catching flies on the fly with his empty right hand, while twirling the chain of his watch around his left second finger, as he walked across the kitchen, was Libber's favourite pastime.

As the assault continued, Flight Sergeant Libber dispatched at least twenty more scorching strokes upon the unfortunate Amos, before I, having hurdled over the bain-marie, came between the two of them, hoping to appeal to some compunctious sense that Amos had suffered enough. As Libber raised his arm to strike yet again and because I was between the two men, his chain unintentionally struck my head. Instinctively I defended myself by blocking with an outstretched right forearm, having swivelled my hips to the right with the aforementioned block, then immediately, I rotated my pelvis back to its squared-on position. With all my might, I simultaneously dispatched an accelerated, straight, downward fist directly into Libber's jaw. The startled man cursed feebly for an instant, staggered back for a brief second then slid unconsciously to the kitchen floor.

Assaulting a superior officer in defence of a Black man is tantamount to treason, so I was in serious trouble. I was arrested and immediately incarcerated. The following day found me transferred to a remote camp near the Northern border and 'confined to barracks'. There I joined fifteen other problematic recruits, each indicted for some felonious crime against the State.

Being a 'deviant', like hitting a fellow soldier for whatever the reason and being the conscientious objector that I was, *vis-à-vis* the military in Apartheid, was a naïve posture of rebellion. Naïve because they could have kept me locked away indefinitely. This struck like an undeniable truth and again, I questioned the system into which I had been born. With this reality check, I knew that I could never follow the same patterns again, no matter how harmful the consequences would be.

The bubble of my naïvety burst. This was my baptism of fire. Getting rid of my boots now, is the first step of my moving on.

Nothing can offset solitude.

16

She is wise beyond her ears, for she feels more than she hears.

Irreverent Reverend Tom Groans

I have climbed the stairway from the white-washed courtyard and am standing on the landing that is a bridge between my two rooms overlooking the cobbled courtyard below. Turning right towards the room that is my bedroom, I notice a small, pink, dome-like shape, barely visible and peeking up over the top of the flat plateau that is my bedroom roof. The shape protrudes upwards, perched like a rounded balloon above the roof.

At first I am uncertain as to what I see, but it becomes clearer after focusing that a breast is what I have in view. In fact, the protrusion is two protrusions, a pair of female breasts seen sideways, so that the two nipples are perfectly aligned. A nude Angela is sprawled horizontally on her back with a seeming attitude of adulterated abandon. Table Mountain, crowned with a thin layer of white cloud, is mirrored in her dark glasses. Salvador Dali could have painted this scene. She is pink-white and she is raking her long, thin fingers through her blonde hair. Her body is fully ablaze in sunlight and I inhale her scent. I assimilate her features from the tiny beads of sweat on her forehead, past her flushed and fiery red lips and past the graceful detours her legs take from her groin down to the tip of her toes. I repress the impulse to seize the moment and slide down beside her, to trace my fingertips from her ribcage to the point of her nipple.

'Don't stand with idle hands. Rub some olive oil into my shins, please,' she murmurs. She is clairvoyant. This is not a body of innocence, is what I think. I sense something narcotic, some fatal grain in her today. I bend and pour the olive oil from a bottle into my palms and start rubbing it into her lower legs.

'Ah! This feels wonderful. A-a-a-aah.'

Angela's respiration has slowed. Her broad mouth in this light has the facial expression of someone who feels superior. She has a half-cocked smile that is not quite a smile. It might be a smirk? Her face alludes to possible vice or lack of tack that one might see before conjugal intimacy.

She casually remarks, 'I introduced myself to F and told him that I'm your friend and that I'd wait for you up here on the roof.'

She radiates sensual comfort, but this loving feeling emanating from her proximity diminishes in proportion to one's physical distance from her. She appears more austere with an air of severity the further out one is from her centre and closer one is to her remote periphery. One can feel her ruthlessness and there is a dichotomy about her. One would never get jaded enjoying her, as nothing about her would ever turn stale. One could never have enough of her to receive the numbing effects of saturation.

Manoeuvring her sunglasses onto her broad, deep forehead with its clear, pore-less skin, she clears her throat. She has been drinking beer from a can and is smoking a joint. Her voice abruptly breaks the silence, but there is no movement of her head in my direction.

'Want a spliff?' she coos, exhaling.

'No thanks.'

'Nothing? I'm not into tripping for getting high's sake, but I can tell you that it impacts my reading, for sure. It lets me draw connections between divergent ideas.'

'Which means?'

I expect the talk to go deeper.

'Tripping gives me serious focus.'

'What are you talking about?'

'I'm thinking that everything's somehow decreed,' she says. Her ideas are ricocheting around her head.

'So how can we be accountable for Apartheid if it's decreed that it's just the non-Whites' time to be discriminated against?' I question.

'Maybe it's our time to suffer, but you will be punished for your cruelty,' she reasons and sits up on her blue towel, legs crossed. She swivels to face me and asserts, 'This smoke is my sacrament. It stops your heart from breaking. My dad says the same thing about playing the blues.' She coughs then inhales deeply, letting the smoke stream out of her nostrils. 'If you have freedom to choose, you can choose to not be responsible, because you allow Big Brother to override you. You can sit on this fence you have been standing on, jumping off every so often when it suits you.'

I stretch the muscles of my back. She looks at me and reveals, 'I cannot feel the same way you do, because although I pass for White, I'm still a Coloured. I refuse to become closed down. If this government were a woman, she would not be orgasmic, but would be hypertrophied and in a state of inflexibility. I need to breathe! Truth is like food and truth is like drugs; it opens you.'

Angela has a charismatic effect that makes me forget myself. Such is the magnetic power of her appearance and yet, after that first energetic wave has washed over me, she reverses the attention back to herself in a kind of backwash. Watching her, one might easily be distracted, but I am listening.

She believes in replacing anger and violence with Karma – the Karma Sutra that is – but she will resort to violence if necessary. She lives spontaneously with all the vicissitudes of life, now that all the calculations are behind her, that is, until she needs to calculate again. From an early age she rejected piety for ecstasy and Tantric Yoga.

'Sex also opens one!' she asserts

'What's your point?'

'Fucking doesn't need a point. Fucking just is!' She pauses, taking a drag from the stub of a joint, inhaling deeply and continues. 'Like good grass, fucking is there to blow one's mind, but there has to be a mind to blow in the first place.'

'What do you mean?'

Angela regards me through the thick haze of marijuana smoke, undeterred by my interruption and simply replies, 'So that one may change what's become stagnant, Aaron.'

Marijuana gives her a free hand to trust her intuition.

She immediately rolls and lights another joint, carrying on with the conversation.

'When something becomes predictable, it contracts the mind because there's no growth.' She takes another drag and offers me a hit.

Accepting the joint, I inhale deeply into the bottom of my lungs and then declare emphatically, 'Even God throws spanners into our works, to challenge our concept of Him. He doesn't want to be pigeon-holed.'

'That's why He's a She sometimes!' she chides.

Angela tells me that I capitulate to this intolerable government because the bad guys like me.

'You, Aaron, have been pigeon-holed.'

'I do acquiesce somewhat to the government on certain issues, but if I'm going to live here, I'm not going to throw my life away for anything.'

She laughs at that, remarking, 'You're funny.'
I wasn't joking, though.

*Camouflaged in the dense foliage of passivity, one can retreat
further; in amongst the branches.*

17

People get the tyrants they deserve, for the multitude's silence, which is a weakness, will preserve.

Irreverent Reverend Tom Groans

I find myself talking with amiable, naked F in his downstairs study where there are papers, clothes and tapes strewn about the floor. His voice is deep and smooth and is charming with a casual nonchalance. There is no vestige of doubt in his pragmatic aura.

F is not moral, nor amoral, but morally eclipsed. He is able to turn a blind eye to other people's dilemmas, not out of ignorance, but because he becomes blinded towards anything that would disturb his calm. An erudite and solitary man, he is enamoured with aesthetic beauty, yet there is something emotionally missing, for what he sees as beauty is a substitute for bonding with people. He can intrigue against anyone who interferes with his aims and not out of enmity or dislike for them, but because they are in the way of his ambitions.

He sucks in on his joint and tells me that marijuana acts as a panacea to connect between different ideas. Gesturing to make his point, F philosophises, 'Ag, man, when I love or hate or feel, I don't really need to smoke trees. It's when I'm indifferent and need some adrenalin that I reach for the smoke. Ganja is about processing what you are already familiar with, but don't try to learn anything new under its spell and don't try and explain anything under its influence. Leave that to good, old vodka.'

F sounds like Angela.

His study is like an esoteric bookshop, shelves filled with an extraordinary range of subjects, from magic and astrology to phrenology and Oriental medicine. I was told beforehand that the house is a haunt to an extraordinary range of people, from serious arcane seekers of knowledge, to mad, bad, manic-depressive psychotherapists, prostitutes and Mahatma-Guru types. The house has a multi-lingual stream of visitors constantly flocking in and out, from professors to self-promoters, from ballerinas to bondage seekers. There are always jugs of spiked punch, wine and fruit juices on the table next to the rye bread and cheeses. The smell of lamb or chicken rich in garlic permeates the room, aromas of which are absorbed into the fabric of the rich, velvet curtains, mingling there with the marijuana.

Sexual anecdotes are often heard being regaled and wafted through the house. Walking into F's pad is like watching a kind of hallucination effortlessly lived. Boredom has made F's house necessary, as it is a diversion from ennui and depression, with its gathering together of beautiful, interesting people blended with a kind of blasphemy with taste.

F talks about many things as the evening wears on. He is the main subject of his tales. His story contains a number of key elements, foremost amongst them is that he is a gifted writer whose writings are lesser known than they deserve, though he is a successful editor of a right-wing political newspaper. Is there a paradox? He is editor of a racist, right-wing newspaper, yet always naked in his home even in front of strangers.

F is a person who, both morally and emotionally, anaesthetises himself. Oblivious to others' shock at his almost constant nudity is how he has numbed himself to their reactions.

He tells me that at an early age his mother was uncaring

and would constantly reprimand him. His father, he imparts, was subdued, depressed and insipid. Both parents are now dead. His capacity to feel was dampened as a child and even today he can only feel through visual and physical hyperbole. Romantic theatrical productions with its symphonic grandeur, or a mass of lighted candles around a bath are all romantic substitutes for love, though he also emphasises he prefers hard sex where there is some pain involved.

F was bedevilled as a child by withheld love, but compensated somewhat by the care he received from his Xhosa maid. As an adult he has difficulty expressing emotions, except when brilliantly stoned on grass. He is a physical and sexual force, he affirms, rather than one defined as mental or romantic. In spite of his intelligence or because of it, he always strives for simplicity in relationships, which is his one genuine trait.

He does not hint at anything. He gets right to the point, the sexual point, which is as close as he can get to a sense of intimacy. There is no deeper or binding commitment for him. He says that the physical act of sex, with the sensual pleasures, allows him to lose himself and take on his lover, just as a jockey takes on a horse. It is all for the ride.

I overheard F say to someone on the phone that equality is the opiate of the unequal and that it is a myth, because nothing is equal in reality. He alleged further, ignoramuses should not have a say in, or vote on, something of which they are uninformed. I heard him summarise that those who are not fearful of authority will be perceived as a potential threat to those in power.

Question: Is F a government agent?

Answer: I have no idea. I am sceptical and will not be able to be candid with him.

F saunters to the kitchen, returning with two cups of coffee, asking, 'What about you, Aaron?'

'Me?'

I have been asked to answer for myself. Where do I start? What should I tell him? What do I want him to know?

'My dear, Aaron, the social anthropologist in me is finding it difficult to ascertain why you're so tense?'

He extracts a joint from behind his right ear, which is another contradiction, as doing drugs in this country is a very serious criminal offence. He offers me a hit. I shake my head.

'I finished the army,' I reply and continue, 'Now I play the blues harp.'

'What about your first eighteen years?'

I do not wish to give a report on my past to him, so I remain silent with a shrug. Silence holds the floor as F takes another drag on the joint and says, 'Come on, you English are just as uptight as us Afrikaners. I used to teach Italian to English students during my university breaks, in Italy. I started off teaching grownups. Italian is an extraordinary language. They say it's easy to learn, but its full of complicated grammar and stuff.'

'What's the point you're making?' I interrupt.

'I decided to stop teaching the grownups because they kept asking me grammatical questions so I started teaching younger and younger children and ended up teaching children so young they wouldn't ask me anything. Then I found that sometimes they'd cry. Anyway, I'd give them a cuddle or pat them on the head. One day an English woman turned up and she said that it's disgusting what you are doing, touching that child! A few days later I was with a small child on the beach who I had been told to look after. Could I look after little Maria, or whatever her name was? Anyway, I did. The parents didn't come back when they should have. They have no sense of time over there. It was getting cold and she was shivering, so I got the towel and this woman went past...'

'Not the same English woman?'

'Yes, the same English woman and she screamed like a

deranged hyena, "YOU CAN'T DO THAT!" You know? Everybody was looking around. I was only doing what the Italians do, rubbing vigorously this part and that part of the head, hair and body, etcetera.'

'Maybe your mistake was that you shouldn't have done it with an erection?'

F laughs and says, 'Yes. I wondered about that. I was at the Royal Academy once and someone had done a picture of a young boy, nude, with his little penis and people were saying, "Ghastly!" It's because people are uncomfortable with their own thoughts. They're hypocrites, especially the English!' F has finished his little speech and settles back into his chair. Pounding is suddenly heard coming from the front door. F leaves, returning with an equally tall, handsome collegian wearing an Oxford University rugby shirt. The collegian has an energetic and open smile and is dressed in swanky jeans and expensive, casual shoes. His gold watch is too extravagant for District Six or any other area. I get the feeling that he is as intelligent as F and just as shallow. He is F's height, but more muscular and cut like a tall cyclist. His large, rounded, green eyes plead superficial sincerity with long eyelashes that liken him to Bambi. He extends his right hand towards me, as F makes the introduction.

'Aaron, this is Russell. He's an archaeology lecturer from Oxford here on holiday. He will be staying with me for a few months.' He reaches for Russell's backpack. 'Excuse us, Aaron. I'll be back in a short while.'

Russell has clear, un-sunned skin that one would ascribe to anyone else but an archaeologist.

They leave.

I inspect the room, which is furnished with a well-worn Persian rug, a couch and bookcases along all the walls filled with books by many eminent writers of the past. Three comfortable easy chairs complete the seating arrangements except for large cushions strewn about the floor. On the walls are Picasso prints from his Blue Period and watercolour paintings by lesser-known South African artists.

To my surprise F re-enters the room wearing a casual brown suit. It is the first time that I have seen him fully clothed. His aftershave overrides the familiar fresh-paint and marijuana smell of the house. With a glance, he announces, 'See you later, if you'll be awake. I work at the newspaper most evenings until midnight except for weekends. Bye!'

I finish my coffee, take my cup back to the kitchen, switch off the light and return to my room above the courtyard. I noticed the door to F's room was ajar and that lying stretched out in the middle of the bed, gently snoring was Russell, completely nude. I have this second realised that his is the only bed in the house. I sleep on a mattress upstairs. I drift on through the courtyard and up the stairs towards my room.

The house, in Angela's words, has come of age, hatched in adolescence on the South African national fault-line. It is the perfect distillation of our time and place and stands at a pivotal moment in world history where everything is moving towards liberalism, except here in South Africa. Here, it is reversing. This dwelling has adjoined the fleet steaming ahead towards laissez-faire, with its crew of hippies, beatniks, bebop and rock and roll. This house is a junction, of sorts. It is that fault-line where novel ingredients are being mixed together in a vortex that could fracture the Apartheid culture in a national nervous breakdown. Here, sexual freedom and civil rights take a hallucinated lunge at convention and its morality and this house has the mesmerising attributes of the perverse, defiant hipster. This hipster is now driven to extreme measures not to become a prisoner of the bland century of claustrophobic hypocrisy and the philistine monsters in Pretoria. This house is testament to the frenzied artist committed to live fast in the slow marijuana lane, where the blood vessels are dilated, which in turn lifts moral inhibitions and introduces a sexually responsive state of exotic mind.

Revenge is to strike and conquer.

18

You're always on the edge when looking in; you're
Life's pet, you're being kept!
Irreverent Reverend Tom Groans

I am awakened by a shuffling sound on the flat roof above my
room. A sound is heard again then a dull thud as something
lands on the wall and bounces onto the balcony just outside
my door. I wait in anxious silence. A slight, cold sweat breaks
out in the small of my back. My imagination is alive to all
contingencies, for this is District Six and the area is dangerous,
especially at night.

The last time I felt such apprehension was in the army, waiting
at night for the footsteps to sound on the gravel path just
outside our group's bungalow, waiting for the order to be barked
that yet again, another irregular inspection is to take place, an
inspection that was never satisfactory.

Bringing my memory back to the present, jolted out of
reflecting on my past by the noise outside, I wait. I wait to
identify the sound that has just bounced off my roof. Who
could it be? What could it be? The darkness makes no decisions,
nor do I make any move. My eyes are drawn tightly shut.
Silence pulsates within me.

Flashback! I take myself back in time to the army, when a

sandstorm caused by the perpetual motion of our constant running had finally settled down. When the running had run its course we were brought to a halt by Disciplinary Officer Corporal Blank's barking order. The dust had settled back on the ground of the large red square, our marching ground, un-affectionately known as the Sahara.

Corporal Blank then shouted in Afrikaans that we were to stand still until he returned. No doubt his hoarse voice was the result of screaming for hours. His voice had sounded more vomit than vocal, more devouring than delivering. At the introduction of our small group to Corporal Johannes Demetrius Blank, the nine-month epoch of his absolute control over us commenced. Every day began with a torrent of curses from his menacing, tight-lipped mouth and everyday he plunged us into a relentless grip of ominous unease and constant, superfluous running in never-ending circles to nowhere.

Corporal Blank was a morose and frightening thirty-year-old man, not because his size was menacing, but because of his appearance. He possessed floating irises, where the whites were visible underneath the pupils, which was disconcerting, as he never looked you in the eye.

He was always finding fault with our struggling, incongruous band of miscreants in order to punish us by repeating the pointless, dehumanising drills, which were punctuated by punches to the body and kicks to the legs. He was darkly suntanned and of medium height, with lean muscular legs. His very low brow sat between two tiny ears and above a thin, long nose, which extended like a narrow balcony above a pencil-thin moustache that ran the full length of his thinly curled-up lip. Corporal Blank very often introduced the authority of his metre-long Malacca bamboo cane to us, in retribution for some real or imagined wrongdoing on our part. If one member was at fault, the whole band would suffer with brutal strikes on our tired legs, our torsos and even at times, our heads.

From his youth, Johannes Demetrius Blank suffered repeated humiliation by his father because he had neither the academic brains for higher education nor the physical prowess to play sport at a competitive level. This made him morbidly proud never to help anyone struggling because he had been humbled by one of his own parents too often. With his softer emotions numbed and calloused, his aggressive instincts were honed and sharpened. Blank's defiantly rude personality had taken hold early, in the shadow of his father's infuriatingly wilful example. Any infringement by Johannes Blank in his own house brought severe retribution from his father's leather belt, which instilled in him a dread of any personal transgression. Later, as a disciplinary officer, Corporal Blank would mimic his father's behaviour, passing on this manner of conducting oneself onto those he took under his own, dreadful wing.

Blank's father had always told him that he would grow up to be a good for nothing and he would later prove his father wrong by being good at something, which was instilling fear and loathing into the eyes and ears of those unfortunate enough to fall under his terrible charge. He was, as such, an unhappy, unloved and unlovable person, a servile self-seeker without any introspection, staying self-questioning from his personality to stave off any self-criticism. He had always received more criticism than he could take.

Making sure that we were never cohesive as a unit was the key to containing and exploiting us. They did it by making the whole group suffer because of the weakest link. They made sure that the blame was distributed equally amongst all of us. They were determined that no individual became the designated scapegoat of the company for too long. We remained isolated, each from the other, the objective, essentially to break our spirits and to prevent a coordinated rebellion. In fact, a mutiny would have been useless anyway, as 'Enemies of the State' had, like Mandela, been imprisoned for many years without trial.

A kind of fatalistic euphoria reset our emotional balance once we realised that we had nothing left to lose.

Hysterical laughter was released as a safety valve for us once Blank was out of earshot and it saved us from insanity. This was the spontaneous laughter of the asylum. The authorities wanted to break us so that after so many months of abuse and sleep deprivation, we might confess to what terrorist organisation or anti-government affiliation we might be involved with, if indeed that were the case. I, of course, worked for no one except my own conscience. We were mutual participants in a bizarre production that had gone on for far too long.

The authorities seemed to know what we were doing and what we were saying amongst ourselves every day, so there was almost certainly a spy amongst us. Our days were a monotony of early risings, inspections, curses, rebuking, marching, running, more marching, running, always sweating, running, spitting bile, spitting, saluting, presenting arms, running, always the same distance ahead and burnt brown from the sun, red from the sand, spate of shouts, screams, orders, shouts, heels on heels, lines, circles, triangles, lines incised and punctuated, same stamped earth, heat, humidity, intolerable heat, hunger, anger, tired to the bones, shaken to the ground, always forward, no quiet, no calm, bodies exhausted, boots stamping, boots kicking, boots dusty, bodies twisted, slapping, feet dragging, boots shuffling, shouts cascading around our ears, boots forward, thrusting forward, bleeding toes, bleeding nose, worn boots, worn bodies, over and out!

We felt doomed and under the spell to this vertiginous descent. It seemed that nothing would ever stop. We felt as if we had fallen into a fatalistic mentality where imbalance seemed to reign. We were physically weakened and had morally abdicated ourselves to the bottom of an abyss.

They were always watching us and yet we could still laugh.

Jerry spat at my feet. The brown salivary mass wobbled like jelly at our feet. We laughed at that as well. That was a year ago.

Tonight, here in District Six, there is someone laughing outside my door. I blink, trying to focus in the darkness of the room. There is a knock at the door. A second knock. A third knock. A strong and deliberate knocking is at my door, vibrating in my ears. I light a candle because the electricity is out this evening. I step out of bed and carry myself to the window overlooking the courtyard and balcony, stretching my neck out, peering to my right. Full moon finds the features of a Coloured man of about thirty at my door.

'Yes?'

'Baas, you have maybe a match?'

There is a strong undertone of Afrikaans to his English accent.

'A what?' I am angry but controlled.

'A match, Baas!'

Baas means boss. My visitor is definitely Coloured. I know that I must play this game of his, if indeed it is a game to test me. This is still somewhat their territory.

With caution, I move towards the door, fish knife in hand, sweat in the other. Latch removed. Door opened to toothless smile.

'Toothless' is tall, thin and slightly stooped. Besides the grin, his face is sombre and serious. In a different circumstance and setting he could be the solitary gentleman in the corner of the room, nursing a martini and looking critically at a painting. He is not a mixer, but he penetrates everyone he sees. He is a tragic, suspicious cynic who keeps everything in perspective. Tonight he does not have that kind of potential. Tonight he could be dangerous. His eyes are deep-set and melancholy. He is not an explainer. His lips are thin and pale. He is not the type who complains, just takes in and takes off when he is good and ready.

Toothless notes the fish knife in my hand. My arm is limp

like a dead fish at my side and not really threatening. He keeps the same toothless smile at the sight of it. I give him the entire matchbox, telling him to keep it. He refuses the offer and displays a gummy half-smile. With two disfigured and dirty tobacco-stained fingers, he extracts two matches. They are the only fingers on that hand. He lights a homemade newspaper cigarette, inhales then exhales over my head. I keep my expression indifferent.

'Dankie, thank you,' he says, then exclaims, 'My name is Tom Groans. I'm the Irreverent Reverend, a sinister man, you could say. I've a way and I'm wise. I'm a fly in the sky's no limit. I'm to show you your sin and make a squadron of noise with poise, until this wooden shed you're in groans and moans for the displaced homes. We are afraid in these parts. Our arts, our lives are small, but our calls are high now, wow, to go on somehow! I've no tremor of profound remorse, on this manic-depressive course, which could end in death and that I inhale like Meth. I keep my enemies close, and my friends away, lest they grab my hand and prevent play.'

I am somewhat taken aback and impressed at his creative poetic intellect. There is something Bob Dylan-ish about his delivery and message. I decide to give Irreverent Reverend Tom Groans my own light-hearted retort and watch his reaction. I respond, 'If you love my thinking and I'm your choice, then if I love you, I must love my own voice. When you're my choice and I make you happy, then my self-love fulfilled will be what I see, so do not 'psycho' or 'babble' or ponder my state. I'm not one of those who love those I hate. If I don't love myself and I need to be broken, then this heart I despise, you won't have a hope in, and if you're just bits and pieces, fetish objects to me, then the jigsaw of your puzzle I won't find or see.'

I hold my ground and watch his response, which is a quickened shrug and a smirk and with that he says, 'I don't know what the fuck you're talking about, but I'm deadly serious, man!'

I comeback, 'I'm saying that if you are comfortable in your own skin, you'll be able to give to others.'

'That's bullshit, man! It's the others that are not comfortable with my skin!' He now leaps like a leopard from my door onto the balcony wall and vanishes over my roof, leaving only the trace of nicotine.

Caught up in an adventure that is beyond one's capacity not to confront.

19

He who reigns does pour.
Irreverent Reverend Tom Groans

The days of the last month seem concertinaed together. I have hardly seen F, but often hear his voice when he returns from work after midnight. I see Russell on occasion, but mainly hear his typewriter whipping away with sharp metallic clicks. The last time I saw him, he was sleeping alongside F, sheets and blankets lying in a jumble on the floor. Both figures had muttered as I moved on past the door into the study. It was Sunday and District Six was slumbering late.

On Sundays something special happens in District Six, which is a phenomenon introduced by the hippies who filtered into the vacated apartments and renovated Cape Dutch single-storied shacks left by the exiting Coloureds. What happens is that the rooftops lose their regularity of shape, as people come to sunbathe and barbecue. The rooftops become a kaleidoscopic mosaic of naked flesh. Backsides, breasts, legs and penises co-opt the view. The growth of a primitive cult, a transformation of the scenery ensues and it is a thing of beauty. But this beauty exists at the edge of decay. It is a beauty in and of itself and not because it's opposite, decomposition, is close at hand. It is of interest to the extent that the catastrophe of 'Separate

Development', the separation of people based on skin colour, is juxtaposed with something as beautiful and unadulterated as nudity.

Last Sunday, I had left the sleeping nude figures downstairs and climbed the wall, pulling myself onto the warm, white, flat roof and spread my towel. There was hardly a flat-roofed building without at least one human being on it. Bodies seen everywhere were dressed in suntan oil reflecting the sun. Before me was camaraderie as well as calm solitude, adjacent to carousing, vigil and romance. In the distance, the lone figure of a young woman walking up the side of a road had attracted my senses. My roving camera eye had watched the movement striding confidently towards my direction. It was Angela and I thought, 'Walk; I want to sit and watch in silence. Walk, just for about an hour and let your rhythm dissolve the synthetic fibres that have tried and failed to fashion you.' She then vanished, swallowed up by the crowded buildings.

Always take the scene before you by surprise.

20

Come down to it, everything matters and not a bit!
Irreverent Reverend Tom Groans

My afternoon ritual of sleeping has been interrupted by a mad opera of boisterous cacophony coming from the house beneath me. I dress and drift downstairs. The noise from the study is loud and lusty, so I cannot hear my shoes on the steps as I descend into the courtyard. The door of the study is open and smoke chokes the air on entering the threshold. The scene is a profusion of naked, male and female bodies. The odour is of sweat. A dozen bundled couples are seen grinding away on top of each other on the large cushions that are strewn about the lounge and study. Incense and marijuana fumes coalesce in the atmosphere. The smell is animal. The setting is jungle.

Someone I have never met before, as far as I can remember, introduces me as 'Aaron, the chap from upstairs'.

I nod my head at each subsequent introduction, not catching any names. Eventually, I seat myself on the floor in a corner with a glass of lethal, throat-tingling punch. I feel like a voyeur in the foyer. From my vantage point I have complete control of the view before me. I notice that the door to F's room is ajar, leaving me with the picture of a naked women lying spread-eagled on her back in the middle of the bed. Her position, with arms spread out, feet together, is reminiscent of a crucifixion. Her head is arched backwards, eclipsed by the rise of her breasts. I weave my way into the bedroom, hesitantly peering into the room first, where I catch the sight of F's nude buttocks as he pushes himself off the mattress and disappears into the bathroom. With trepidation, because F is taking a shower, I make my way from the foot of the over-sized bed to the middle of it and stand alongside Angela who is lying prone on her back.

I note the apex of her pubic hair below her smooth abdomen. I am feeding my eye casually. She seems self-contained, almost demure. My voyeurism is un-menacing as she is undisturbed. I am more emotionally than sexually aroused by such a gorgeous sight.

Unexpectedly, without opening her eyes she simply pats the bed alongside her and says, 'Here!' So I sit. She once said that she could smell my presence, 'So,' she says, 'Has your cock lengthened?' She reaches out and up and touches my jeans below my belt. The act is simple. My answer is, 'No!' I reach down and kiss her untidy head. I browse her body noting her partially exposed labium protruding past her trimmed pubic hair. I bend and kiss her mouth. Her tongue darts between my lips then retreats just as quickly. There is a hormonal charge that nerves through me. Her breath is magnetic. She opens her legs a little and the dampness reaches my nose. Her nipples stand firmer. Her lips also have filled. I feel the subtle vibration of her lungs quietly shuddering for more air as a little sweat starts to surface on her upper lip. I have to pull away. I lie back on my elbows and stretch my neck back, adjusting it. Like gravity, casual sex with Angela is almost irresistible, but I resist. I don't like to perform in front of observers.

One can isolate oneself by going to a remote spot or, like Angela, withdrawing into the centre of one's being, whilst in the midst of a crowd. The full light of a tall candle flame bathes her pale, oval face. She manoeuvres both her arms above and behind her head in an extensive stretch, like one would when about to dive into a pool. She smiles. She is comfortable wearing nothing except the light. With two casual fingers of her right hand she lightly plucks her right nipple for a moment and opens her eyes as her mood returns to normal.

She notices me examining her pubic triangle of hair cut like an inverted pyramid and says, 'This is my holy trinity!'

'Which is?'

'The trinity are: good attitude, because spirit is substantial. Secondly, one should enjoy the flesh and not negate the body and thirdly, to realise that it is a blessing if one is emotionally intelligent enough to understand these first two points!'

'I like that!'

'Fuck faith in someone else's ideology!' she curses.

'I could have faith in this.'

I smile, stroking her ankle and continue. 'You look quite magnetising lying here like a sacrificial lamb.'

'I'm no sacrificial anything!'

She is spread out on the sheet, directly under a 4-foot oak cross, which is mounted above the headboard. A large mahogany Jesus with sad eyes and a crown of thorns is nailed to the crucifix. Wooden Jesus has an expression of anguish. Above the head of Jesus and carved into the vertical beam, are the words, *King of the Jews*. I glance up at mahogany Jesus then back to spread-eagle Angela. She notices my curious expression and comments, 'The crucifix appears to be incongruous here, but in F's opinion, Jesus suffered for the sin of allowing himself, as a man, to be seen as the Godhead.'

'Well, Aaron.' It is F's voice as he enters the room, this time with a towel wrapped about his waist. He continues talking as he towers over us, while looking with deliberation at Jesus on the wall. 'A glowing light is always costly, like our Messiah over here. Illumination comes only at the expense of that which produces it. An un-illuminated candle doesn't burn. I must emphasise that by a "new way" I mean "pushing the envelope", breaking new ground. We cannot be of service to others without an initial cost to ourselves. If we're very lucky we might receive the energy back that we have expended, but that is rare. Searing suggests suffering. You can ask any wick on the shelf.'

Angela arches her back and breathes in deeply, then exhales and says, 'We are liable to think that we do the most good when we are robust and powerful.'

'I agree!'

F leaves the room and Angela dismisses what I say with a flip of her hand. 'On the contrary, Aaron, because when we ache, the pain allows reflection.'

F re-enters the room to take out a small bag of hashish from the bedside table. He leaves again, saying, 'Pain allows appreciation. When you suffer you live in the moment!'

'I don't see F suffering!' I utter as he enters the room once again.

'No, darling chap, you might not see my suffering, but it's there. I suffer at times from a mild depression of not being able to make any meaningful, emotionally committed connection.'

Angela, swinging her feet to the floor, stands up, stretches and strides into the bathroom. F seats himself near the head of the bed, placing a pillow in the small of his back against the headboard, and leans back.

'Aaron, you know when you go to a bad movie in order to see what a director should not do?'

'Yes, it's called a negative example,' I answer.

'That's what my crucifix is. It's a negative example of what one must not become. The message of this image is not "Why hast thou forsaken me?" but why have we not forsaken this false man the way God did? A Hitler could only arise in a society that has elevated a human into achieving God-head status.'

'This government has God-head status!'

F laughs cynically.

'Here in South Africa, it's the reality of power, but not to be worshipped, idiot! Our government is just the lesser of bad alternatives.'

Angela comes back into the room. She has nothing on. Her hair is sopping wet. She lowers herself between F and me. I observe her as I would sketch her, as opposed to a static photograph. Seeing her is a process of scribbling and scratching out, as she reveals different aspects of her personality.

My sketch of District Six is also metamorphosing.

21

I'm ghetto, District Six ghetto and my pen is my stiletto!

Irreverent Reverend Tom Groans

There is an assortment of vehicles parked outside the house. The front door is open and the sound of French is being spoken. I enter the house, walk down the corridor and turn right into the study. There is a gathering of about eight males, all chattering excitedly, bobbing about the room, slapping each other on the backs the way baboons nip at each other, while sipping wine from F's coffee mugs. Another troop of Frenchmen approach the study through F's bedroom, followed by F himself.

'Everyone will introduce themselves to you in due course. They know who you are. My friends will be joining me for the next four months or so. They're affiliated with a French television company and plan on making a documentary on Cape Dutch architecture, starting here in District Six, before the area gets too "gentrified" and loses its character.' He gives me a wink and a nod and discloses, 'At least that is why the government gave them permission to film.' He nods and winks again then paces the room offering refills. After much drinking, the Frenchmen drift out to their vehicles to fetch their film equipment. F is wearing underpants with an apple design on the front. The words *Eat Me* are written inside the apple. He sits facing me in his easy chair. He has had much to drink and his eyes flick over my face. His mouth peels back in a relaxed smile. I wait for the question that is a couple of months overdue.

'So, tell me about yourself?'

I cannot help but laugh. The bastard has a memory like an elephant. Sipping the wine, I feel the weight of a few drops on my moustache. I feel it tickle my skin beneath and wipe away the sensation.

F coaxes, 'Open up, boy. What do you want to do with your life?'

'I want to write.' My answer is a cliché.

'Well, Aaron, the only two subjects of importance are power and hypocrisy. Power is not something you have intrinsically; it is something that you get, depending on your particular strategic position. Power is about selfish survival and as for hypocrisy; the past generation presided over things with hypocrisy. I revolt against this. The army-length hair, the collar and tie, the suits, the uniform of the gentleman all hide their true attitude. I'm not exemplary, nor consistent and smug like our parents. I live according to a philosophy that being honest is everything and convention blocks access to the truth. Everything is cyclical. What goes up will go down and vice versa.'

'Being honest with yourself is one thing, but what about being honest with others?' I jibe.

'That would be on a need-to-know basis.' He smiles.

'You wouldn't make a very good friend.'

'I have very few friends and I'm straightforward to everyone, as long as they mean me no harm.'

I change tack. 'What about love?'

'Aaron, I love everyone who is not my rival.'

'F, you can't love this abstract everyone. To love, you'd need to have had an intimate, warm relationship with your parents or a parental figure in the first place and if you'd had that kind of relationship then you'd be able to be empathetic.'

'You are a naïve idealist. You ask about Love? Again, I repeat, if they're not my enemy I'm cool with them! Anyway, you can only be empathetic with those you agree with; otherwise you're not empathetic, although you might be sympathetic. Sympathy is more general. I think that you can only love those you understand and agree with, because if you didn't agree with them then you wouldn't get their point of view. You can't love God because there's no way you can empathise with him. You might be afraid of God, you might be in awe of God, but you can never love something you don't understand.'

'So, we're at an impasse?' I ask.

'Correct,' he broadcasts loud and clearly as he lights up a broken bottleneck that is filled with bright-green, fresh, pungently sweet marijuana. It glows a deep red as he inhales slowly and deeply. With deliberate concentration, he holds in his breath to let the drug permeate. Slowly, with lips pursed and used as an escape valve, the circulated smoke is blown patiently out of his mouth in an even, quiet, slow-pumping tempo. F arches his head, blowing the last of the grass out of his insides in the direction of the beam above him, whilst closing his eyes in a blissful pose. Whispering up into the ceiling, he says, 'Anyway, I love you and I can't imagine my life at this point without you!'

I am a little shocked to say the least, but I know how it is with drugs and so respond, 'I think it is the marijuana talking,'

'No, you conceited arsehole; it's me talking to the marijuana!'

I am much relieved.

F continues his ruminations. 'Who is right is who has the right of way. When I was at university I had a religious crisis. I couldn't just accept the bible's maxims as unchallengeable, divine revelation. I couldn't merely demonise new scholarly insights from recent history, as well as intellectual analysis and demote them to some distant corner of my psyche that would have no effect on my faith. "Thou shalt not kill" and the thousands of other adages, I couldn't accept with intellectual integrity as coming literally from heaven. The human experience, like our early negative experience with the Blacks over the past few centuries, has to be present in how we react today towards them. This recent, living history here in South Africa is always present in how we reconcile, filter and interpret divine revelation today. Divine inspiration is not just to us, but also through us. Open interaction and discourse with God is also required. And while we're on the subject of perspective, I'm appalled at the spectacular loss of perspective by the liberal-leftist circus, with their hysterical carnival of fake emotional support for anyone and anything black. They're bereft of all self-restraint and are just self-indulgent, sentimental show-offs where the show is all about them.'

'F, I think your attitude of sitting at the same board meeting with God, where you and He are interdependent, might have made you a bully. Maybe you're even a psychopath.' My voice dances lightly on the word 'psychopath' in order for F not to be too insulted and in order that I might receive some kind of response from him.

Unperturbed, F responds, 'Every bully has a bullee: those who want to be bullied, those who are craven and cowards, who want other people's directives. I have good self-esteem. I'm just their "craven" image. As for being a psychopath, well, maybe I am. If I were placed in a position where I had to kill one person out of a choice of three people, most people in my position would find this a difficult dilemma, but not me. I'd make a simple mathematical calculation. So, maybe that makes me some kind of psycho. I have no moral dilemmas ever!'

'Maybe your self-esteem is too high.'

F merely shrugs and takes a huge, deep hit on his bong while sliding lower in his chair.

I have said much more than I had intended. I look up and he is slouched and faking sleep. He loves a game. His eyeballs then flicker and open.

'Very interesting,' he says.

He must mean that he finds his own thoughts interesting, as I have said very little.

Maybe he finds my narrow-mindedness interesting.

I am suddenly reminded of Jerry Jacobs, a friend from the army who, like F, would emphasise the word 'very' when saying, "very interesting!" What surprises me is how much like Jerry Jacobs F looks facially and especially how he sounds, except that Jerry did not abdicate logic one moment, to use it at another time when it suited him.

F jumps out of his seat and in mock ballet, spins out of the room, through the door towards the Frenchmen who are now congregating in the kitchen.

To be caught up in the rigmarole will leave you half, not whole.

22

To know a veil is pointless.

Irreverent Reverend Tom Groans

Angela, with only a towel wrapped around her wet hair, sits cross-legged on the mattress in my room. Her profile holds me in its perfection. It is now my time to shower, so I kiss her forehead then the bridge of her nose and make my way to the bathroom on the other side of the balcony.

On the outside of the door to the bathroom is a beautifully handwritten note. I search for the signature at the bottom of the note before reading its contents. It is from Angela and it was obviously written sometime in the past half hour. The note says:

> *My gorgeous Aaron,*
> *Be as happy as you can be. Life has a way of turning things on their heads and one day the 'head' might be the 'butt' of one's jokes, just as next time, Aaron, I'm on top! Remember that pleasure and communication should be the primary focus of all engagements!*
> *Love Angela xxx*

I shower and return to my room, where Angela is stretching. I hug her from behind. She turns and bites my shoulder.

'Aaron, F is correct. There is no such thing as human nature; we are all so different, but there are human natures, plural, even within one person. We have to be consistent and acknowledge that there are other people, equally intelligent, but unlike ourselves, who are also as dynamic. If there is a double standard, such as one standard for us and another standard for others and we have no consistency, then we will get the kind of anarchy we have here.'

'I agree. You know why F says an Ideal Home Exhibition is called an Ideal Home Exhibition?'

'No.'

'He says it's called that because an ideal home can only be found in an exhibition.'

'Aaron, every human being should be able to pursue his or her own ambition as far as their own ability will carry them. It is not perfect, but it is an ideal that we must uphold. It is not an argument that non-Whites in this country are not slaves and are paid the same competitive low wage as other Third World countries. They are paid, but their ability to control their own lives is seriously impeded by not having the vote, by not having access to the same high level of school education, thereby limiting their future work scope. They cannot live and therefore work wherever they wish. They do not have a strong financial power base. They cannot even build up good equity on their properties because their properties are in cheaper areas. Is this an ideal only for the 'non-pigmented' Whites who make up a small percentage of this population, who own eighty-five per cent of the land and the best land at that? No one is talking about being perfect, but we have to do much better than this.'

'You're right.'

'Aaron, one has to treat people the same way as when attending someone who is dying, because we are all in the process of dying really. One has to be able to listen, support and not invade their privacy. Don't push this argument too hard with F, though; he works for a Nationalist newspaper.'

'I won't. Tell me why are you involved in this house with F? It doesn't make sense. I at least did not know who I was moving in with.'

'There is method to my madness, Aaron, but keep our conversations to yourself. Over the next few months, just look and keep your mouth shut for all our sakes. Here in South Africa people have abdicated their power to Big Daddy. F said there is only "relative" power and I suppose he also meant "relative" morality as well.

'Everything for F is a charade, a game, pretence, a deception. He is a player who pantomimes a different persona, even a different moral persona, depending on the situation he is in. Even his sexual persona is an intricate game. I will leave my short essay about F's personality with you tomorrow afternoon. I'm not even the type of girl F likes. I have hips and breasts. I'm here because F loves my face and also because I introduced him to Russell.'

'So, F is just "bi"-ding his time?'

'Yes, while I bide mine in this perfect locale, this house, which being under F's unsuspecting jurisdiction should give us perfect cover.'

'Perfect cover for what?'

'For being able to manoeuvre around the district and Cape Town with impunity and to have a base that's in the most central location.'

'Impunity from what?'

'To do my thing! Now, that's all you need to know.'

It is important to have a perfect cover from an imperfect past.

23

The boundary that keeps you in is the boundary that keeps you out.

Irreverent Reverend Tom Groans

Angela's essay on F:

F's preference for a sexual relationship with another man, despite the fact that he could secure female partners, is not indicative of a clear, articulated choice because the only sexual relationships F recognises are the same sexual relationships that society recognises, namely those between heterosexuals.

His female persona, consequently, allows him to have sexual relations with boys that he could not otherwise conceive between two males. F's male persona allows him to perform with a girl, but because he is all 'girl' himself, the girl he is with has to have 'tomboyish' traits. All the while this 'tomboyish' girl, who is attracted to girls, can feel something for F, this effeminate man. Meanwhile, effeminate F, to get the partners he wants, has to have some appearance of masculinity, such as a fast sports car, in order to be compatible with the sexual prohibitions imposed by society.

These two faces of F, male and female, are essential to his sense of self because it allows him to fashion identities that at the same time assimilate and circumvent the values of the patriarchal society in which he lives.

It is important to manoeuvre for a larger personal world.

24

We all live as one nation, under one skin!
Irreverent Reverend Tom Groans

Two heads of hair and their respective bodies lean against opposite verticals of the door to F's room. I peer through the gap between them into the room, which is bathed in bright theatrical light. A visual current between the view and me connects in the room's centre, where, with imaginative renovation, it has been transformed from a regular room into a 'bordello of filth', as Russell likes to call it. Waves of heat and debauchery sweep over me, coming in tantalising cadences to enhance the already vibrant energy. The spiciness of nudity in the pornography being filmed and the various couples in the throngs of ardour does impart a prick to the visual current of what is obviously sensual pleasure, whether it is debauched or not. The added spiciness is the joy that is tangible, for at the very least they are being well paid. Any excruciating inner examinations of their psyches have been left at the door.

There is an exposure of stiff-necked penises 'way out on a limb', but I find nothing repellent. Sex is occurring with the minimum of ceremony and it is base and it is vulgar but, the rapture is real. There are duets, trios and solo performers, all kowtowing to every conceivable agile position. Two middle-aged men in their forties are the oldest of the sixteen people in the room and they are 'wheel barrowing' two girls from the rear with such appallingly loud artificial snorting that the three young men in front of them have lost their erections amidst the din.

My first thought is that it is deliriously comical. I find there is nothing loathsome in the trembling going on. The hysterical paroxysms captivate the lover's fever pitch and progress at great speed towards naturalism's orgasmic triumph. There is no pathos in this room and certainly no solemnity, only the florid movement of heightened sexuality.

All the 'fuckers', as director Jacque likes to call them, are light-skinned Coloureds from the area. The permit for a documentary was the ruse to make a cheap porno movie, using the Coloureds in the area and beautiful Cape Town as the setting.

F must be getting a kickback of sorts. But these Frenchmen are friends of Russell, so it might be he who is F's kickback, I surmise.

The making and distribution of anything pornographic in South Africa is a crime, as is overt homosexuality. Certainly F would lose his position at his conservative newspaper if his bisexuality were known. Has F been blackmailed by Russell? I have noticed that they have been less demonstrative towards each other of late.

Meanwhile, in front of me there is a wilful exuberance of buttocks and backs yielding to each other, carried away by the accentual rhythms of Wagner from an LP in the corner. There is no clear contrast between up and down, forward- and back-thrusting, just lots of staccato fits and starts, with the elasticity of impetus. There is no storyline. It is just what the director, Jacque, known as the Doctor, ordered. There is a careless lightness to all the 'fuckers'. I can see the relaxedness of the sweating, fornicating bodies superimposed on the odd stiffness of erect penises and it has an effect of inherent contradiction and perversity.

The film is to be called 'Punch and Judy' and all the men, before they disrobe in order to engage, are dressed as stiff English Morris dancers, while all the women are dressed as the Swan Queen from the ballet *Swan Lake*.

The film graduates in erection terms, from pantomime to real-life fucking, as Doctor Jacque puts it. Every now and again he shouts in his thick French accent, 'Cut! Shall we start again?'

Here we have a conversation between the Doctor and his actors:

'Enjoy, my darling. No frowning.'

'But, he is so big, Doc!'

'Love, when you've been in the business a little longer, you'll see that you'll expand!'

'You! Yes, you! What is your name?'

'Dubin, sir.'

'Well, Doberman,'

'No. Dubin, sir.'

'Well, Dubin, how about more oil for foreplay? Get her stimulated man. Girl, if you can't get excited then just act like you are excited. No free fucks here and don't worry about your hair, everybody looks good coming!'

The male actor watches as the Doctor, trying to show the girl what to do, takes her part. He shows her how to turn the hand around the boy's penis by twisting the wrist then turning the arm at the shoulder and then extending the arm without letting go of the penis, so the girl now has room to move to another position. Doctor has done such a good job of demonstrating that the boy has just prematurely ejaculated. There is some embarrassment and laughter all around.

Doctor Jacque tells everyone to listen up, because he wants everyone to fornicate to the beat of the music. 'Keeping beat to whatever rhythm one wants is a decidedly human characteristic,' he says. 'Animals can only perform the instinctual beat that they have been programmed with. They do not keep perfect time.' Doctor has become philosophical and says, 'Having grace in movement gives that grace extra power and it's this extra power that is intoxicating to behold. Enjoy the music folks!'

I know that Doctor Jacque's philosophical dissertation is wasted on the 'fuckers', but it is not wasted on F, who is beaming a broad smile in the corner of the room. F loves talk of referential power. The power of those in power here in District Six is excessive, even though the Whites in power might say it is necessary in survival terms. They might also feel that this power they have is beautiful precisely because it is extravagant like a dance or choreographed sex, having nothing to do with survival at all.

It is a deadly dance.

25

It is Black or White at both poles, not many shades between, while the equator to a bi-polar equates to not being seen.

Irreverent Reverend Tom Groans

The French director, Doctor Jacque, stands with F, Angela and Russell on the roof of my shower room on the other side of my balcony that overlooks the courtyard, all four of them silhouetted this evening against the full yellowness of the moon. Doc Jacque's body profile is solid but short, with a well-developed barrel chest from where his booming, director's baritone voice is emitted. Jacque has two prominent buck teeth. He gives the impression of being a well-fed rabbit. He is premeditated in his thinking and needs to be sure of something before he ventures into it, so being involved in porno in conservative, Police State, South Africa is really a stretch.

Watching them, a bat bursts past me, flapping just above my head and I instinctively duck, even though there is no need as their radar for evasion of contact is precise. It is the motion of movement inches from my head that recalls a vivid memory from my army days, when Disciplinary Officer Blank's radar was also precise, with the added intent of striking the top of your head with the open palm of his hand as he strode past.

In my mind's eye I reminisce, taking myself back a year ago to my army base. The silence is disturbed by the sound of my surname being called.

'Aardwolf!'

I turn to see the sinister features of Corporal Johannes Demetrius Blank, after hearing his bark, which always precedes a plea for his sake to place a rope around your neck and jump.

'Aardwolf! The major wants you NOW!'

I run double-time across a marching ground to the major's bungalow office. I enter.

'I want information, Aardwolf! For your sake! It will save us all a lot of time.'

Major is a walrus, a small walrus with big ideas. His nose overhangs a small nervous mouth that has an overbite with small mousy teeth that love to chatter. His pointed chin points upwards towards his downward bent nose and gives him a circular appearance. Like clockwork, I read him like a book. He reads me like a page.

'Aardwolf, would you like to know what we have on your little group activities? Choose any day you like. Take last week for instance. You were AWOL last Tuesday night at 2200. Don't look surprised. This is not a prison, but you are confined to barracks, which means you cannot leave without permission! You went AWOL by going under the barbed wire by the south end of the base and were picked up by a car that dropped you at the corner of Berg and Mathew streets where you and your four buddies walked to 17 Klipstraat. The house at that address belongs to the Goldman Family. There, you all listened to music with the Goldman kids, but after a while you disappeared into the study adjoining the lounge and talked to Mr Max Goldman for an hour. Tell me, Aardwolf, what did the two of you talk about?'

'We talked about sport and about my family, as he is a distant cousin of a friend of my parents,' I answer. I hold the major's stare, trying not to show that I have lied about the conversation that took place between Max Goldman and myself. My lie has a benevolent excuse; Max Goldman is anti-Apartheid.

Walrus closes my file in front of him, gives me a once-over look and orders me out of the room. The interrogation has me scared. An informer prowls close and any one of my four colleagues could be him.

To take as much latitude as one's longitude will allow.

26

Those with rank are indeed rank and the file just file,
as I manoeuvre through their guile.

Irreverent Reverend Tom Groans

My particular failure in the eyes of the military was due to my heretical contrariness to their orders and my objection to fighting for the values of Apartheid, rather than because I had been complying with the enemy, which I had not, and of course because I had punched a superior. However, my liberalism took the form of a tiny bit of a gesture that added little more than a hiccup to the easy flowing sequence of South African Apartheid rule.

What I found out after I had returned to my bungalow was intriguing. I asked my friend Jerry if he had told the major about my going into Max Goldman's study alone, while the others, Jerry included, had sat in the Goldman's lounge with Max's two sons listening to music. Jerry had closed his eyes, allowing his face to drop to his chest and shook his head in the negative. No, Jerry had not told the Major anything. That was a massive problem for Jerry, because he had been ordered to report on everything this particular group of misfits did, as part of a 'plea bargain' deal he had done with the District Attorney in South West Africa the previous year.

*

Prior to the army, Jerry had been caught trying to sell three diamonds to two female members of the anti-Apartheid African National Congress Party, whom he had befriended one night at a party. All this had happened to Jerry six months prior to his military call up and post-matriculation, when he was working part-time for a diamond company in South West Africa. Jerry had cooperated with the police in South West Africa, telling them everything they already knew, while claiming ignorance about who the two girls were working for, which was the truth and besides that, he had told the secret service that the two girls were whiter than he was, so if they were working for the terrorist group, ANC, how was he to know, they being both blonde and blue-eyed?

The two girls had shown every sort of interest in Jerry. They truly liked him. It was more than just money and sex to them, but the money was the initial thrust of their interest in Jerry. 'Thrusting' was Jerry's initial interest in the two girls. He had sex with them one-on-one and also simultaneously. The two girls, named Leah and Monique, had said that they had a contact that could get rid of the stones for a good price. The idea was that Jerry was going to sell the three, highly-prized, pure-white, Angolan diamonds to the two girls at a relatively low price and then the two girls in their own turn would resell them to their contact at a much higher price. What Jerry did not know at the time, but what he later found out, was that the money the girls eventually would have received for the stones would have gone into the coffers of the anti-Apartheid ANC, to buy weapons for their fight against the Apartheid Government.

The district attorney had given Jerry no jail time for the illegal possession of diamonds in exchange for having him spy on his fellow conscripts when he went into the military service. So, Jerry's disjointed gesture of not complying with the plea bargain was more serious than my misstep of just being insubordinate.

If Jerry had not told the authorities of my alone time with Max Goldman, as he should have, then who had informed on me and who had informed the authorities that Jerry was not living up to his end of the deal? It left the three other 'friends' of mine as suspects. Hendrik, who was the lone Boer or Afrikaner in my group, seemed the obvious choice.

Events can move in all directions with remarkable speed.

27

Does his suppleness lie mainly in his head, or in the
belly of his beast, or in his penis instead?
Irreverent Reverend Tom Groans

Who was Jerry? Who were the two girls? I wanted to know.

Jerry used to tell me that he was a serious womaniser of modern technique, which meant that he was interested in women and could engage himself in them. He was a devoted listener, whose good manners were trimmed in the buoyancy of a wicked but light sense of humour. Jerry was always modest and gentlemanly in the company of the opposite sex, even when he had an erection. Had Jerry not been in the army, his shorn head would have had straight, lank, blonde hair, dissipating any melancholy his otherwise hatched-type, strong features would have suggested. Jerry was premeditated and sober.

Jerry's father had been successful but domineering and had instilled in Jerry, in no uncertain terms, that if Jerry did not behave exactly in a way that enabled his father to have peace and quiet in the house after a long day at the office, that he and his dog, would both be kicked. With Jerry's strong nervous system, he refused to submit. He turned his father's ironic sarcasm back to its source and against hypocritical paternalism wherever

111

it raised its ugly head, whether it was an individual or a company such as the diamond group he had worked for, who exploited its own workers, or the army hierarchy.

Jerry became a master at caricaturing his father's shrill, dry, clipped falsetto voice. He added a nasal tautness to the falsetto that had urgency about it, coupled with a nervous keenness. There was the suspense of his mimicry's sudden outbursts, something that could surprise the 'out-of-towners', letting everyone know that no one gives a shit about them and that they had better get used to this impersonal, cold, selfish armpit of a hell-hole.

There was nothing pretentious about Jerry. He was unspoilt in his prodigious expressiveness, being able to project his anger by transforming himself into his tormentor and mimicking him. There was nothing fake in this transformation and Jerry would lose his own personality wholeheartedly in the 'other', for he understood what stood beneath gestures.

Jerry had a kaleidoscopic succession of embittered, angry, frustrated characters that he could arrange in a sequence like a fashion parade. There was no reality that he left unturned and no secret emotion he did not caricaturise. All of his characters were in some way automatons, or amoral drill-sergeants, empty of emotion, but full of conviction, like his father, and he committed himself totally like a virtuoso to what he was pantomiming. Thus was his skill, that he could loosen any situation by its paradox. When he was 'himself' again, he was honest and deadpan, like a horse out to pasture. He was stable.

Had Jerry been hoodwinked by the two girls? Had he just been unlucky to be caught?

Being reluctant to seek information, which one would personally rather not know, could be short sighted.

28

He's unredeemable, a man going down; not fleet-footed enough to leave the ground.

Irreverent Reverend Tom Groans

Jerry described the two lasses to me, Leah and Monique, as he packed his belongings for his departure to some military or state jail. Because of his failure to live up to the plea bargain deal of reporting exactly what had gone on in the Goldman house, he found himself stuck in another new predicament of incarceration.

Because of Jerry's strange sense of humour and his love of punning, he decided to call Leah 'Dire'. So, in Jerry's head, Leah became Dire Leah, but the name was totally incongruous with her delicate beauty and finesse. For some reason, only known to him, he found that hilarious. Monique he nicknamed Mono. The two blonde, blue-eyed girls were first cousins, whose mothers were identical twins. Actually, they were also half-sisters, as Leah's father had impregnated Monique's mother, his wife's twin, his sister-in-law. The half-sisters looked identical.

They were equally tall and powerfully built with an athletic grace and spring in both their steps. Their strength rippled down the extended contours of their long elastic legs. They moved with ease and simplicity from a calm centre and were quick and pliant like the graceful architectural play of flesh that they were. There was no fragility in them emotionally.

Both girls had natural wit and like Jerry, an enthusiastic sense of caricature and could parody virtually everything they looked at. They both had a tendency to make 'banal' anything that everyone else took seriously.

Leah, or Dire as Jerry liked to call her, was the more cerebral of the two and had received a degree from an Oxford university, as had Mono. They had both also been star athletes, Dire Leah in the long jump and Mono in the high jump. Jerry said that they were the best field athletes in the world with breasts. Their breasts were very large for tall girls, with both pairs pointing skywards. All four of their mammalian glands stood proud of their sternums like a multiple, fascist salute.

Leah used to tweak and squeeze her nipples with quite a bit of friction, between her fore finger and thumb, whenever she was daydreaming. She was not self-conscious about this habit of hers and did it the same way guys do when they play with their testicles. It relaxed her. Jerry said he used to wince when he watched her tweaking as he anticipated pain, but there was only pleasure in it for her. Mono used to scratch her Venus-mound through her jeans as a way of relaxing and appeared equally as unself-conscious about doing that.

Jerry said that Dire Leah had a great sense of humour. She thought that Jerry's penis was better looking than Jerry himself, but that he, Jerry, had the better personality. It was the personality that interested Leah. She felt it was the ability to open up emotionally, with its accompanying open musculature that allows one to feel with another person. Naturally, she felt that one had to be intellectually intelligent as well, in order to understand most of the vast implicit aspects of the other person that lie beneath the surface content: that huge content of stuff that is implied, that tells you where the other person is coming from. Most of the contents of a good joke are implied and not elaborated. A mutual 'I get you!' is what brings the knowing smile, is what Mono thought. Meanwhile, Leah's philosophy embraced the idea that 'an open body equals an open mind' and that human beings can be understood neither as substances with fixed properties of moral thinking, such as one's intention and duty governed by the norms of the good and the right, which we do have as well, nor solely as scientific subjects interacting with a world of objects governed by truth. In truth, she would say we were often untruthful and schizophrenic, wriggling this way and that, trying to find out our authenticity, or who we are and what we want and not what society, such as our families, want from us.

Openness for Leah meant thinking in an untraditional fashion, as orthodoxy in her book implied being stuck in a rut, as one can only discover something when you have pushed through the accustomed, already-acknowledged norms. Moderation equalled mediocrity and a certain bland sameness to Leah. Insipid mediocrity was anathema to her, as it represented what is average and that which sits in the middle, at the half, in a half-hearted way, without putting one's guts into anything. Yes, creativity came with openness and a body that was muscularly pliable and therefore 'open' had less emotional armouring. A simple, unsophisticated life, she had said, had never broken any rules in order to advance.

The thesis that Leah was working on at university was about the four convulsive behaviours of human beings: laughter, crying, yawning and orgasm. Leah said that all these partially involuntary, convulsive ways of behaving require the shaking and heaving of the diaphragm. The degree of the diaphragm's tightness, the degree of its hypertrophied closed state, with its parallel degree of inhibition to laugh, cry or orgasm, tells to what extent the mental state of the person is impaired. Is this person empathetic? Is this person sympathetic? Are they open to feel, is what Leah always used to question.

There was one other thing Jerry had mentioned about Leah and it was about a distinguishing feature that she had on her body. On her perineum, which is the area beneath her, in front of her anus extending to her vagina, Leah had a light blue birthmark.

It was in the shape of either a question mark or an ear seen sideways. What was ironic about that question mark was that the two girls were one big question mark as they disappeared out of Jerry's life as quickly as they had arrived.

Jerry told me about how he got involved with the two girls, as he was packing his bags to leave this army hell-hole for a worse place. He had met the two girls the evening of his nineteenth birthday, where he had been nursing a beer alone in a bar in the city of Windhoek, the capital of South West Africa. That first night they all became lovers then over a few weeks they became friends and over the next few months, they all became co-conspirators in the crime to sell illegal diamonds.

Jerry said he must have been insane at the time to have even considered doing it, but such is the magnetism of sexual attraction. He did not know for whom they were working during his time with them, nor did he enquire, and only found out from the authorities upon his arrest that they were members of the banned ANC.

Now, here, back in the army, he could not trust anyone, myself included.

To be surprised requires no experience or training.

29

The hunted, who with a little strength and a little knowing and after a certain tending of the wounds, become as a branch, against which the wind is bent.

Irreverent Reverend Tom Groans

Jerry had told me several months earlier about how he had been arrested in South West Africa, but he had understandably left out the plea bargain aspect of it. This was his story:

Up until the existential moment of meeting the two seductive first cousins, Jerry had been considered by himself to be either one basic ingredient of inelegance, or a single facet of un-established youth. These sometimes mutually exclusive attitudes had continued to coexist side by side in Jerry up until his nineteenth birthday, which he was celebrating by himself in a Windhoek blues pub when he was approached by the two girls at the bar counter, while the sound of Bessie Smith's mournful blues blew through the room.

The girl called Leah, having noticed Jerry inspecting the walls of the pub, which were covered from top to bottom with the sleeves of early LPs and EPs, came up to Jerry and said, 'Nice artwork. No?'

'Yes, really brilliant designs, some of them!' Jerry had

responded, before he turned to look at the stunningly beautiful girl at his ear.

When Leah had come into focus, Jerry's breath was almost taken away by the mesmerising sight of her. Michelangelo could have carved her out of marble.

'You know these album covers are all bullshit, don't you?' she almost shouted above the music.

'What do you mean?' Jerry asked, raising his voice back to counteract the noise level in the room. He was surprised at her bluntness.

'Well, up until the Second World War, the blues had been considered by Whites to be either one basic part of jazz or a facet of American folk music. It was in reality basically Black music, or dirty music, if you will. There was self-denial on the White elite's part, but sectors of the hip public were starting to groove to it and to accept it as a separate, self-supporting entity with its own strong life force,' Leah said.

'So what's that to do with the sleeve covers on the walls here being bullshit?' Jerry inquired.

'The bullshit is in the presentation on these album covers. Not only were they on Folkways labels as a folk artefact, but the album sleeves were decorated with folksy motifs or decorated displaying tacky female pin-ups without the black singer's faces on the covers. There was no such thing as crossover.'

'Just like here in SWA and South Africa, we have no crossover, if you know what I mean,' Jerry blurted out.

Leah then produced a bottle of semi-sweet, red Madeira with two glasses that took whatever blues there was in his extravagant, spirited little head clean away. Jerry, in his oscillating mind gave a silent war cry – 'Whoooooooop!' – at the luck of being seduced by this beauty incarnate and if he had been alone, he said he would have jumped up and down.

That conversation let the girls know that they and Jerry were on the same page politically, certainly regarding the Black-White issues at hand. What put Jerry's mind at rest about what the girls were all about was the fact that, although these girls might have been left-leaning liberals, they were not so left-leaning as to juxtaposition themselves with the government's arch-enemies, the Communists. Both girls were avowed Capitalists and on more than one occasion decried Marx's *Das Kapital* as being unreadable. On more than one occasion they mentioned that the Communists had killed four times as many people as the Nazis. Communism in all its forms, they mentioned, has always had no idea how to run any economy and will always foster a revolutionary elite that again and again will exploit through tyranny, the majority underclass. Communism they denounced as having no class, in a meretricious sense.

Where is natural selection? was a slogan written on the front of a T-shirt that both girls wore. A society reduced to the average common denominator was anathema to the girls. Capitalism for sure has its victims, they said, but nowhere near the disastrous level of Communism, which will always bring apathy to the workforce in its wake. They also concur that in the long run, if the majority's debts are not eventually forgiven in a Capitalistic world, revolution by the underclass majority against the minority elite will occur. The human instinct for acquiring more than we can afford, in every sense of the word, being our Achilles heel on this planet is also something that they both agree about.

Over the next couple of months the girls had sussed Jerry out and not only grew to understand him, but to really like him as well. In fact, the two girls and Jerry became very close; yet, not even Jerry could they trust unconditionally. The authorities use blackmail all the time and even the most principled individual can be turned when a gun is held to their loved one's head, or when their own freedom is on the line.

He realised almost immediately that the high-standing nature of the girls did not preclude them from getting to the low-down nature of his lusts and he was soon thrusting upon them in dignity, digging into their nitty-gritties without indignity, with all his considerable sincerity buoyant with hormonal excitement.

The girls had known that he had rented a small apartment above the apartment house belonging to a certain Paul Clithero, the taxidermist, part-time diamond cutter and former convict. Clithero had been convicted and jailed twice before. The last time he was convicted was almost thirty years ago, for having stolen gems in his possession. Surreptitiously and stealthily, the girls knew that if Jerry befriended Clithero and came up with the idea that he, Jerry, needed quick, easy money, then Clithero would in all likelihood give Jerry illegal diamonds to sell.

Clithero knew Jerry worked for a diamond corporation and therefore, he knew that Jerry knew something about the value of stones and might have had connections.

The beginning of this plan did in fact eventually happen. Jerry did get the illegal diamonds from Clithero. But the girls didn't want to deal with Paul Clithero directly because, to the police, he was a big red flag.

Paul Clithero was a light-brown man in his late-fifties, with a very curly, almost wiry, full head of grey hair. His skin was leather-tough from a life spent in the African sun and was a folded, coppery brown from his genetics, which had some distant Hottentot blood in it. He was without consideration considered White by the White community in which he lived, but, to those who knew better, his sunken, dark-brown, almond-shaped eyes and the exaggerated height of his bony cheekbones were a dead giveaway of some native lineage. Clithero's appearance had a reptilian resonance, particularly when he wore his circular, horn-rimmed spectacles. A cigarette was always hanging from his dry lips. There was no *joie de vivre* in his intent eyes.

Paul Clithero lost his teeth in a brutal beating he took in jail three decades ago. He was brutally gang raped for over an hour, the rapist-convicts having used petroleum-jelly to make the ferocious penetration easier for themselves to enter that 'dark side of the spoon'. Hence, the genesis of Clithero's most popular expression: 'There's no problem that a little grease won't aid!'

Having painted a picture of some kind of monster, contrary to the image of him, Paul Clithero was kind and warm towards those he liked and he liked Jerry for three reasons: he liked the fact that an English boy from Durban would come to unbearably hot and alternatively freezing cold South West Africa in order to fulfil his desire to photograph the topography, animals and indigenous natives of the region. Clithero also admired Jerry for working at a local diamond mine, in its administration department, in order to earn enough money to pay for three years at an agricultural college in Somerset, England. Jerry wanted to attend that esteemed college after finishing his one-year compulsory military service that was to start in six months' time. Thirdly, the reason Clithero liked Jerry, was that Jerry loved listening to the blues, whose riffs would seep through the floorboards into the house below. The sultry sounds filled Clithero with a nostalgic longing for the past, when he had had all his teeth and when he had kept himself in better physical shape, because back then there had been a woman in his life.

That was a long time ago and even her image in his mind had begun to fade.

Paul Clithero had a contact in a central African country that passed on uncut diamonds to him, stolen from docked diamond dredgers that had worked the gravel from the beds of certain rivers in that dangerous, lawless, mid-continental region. His perfectionism peaked when it came to recognising gem-quality diamonds in the rough, uncut stage and he was a master at cutting and polishing them. In fact, the cut is nearly everything when it comes to diamonds, just as much, if not more than the size and clarity of the jewel. He would often tell Jerry that only about 2% of the diamonds reached absolute perfection, that the quality of diamonds and women can be recognised by their colour, the brilliance of their unique optical refraction and the dispersion of their marvellous lustre. He would tell Jerry that he liked women with 'spunk', who were endowed with a type of hardness, like a diamond, and who had strong convictions, whilst simultaneously having the transparency to draw one in, like a perfect gem.

Jerry had counted on Paul Clithero having confidence in him. Jerry thought that the reason he would give him for needing so much money so soon to study abroad was not only a good reason, but it was in fact the truth. The fact that Jerry had a source to take the diamonds off him was a boon to Clithero. But Jerry never mentioned the two girls or that, to all intents and purposes, it was the girls who had set up the whole operation.

Three gems, each six carats, were hidden in three potatoes that Jerry was to have handed over to Leah in the restaurant toilet where she was to then examine them with a magnifying glass and when satisfied, hand Jerry the money in exchange, while Monique remained at the table as lookout. The reason this particular restaurant was chosen for the diamond exchange was threefold. Firstly, even though the girls and Jerry were lovers, the girls did not want anything illegal at their place of residence and anyway, their apartment had only one exit out the back in the off-chance of a raid. Secondly, because of Paul Clithero's criminal record and the fact that Jerry worked in the diamond industry, the authorities were aware of Jerry, so anywhere out in the open as a point of exchange was also out of the question, especially in a country that has eyes everywhere. Thirdly, this particular restaurant had three exit routes out the back-kitchen end, two of which gave the girls the option of escaping into the bay, for they were also great long-distant swimmers and the third exit, which they eventually used, was a sub-terrain passageway that lead from the dry-goods storage room through a hole in the floor, which was usually covered by a 50 kg sack of rice, through to a complex network of storm-drain tunnels that lay under and criss-crossed the city.

Monique had sussed the place out a month earlier, having been told about the storm-drains by a cook at the restaurant, who happened to be a card-bearing member of the hated African National Congress. Because of the trust issue, Jerry was never informed about the tunnels or escape routes the girls had in mind.

Jerry had described the atmosphere surrounding his arrest in detail and this was his description of the event:

The two girls and Jerry are sitting at a table in a restaurant in Windhoek. It is a very hot and humid night. Jerry has his back to the door and is about to suggest that Leah and he go to the toilet to exchange the three diamonds, which are inside the three potatoes lying in his pockets, for the cash in Leah's purse. The two girls are facing him across the table. There is the faint sound of activity behind Jerry in the vicinity of the front door, but before Jerry can turn around to look, he notices that both girls are already aware of the disturbance to his rear.

There is a glint of a reflection of danger in the rich blue of their eyes. Their heads drop in unison onto their sizeable chests, but their eyes peel upwards, their heads still down, like racers in the blocks. In an instant, both of them, with raucous abandonment, give a belly scream and explode out of their seats in rapid time, simultaneously rotating out of their chairs, pushing the table into Jerry who is still facing them. Instantaneously, with synchronicity, both girls' pairs of legs quick-flex at the knees, exploding their thighs that extend their bodies over the table that was behind them, but is now the hurdle on their flight path to the back-kitchen door. The air is carved away ahead of them. Their arms whip whatever is in their way out of their path. Everything is thrust aside and backwards. They have blasted themselves into space at a feverish pitch. Their hands clutch the air like palms in water, propelling their bodies furiously forward. They are a mass of movement while, to Jerry, they are almost invisible in a singular way. The vibration of their combined energies tremble through every limb of their bodies and pulse the atmosphere, howling through Jerry's brain, inexplicably paralysing and perplexing his head, scattering his equilibrium and anchoring him to his chair. He does not even make a move to exit the room even though it is he who has the diamonds in his pocket, as he had not handed them over to the girls because they had said to wait a few minutes.

The effect of this sudden eruption of the girls has a greater impact on Jerry than merely physical. The surprising awakening of brute force in the girls has submerged below his consciousness and like a lethal dose of venom, has sapped him of his energy. He feels circumvented and impotent in the calamity of the moment. He feels light, as if his body has been spirited away in the undercurrent of the drama before him. He feels unaccountable for his inaction. An invisible trail of witchcraft has left the room and laid him under its spell. He is surrounded by the secret police, their guns drawn.

A deep commanding voice announces, 'You have no right to remain silent!'

Everything you do not say will be held against you.

30

Touch is the official tongue of those who prefer silence.
Irreverent Reverend Tom Groans

It is a warm, dry afternoon in Cape Town and the fan is turning fast on the ceiling of F's sitting room where I meditate on the disembodied pornographic scene before me. The scene is of body parts as topographical performance pieces, of body-contours depersonalised, oozing and heaving like volcanoes, or thrusting and pummelling like earthquakes. The vision is of disassociated people only connecting with their fluids, only integrating with their sexual organs. There is nothing to hold onto when one is so well greased. These are aesthetic intimacies without any emotional exertions. These are the pleasures of surface non-commitments, where display is the play of the day and where image is the sign of our times.

What I see before me is sexual release as a safety valve for frustrated pressure that has built up, or maybe it may have nothing to do with all my philosophical ruminations and that everyone today in the room is quite happy and just fucking for the money.

In the midst of all these robust busts, fluctuating penises and sexual magnetisms, the main 'actor' makes his appearance. He is 'hung like a rhino', according to the director and is about to work wonders on the female lying there on the double bed. Her belly and breasts are exposed through the front of her long robe of purple-coloured silk, which is richly embroidered with miniature black and white figures of couples engaged in coitus.

The male actor is a muscularly firm, long, graceful and handsome Coloured man in his early thirties, who looks a little out of sorts today, as it has taken him half an hour to get erect. Today, only his penis has a look of dignity about it, as he walks with a solemn stride into the room.

Hunger is the actor's nickname. Meanwhile, he mounts the bed enthusiastically like a tall jockey and embraces the eager female between her open, sweaty knees and parts her plump but hardy thighs, like one would a roasting-hen before stuffing it. Off they go in tormented, agitated fits, she shrieking and he umphing and aahing. They become insensible altogether. Her eyes wander into the back of her small, shapely head. This agitation of the main couple has the focused attention of the other rhyming couplets as they imitate their actions in an astonishing spectacle of supernatural appetites.

This delirium peaks in mutual multiple orgasms, diffusing the magnetism in the room until an effect of calm tranquillity takes effect.

'It is all an act at first, you know.' Angela's voice from behind startles me. She places her arms around the front of my body and continues, saying, 'This is convincing proof of the power of magnetism.'

'This might be convincing proof of the power of money,' I throw into the fray.

'The couples that we are looking at did not even know each other this morning, actually not even an hour ago and yet, look at all the passion they show for the person they're fucking. They have all created images in their own heads of the other's gorgeousness in order to get excited. Blow-up dolls were rejected because they do not give good eye contact. Yes, it is fantasy and yes, pornography may give unrealistic expectations to its viewers, with its perfect bodies reacting with over-exaggerated responses, but when a religious cleric talks negatively about pornography selling fantasy…holy shit! Is that not the pot calling the kettle black? I don't go to church and accuse the priests of disseminating fantasy. What's a bigger fantasy, the bible or me fucking the teenage babysitter? Fucking the girl in pigtails is far more likely to happen than being resurrected and your penis is certainly more likely to be re-erected! The priest is correct, that porn is better than reality, but that says more about shit reality than about porn. Aaron, it is the power of self-propaganda, being stimulated! Even governments know that one unbeliever may weaken the potency of its hypnosis and destroy its efficacy.'

I note that Angela can illustrate all her philosophies using sex as a metaphor.

'I am a palmist,' she whispers in my ear.

'You mean a psalmist?'

'No, I always say what I mean and I said that I'm a palmist,' she says, grabbing hold of my hand. Quickly, while still holding hands, she palms off to me a small newspaper clipping that she has curled up in a tight fold in her fist that I now gently grab and squeeze into my own palm in a sort of passing the baton, relay-style. Angela releases my hand, pats my back and says cheerfully, 'See you tomorrow.'

I head back up to my room, open the door and switch on the light in order to read the article clipping that Angela has handed to me. Angela has only torn out the small headline and first few lines. The third page headline in the newspaper, in large, bold, black letters, reads, *MURDERED MAN NAMED.*

Underneath, the first few words in smaller print are:

The white male, found murdered in a park by three bullets to the back of the head several months ago, has been named as Captain Johannes Demetrius Blank, known as Captain J.B., formally of Hout Bay in the Cape and lately of Pretoria,

Transvaal. Captain Blank was holidaying with his family at the time of his murder. Captain Blank had worked for the Bureau of State Security the past six months, having risen quickly up the ranks, after working eight years in the Transvaal Military Prison system as a Disciplinary Officer...

The rest of the article Angela has discarded.

I feel myself swallow deeply and I start to sweat under my arms. My pulse is racing as I try to make some sense of this revelation that Angela has thrust before me. What is her connection to the late bastard Blank and how did she know I knew him? It was public knowledge that an unidentified man had been shot in the park. The authorities had obviously known who Blank was, but had remained silent while an initial investigation took place. The body had been discovered one hour after its death by four junior schoolgirls who had become fascinated by a flock of seagulls eating sandwiches out of the reclining man's hair and chest. It was in all the papers.

Angela had very secretively slipped the notice into the palm of my hand, so as not to be noticed. The message was specifically for me, no doubt. She could have come up to my room and merely handed me the clipping. Possibly, she was playing it laid back in case someone was watching her, as the newspaper had only this evening come out with the victim's name in it, so maybe she didn't want to rush up to my room immediately.

I am going to play it cool and let her come to me. I will do the fishing and give her some slack. With this notice confirming my pathological former disciplinary officer's violent death in the park, my life suddenly seems to have come full cycle. Jerry must be smiling, I speculate, because Angela, however she is connected to this late, psychopathic moron and therefore connected to both Jerry and I, has done us proud.

The authorities initially thought that Blank had been shot once, as there was but one, irregular entrance wound, but during the post-mortem, three bullets were found imbedded, with the second and third bullets almost perfectly, but not quite, lined up behind the first one, like slightly misplaced metal vertebrae.

Quid pro quo, what comes will go.

31

We're filthy, on a filthy land, we waddle over waddled sand.

Irreverent Reverend Tom Groans

With the shocking news of Blank's death vividly buzzing about my imagination, I undress and with a towel draped around my waist, walk across the landing to take a warm shower. Returning to my room having washed, I am captivated by Angela holding a yoga position on the mattress. Her presence is clear in its three-dimensional distinctness, for her outline seems clean cut. Angela's naked figure is standing or more accurately, she is bending over backwards in a backward arm extension. Her torso and long, slim neck also hang, with both her lean muscular shoulders also pulled back. She appears as if caught by camera midway through a backflip.

I appear upside down to Angela, as her head is also pulled downwards in a continuation of the overall arch effect. Her hands are touching the sheet behind her. In this exposed position, her spine has a sharp vibrating edge to it, like a bow pulled to maximum that is about to spring explosively to neutral. Her stomach is smooth and as tense as a taut elastic band. She holds what would normally be an awkward position, gracefully and with elegance. In this position of sustained non-movement, the sweep of her rounded body has a visual and kinetic harmony, like a well-constructed and beautiful poem. Angela juxtaposes strength with an elasticity easily sustained.

Looking at her, I feel my head clear. Her openness echoes some excitement I have inside me somewhere. I identify and feel with her. Maybe it has something to do with energy, for I have never been that limber, nor have I ever been that simple in my suppleness.

I note that Angela seems to occupy a much smaller area of space than her tall, broad frame would suggest at this particular moment in time. At other times, when she is exposing her acute philosophical views or if in discussion, it is as if her intellect requires more expansiveness and she seems to take up more room.

She springs back up to her standing position, looking down at me. I am seated beneath her on one of the pillows, as she slowly rotates her neck, cracking her cervical vertebra back into position. At the same time as she is doing this rotation of the neck, she rather nonchalantly, in a matter of fact way, is playing with her nipples with her forefingers and thumbs, in a way that I have never seen done before. In fact, Angela is quite brutal in the way she is plucking and stretching them. She is also oblivious to everything around her in this personal activity of nipple aerobics.

Suddenly, like I have been hit on the head, a realisation strikes me. It is a stroke of extra sensory power, an existential moment that brings everything into focus. It is the nipple thing that did it, coupled with the newspaper notice of Blank's murder and all I can do is let out that universal monosyllable of surprise. 'aah!'

Angela is quickly shaken out of her daydream, clears her thoughts and says, 'What?'

I realise that I should have kept that exclamation to myself, but then I ask in as relaxed a way as possible, 'Angela, what is your family name? Your dad goes by the name, Pound

Current?' I have still not mentioned the article she handed me earlier.

'My family name?' she asks suspiciously.

'Yes, your family name?'

'Why do you suddenly want to know my family name, Aaron? Did this desire to ask this question all of a sudden shock you into asking it? Because all I heard was "aah!" then you ask this strange question.'

'No…I just this moment realised that I had never asked you your full name.'

'I can tell when you're lying, Aaron. I'm a very smart chick.'

'No, I'm not lying and if I am lying, what am I lying about?'

'Why do you want to know my name?'

'You obviously have something to hide, to blow up such a trivial question, into the kind of question the Inquisition would ask.'

'All right then, my surname is Ways.'

'As in "A-ways we go!"' I joke.

'Exactly! A. Ways. In fact Aaron, my full initials are A.L. Ways, as in Always.'

'What does the L stand for?' I ask, but I already know the answer and it was the nipple thing that clued me in. Now, the Angela-Captain Blank-Jerry Jacob and I connection makes sense. I speculate that Angela either did the killing or was involved somehow in the dirty deed done to belligerent, bilious Blank. And suddenly I know that I am in trouble, to say the least; especially if she is working for the dreaded African National Congress. She is a spy in the house of porn and I might be in a jam.

'The L stands for Leah,' she says in her clear, concise way.

'As in Dire Leah, I presume?' I jest to see her reaction.

She holds my gaze and without batting an eye says, 'As you know, Aaron Aardwolf, I've heard this nickname of mine before. Dire was the nickname given to me by our late friend, Jerry, in South West Africa.'

I catch my breath, as I feel a cold sweat on my temples and a sharp muscular pull in my stomach, while all I can mumble is, 'What?'

'You don't know, Aaron?'

'What do you mean by "late" friend?'

I am shocked. I am shaking.

'Oh! My God, Aaron! You didn't know that Jerry died?' Angela whispers.

I am stammering. 'How would I know? The last time I saw Jerry was at our camp and he was packing his kit for jail. What happened? How did he die? How do you know my connection to Jerry?'

'He killed himself with a drug overdose, Aaron. I'm really sorry. I eventually made contact with him via a Black connection I had in his camp. He told me all about you in a long letter he had written, which he had given to one of the Blacks from your barracks, who in turn had smuggled it out of your camp the day he left. The Black man who was working in the officers' mess that you defended by punching out that officer, posted the note to my post office box number. Me finding out that a certain Aaron Aardwolf was staying in this house in District Six was unbelievably serendipitous, a needle in a million haystacks! Jerry had kept my post office box number and given it to that Black man in case of an emergency. Jerry knew he was in emotional trouble before he left that camp. He killed himself in transit to jail. Jerry would never have survived the brutality of another extended period. It is this Terrorism Act of 1967, which gives the government limitless power to jail whomever they want, indefinitely and without it ever going to trial that disturbed Jerry.'

I am hardly listening and remain dumbfounded, a little dizzy and out of sorts.

'Isn't it ironic, Aaron, that you and I are here in District Six and it's this number six that is the crux of this matter, as it's Section Six Law that allows any police officer, at his own discretion, to detain anyone that he thinks is a terrorist until such time that he, the police officer, is satisfied, and quote, "until no useful purpose be served by his further detention." The government or should I say, the Secret Service, are under no legal obligation to ever let you go, or even let your family know where you are. This is Section Six Law and this is District Six and lawless.'

'You trust me, Angela?' I watch her face carefully, searching for an honest response.

'I trust in your common sense,' she says in as light-hearted a way as possible, under the circumstances, but there is a hint of a threat and an abrasive assertiveness in the timbre of her voice.

'Am I in trouble or not?' I am half-serious at this stage of the proceedings.

'Aaron, this conversation never happened. By the way, Blank did his apprenticeship on you guys in the military, an apprenticeship in brutality. He proved to his superiors that he could take no prisoners and that he had no conscience about beating or even killing someone as an appropriate response to a personal insult.'

'Like you, maybe?' I am being facetious and brave and drive home my point. 'You believe that when it comes to honour, killing is not a crime either, right?'

Angela ignores me, giving me her expression of 'Are you stupid, or something, comparing apples, with oranges?' She continues her train of thought. 'The powers that be moved him quickly into a position that was perfectly shoe-horned for him. They promoted him to a position of company leader of an interrogation unit or for want of a better title, Murder Squad. I had a more personal motive for hating the asshole and that was because of his treatment of Jerry.'

'A vendetta is still a conflict involving honour, no?'

Angela dismisses my comment with the flip of her head, giving no response to my statement, and exclaims enthusiastically, 'Are we going to fuck or not?'

She lies on her back in front of me. I am still seated on the pillow.

'Yes,' I say as I remove my towel from around my waist. I am looking forward to giving her a perineum massage, so I can check out the birthmark she supposedly has, the one that Jerry talked about. Is it the shape of a question mark or an ear seen in profile? That is the question. Also, will I suffer the slings and arrows of outrageous fortune and will I have to take arms against a sea of troubles?

Reach for her as one would a priest; bring her back to your confessional, she will exorcise your lies and clear your head.

32

*We're sodomites; we do the planet, we bugger with
a robber's habit!*

Irreverent Reverend Tom Groans

Angela 'Dire' Leah Ways lies on my mattress looking at me
with an easy half-hint of a smile on her pink lips. The mystery
surrounding the exact shape of her perineum birthmark was
solved a little while ago with one warm kiss, followed by an
informative peek. The birthmark is in the shape of a question
mark and about that there is no question.

'Aaron, Jerry had written in his letter to me that what had
got him into hot water with the major was that he had not
told him of you spending time alone with Max Goldman when
you all went to visit the Goldman's home. A mole had informed
on the two of you. You do know, Aaron, there's talk that Max
Goldman is a supporter of the ANC, that he is one of us.'

'You mean he's Coloured?' I joke, getting my equilibrium
back. Max is Jewish and is a distant cousin of a close friend
of my family.

'No, stupid!' she says, dismissing my obnoxious remark.

'Do you know Max personally?' I ask.

'I've sat in on one of his lectures at the university and I've
read two of his books on the questions concerning morality.

It's been suggested that he has some connection to our military wing, Mandela's 'Spear of the Nation' movement. Years ago, in a lecture at Cape Town University, he had said that a campaign of sabotage against government establishments in order to overthrow an oppressive regime was far more acceptable than a terrorist war that kills 'soft' targets. I'm sure the government is watching him like a hawk. One of Max's close friends from Cape Town is a Coloured friend of my fathers. This Coloured friend of ours happens to be on our Coloured Representative Council, which as you know is a big joke because under the government's "separate development" theory, we are meant to make our own laws, but in reality we have no power, no money and no land. This is where we want to be and I'm stubbornly holding on for as long as I can, for my advantage is that I can pass for White. Aaron, you and F are in fact living in what was my darker cousin's home and she and her family lived here only two years ago.' She changes direction. 'What did Max Goldman tell you that day in his home that the major wanted to know about?'

'The abbreviated version of what he said was that he had heard through my family that my poetry was very good and that I should take a good hard look at this despicable system we live under and attack it surreptitiously using metaphor and innuendo to influence the next generation. Max said that religions are really governments disguised as benign dictatorships and that they also tell "noble" lies, which they see as a necessary thing to educate their ignorant "flock" into seeing things their way.' I take a breather and note that Angela is listening intently. I breathe in deeply and continue. 'These little deceptions force-fed over time, Max said, hypnotise the listeners so that over more time bigger deceptions can be self-fed.'

Remembering back to my army days when I had first met Max, I recalled that what struck me initially about him was that he appeared to be an impulsive idealist who had a lot of faith in his intuitions.

'Aaron, are you with me?' Angela's voice shakes me out of my reminiscing.

'Yes, I was just thinking.'

'Thinking about what?'

'Oh, I was just remembering Max. Tell me, how does F come into the picture?' I am curious.

'My dear Aaron, F is not in the picture at all; he's on another path altogether. He knows nothing and we will keep it that way, will we not?' It is more an instruction from her than a question to be answered. She lies on her stomach and motions for me to sit on her buttocks in order for me to massage her lower back, and says, 'Talking of paths, have you seen the graffiti written on the wall facing your balcony, down the adjoining alleyway?'

'No! I hadn't noticed anything written on that wall the last time I looked. It must have been written within the past two days,' I reply, while applying olive oil to the sacroiliac area of her upper-buttock/lower-back region. I finish the half-hour massage and venture onto the sun-drenched balcony, peering into the alleyway. Written in black paint are the words:

Bar, bar, black man, have you got your pass? Signed, *Irreverent Reverend Tom Groans.*

Remember. Now remember to forget.

33

Man tries to tame Nature's feminine wildness, to halt the great flux of its drive.

Irreverent Reverend Tom Groans

Angela's musky body odour exudes from around her neck and underarms and is an affective stimulus that moves me emotionally into a nostalgic state of arousal. This aromatic odour represents anticipated gratification. Her breasts also literally inflate like a balloon when she gets aroused. I can only imagine how strong the subliminal impact is that Angela bombards me with, because the conscious points that I am visibly battered with are more than strong enough.

One of the main reasons I am attracted to Angela is that we share a mutual dominant emotional prime mood – optimism – which is the centre of both our equilibriums and to which both our personas return from any emotional digression.

Both of our bodies have a similar muscle tone, which makes perfect sense because mind and body have the same symbiotic relationship with each other as well.

A definition of Angela is like any answer, it comes only with hindsight, at the end of a period and now I feel I am in the middle of her sentence. At this moment I am reading her like Braille. I have never seen Angela angry, but I have seen her frustrated as she suffers fools and foolish situations badly. From what I have seen, the one organ she uses as an outlet for this neuromuscular expression of frustration is her vagina. She gets an overwhelming desire to fuck and I mean fuck, not make love. Animals when they get frustrated need to defecate, some throw up, some hyperventilate, but Angela fornicates because her internal organ is involved in her emotional process and the orgiastic release flushes the lactic acid out of her system and brings her muscles back to kinetic homeostasis. She is a penis whisperer.

I start off making love, but end up fucking with her.

Angela does not fit the military-spy stereotype characterised in popular literature, as she is neither a fanatic nor an ascetic. I have written some good poems of late and she has been my inspiration, so I turn to her lying relaxed in a foetal ball at my side and say, 'Angela, you might not know it, in all my writings of late, you have been my muse.'

'I'm your horse?'

'No, you're my stable! I'm joking. M.U.S.E!'

'I'm ragging you.'

'You don't fit any mould, Angela. You're unpredictable.'

'You mean I'm not the stereotypical tall, blonde, blue-eyed bimbo?'

I ignore her comment with a smile and continue. 'I read once that the stereotype sets the standard against which one assesses one's experience. In other words that the expectation is self-fulfilling and that it is this discourse on the stereotype seen in movies and read about in novels, etcetera, that creates one's goals and passions and desires.'

'They got it wrong in my case. Discourse didn't create my passion.'

Angela is relaxed and for once, I can tell that she is not in a philosophical mood, so I change tack. 'So, what does F know about you?' I ask.

'F knows that I'm from somewhere in Cape Town and that

while studying at Oxford I befriended Russell and met Russell's friend, Jacque the director, there as well. F knows that Russell was wanting to film in Cape Town and needed somewhere central to stay. I'm well acquainted with this house that you are all staying in, as my family had lived in it for the past hundred years before the expulsion, as I mentioned to you earlier. I knew that besides F, the large house was empty, but that your two rooms were being rented to an Aaron Aardwolf. Anna, the cleaner who cleans for F every so often, told me. Anna's an old family friend. With your connection to Jerry, it was pure coincidence that I should run across you in Cape Town. Unbelievable really! I then sought you out! As I said earlier, Jerry had mentioned you in his letter to me. After investigating F, I became well aware that he was a dandy and would like nothing better than to meet a cultured homosexual like Russell, who also happens to be beautiful. The first day after meeting you, when I came to the house, I presented F with a photograph of Russell reclining naked on a deckchair on some white-sandy beach in Greece. I asked F if he had any spare room, even if it were the size of a closet, which Russell could rent. I knew that F would be intrigued, if not by Russell then at least he would be attracted to me. I knew that for a girl I would be appealing because I have got what he has since called "fly-half rugby player legs". I knew that F was a Nationalist editor of a right-wing newspaper and that he would be a perfect cover for our plan to film a documentary on the desecration and disintegration of District Six for anti-Apartheid propaganda to be used abroad.'

Angela takes a breath and I interrupt.

'Hold on! What documentary on the disintegration of District Six? I thought Jacque is making a pornographic movie under the guise of doing an architectural documentary on Cape Dutch architecture?'

Angela shakes her head at my naïvety and I elaborate.

'This is what Jacque got the visa for in the first place? I

thought that Russell had in some way blackmailed F, if that's not too strong a word, into turning a blind eye to the erotic goings-on, if you know what I mean. Are you telling me that you've hoodwinked F by using the pornography itself as a subterfuge in order to film something far more dangerous?' I am flabbergasted at their audacity and courage to conduct a double 'red herring.'

'Yes, the house is a Trojan Horse, or should I say Trojan House? The enemy has crept in. There is no money to be made in documentaries on either architecture or politics, but there is plenty of money in the selling of sex,' she admits.

'Another ruse?'

'Yep. The rooster is here!' Angela announces, looking past me towards the door, which opens to reveal a bare-chested F in his jogging shorts and sweating from having just returned from a run around the block.

F is a little winded, but smiles and says, 'What's up?'

'Nothing!' Angela and I say in unison.

Nothing can be full of much.

34

Trust Never Sleeps
Irreverent Reverend Tom Groans

Diminutive Officer Arcane lay on his side, curled up in the foetal position, fully awake, while his 6-foot wife lay stretched out alongside him, gently snoring, her long blonde hair cascading this way and that over her gorgeous face. A giant bell was ringing in his head like someone hammering on an empty milk canister. This noise was all in his imagination, but it was disturbing his desire to just fade away for the evening and go into deep oblivion, somewhere beyond rapid eye movement sleep. What was bothering him was the enormous faux pas of his career, when he had neglected his duty and responsibility to protect the psychopathic Captain Johannes Demetrius Blank that led to his murder in the park. Not that he could have prevented the killing per say, but he might have been able to identify the shooter. He was distracted the day of the killing by his son's shooting out of their neighbours' porch lights and so had compromised his position as bodyguard. He should have been more alert.

As he lay there on his side, with the noise of his subconscious thudding between his ears, he began to reminisce about that fateful day, as he had circled the park, having followed the captain before he made the unfortunate decision to return to the police station early instead of entering the park and keeping company with the doomed Captain Blank. And then, with alarming clarity, it seemed as if a giant fish had swept itself into the little net of his mind. He made one of his creative excursions into the un-virgin territory of the ragged reef of his truth, as if a tape had triumphantly been turned on in his head. He remembered with his photographic memory everything and everyone he had passed that fatiguing day on his way to and from the park. The noise in his head had quietened down and the blonde girl with the yellow helmet and large, over-sized sunglasses, reading a map and smoking a Camel cigarette while standing alongside her scooter, came into focus. Why had he not zeroed in on her before?

He remembered back to his first reaction that day, when he first set eyes on the girl with the map. She reminded him of someone, but then he became distracted by his son's problem. He had first dismissed the girl as being non-threatening, while he had also noticed in that glance, even though her upper face was obscured by the frame of the glasses, that she had resembled his own wife, or more pointedly, how his wife had looked two decades earlier. His wife and this girl both had the same full-lipped broad mouth. They were also both blonde and very tall.

Now reminiscing, he realised that not only had the helmeted, tall, blonde girl reminded him of an earlier version of his stunning wife, but, in retrospect, she reminded him of a girl in an out-of-focus photograph that he had seen on a wanted poster, on a wall of a Windhoek police station in South West Africa about a year and a half earlier. The blurry photograph was of a tall, blonde girl and a young male cohort of hers. The man, in his late teens, was eventually caught in a sting operation, but the girl, who went by the name of Leah, and another blonde girl, miraculously escaped that day.

Officer Arcane had superimposed the girl in the out-of-focus photograph and the blonde by the scooter in the fertile oasis of his mind's eye. With both of them in this juxtaposition he became convinced that they were one and the same terrorist. The shooter was the one on the scooter, he was certain.

Peter Arcane, forever playing with puns, was determined to follow through on his hunch and become the 'cane' to this girl's 'able' body. He smiled to himself. He had little sentiment for his nemesis, whom he was now 100% sure was the same terrorist who was involved in the illicit diamond dealing in South West Africa and who evaded capture in Windhoek.

Arcane saw Leah as something akin to a diamond, in that she was just a beautiful, brilliant illusion. The mystique of diamonds themselves is all an illusion, endowed by marketing people who have converted them into universal tokens of power and romance. The trick has been endowing the crystals with romantic sentiment so that those who buy these gems never sell them because of sentimental reasons, enabling the market never to get flooded.

Leah is easily marketed, Arcane surmises, because of what society considers her rare façade of beauty that people would like to hold onto. As far as Arcane is concerned, her beauty is only skin-deep, but he acknowledges that she is as dangerous as a diamond and that she cuts just as deeply. He reasons that this Leah creature, whoever she is, has been endowed with an additional bogus sentiment, that of being some kind of Sister Teresa, who is prepared to give of herself to others even though she is a fortunate White person, for the good of the oppressed Blacks. Yes, Peter Arcane thought, she is exactly like a diamond in that she is a false, romanticised product and all because she has the correct cut, colour, grade and size. What he does not know is that she also refracts like the precious stone, as she is rainbow-coloured in her DNA.

The poet sits on the burning deck,
picking his prose like mad!

35

He feels comfortably unclean.
Irreverent Reverend Tom Groans

Irreverent Reverend Tom Groans has pitched himself onto my balcony from the roof and has landed at my open door. This is toothless, manic-depressive Groan's second uncalled-for visit. I hear the thud from my bed where I am reading a book. He pokes his head into my room.

'How's it going?' he says in colloquial English, with his Afrikaans accent and then without a response from me, says, 'I walk a slackened tight rope every day to stay afloat. You can take away my thoughts, if your bad treatment is successful, for you have no conscience to get rid of, except me. The racist description of me is your prescription. Your injunctions prohibit. I exhibit pathologies without apologies. The procedures here have let me know I'm diminutive. I don't have to be told I'm diminutive, but you have told me that I'm diminutive. Now, I'm diminutive without being told, because I scold myself. I tell myself that I'm mental health! I'm Bi-Polaroid in black and black and I can't get my light colour back. You, though, are on the side of a Monster and are blinded by choice, because you choose to ignore your inner voice. You love a Monster and are blinded by praise, for you choose to ignore its evil ways.

146

You love a Monster, with all your ardour, because you serve; you aid and harbour!'

Irreverent Reverend Tom Groans turns abruptly and jumps onto my balcony handrail then onto the roof and deserts me.

Know to have your resignation and application ready.

36

Her spirit feeds her, she's in-fed
Irreverent Reverend Tom Groans

Small, weather-worn fishing vessels are beached, having been pulled up onto the crushed-shell and sandy shoreline that makes up the fishing-boat area of dockland. This is the part of Cape Town harbour that has not been concreted over as of yet and the beach infuses a distinct fish and seaweed mix into the air as the soiled ground evaporates the on-going fermentation that the sea and fishing boats continue to throw up, as they have done for the past two hundred years or so.

Angela has come down to the harbour to meet her brother, a Coloured fisherman who can also pass for white, although he is a shade darker than Angela. It is through the fishermen that Angela passes on her information and videos that she has accrued on her dangerous rounds.

Her brother's boat should be arriving in one hour's time.

Angela likes to come to the docks before all the hubbub of activity overtakes the place. She takes in this ambiance as the thick ocean fog lingers over the sea and coastline.

*

Suddenly, all her senses have instantaneously triggered a warning to her sixth sense, her District Six sense. She must be on the defensive and be alert. She is a wanted person by the government and right at this moment a sound slightly behind her, to her left, seems out of place, as the area is usually deserted at this hour. Only the ocean in front of her has she eliminated as being safe.

Angela rotates her head slowly to the left, then to the right, with no other part of her body moving. She does not blink. Her peripheral vision has picked up something that was not there a moment ago. It is the figure of a medium-sized man, about 5 foot 10 and weighing 170 pounds or so, who is wearing a mackintosh and an Australian cowboy hat. The man is about 100 yards away and is standing facing her in a misty silhouette, smoking a cigarette. The smoke from the cigarette hangs about his face like a shroud in the heavy fog.

Her focus burns into the figure, assessing his identity. The two of them have not made a move for what seems like forever, but in reality is only five seconds. An expectation of some action electrifies the space between them, at least from her perspective that is, because she knows well that a cat and mouse game in this country can mean life or death.

Someone once said that 'a great silence has a mighty sound', well, this was it.

The form of the man has dropped his cigarette and is approaching Angela in a carefully studied way, the way a great cat approaches a dangerous prey. Angela has decided that the distance needed for her to verify who the person is would be too close for comfort and that she must throw caution to the wind and get out of the situation. If he follows her, then she is correct in having run and if he does not follow, so what? She will have erred on the side of caution. With a swift, cylindrical turn, her pelvis and hips swivel to her right, turning her away from the figure whose image is still cautiously moving forward towards her. The fuel of her adrenalin emits a burst of air from out of her mouth, like out of the exhaust pipe of a car, and with that grunt she jack-knifes and is torn loose into her shuddering stride almost immediately. She is off the beach and onto the concrete road in full momentum, accelerating all the time, gliding into the next gear. Only now that she is in full motion and has regained a state of focused calm, with her white-knuckled fists flying out and back at her sides, synchronised with her furious legs, does she for the first time glance back to look and see if she has a pursuer.

It is now clearly evident that she does indeed have a pursuer.

He is being out-distanced by her and quickly. Another glance back and she notices that he has slowed almost to a standstill and is talking into what must be some kind of walkie-talkie. The Bureau of State Security, otherwise known as BOSS, must be after her. Someone must have tipped them off, or she has been recognised somehow, even though she thought she had been as careful as possible.

The quiet routine of the evening has broken down. Angela has to clear her head and get some coherency into her thinking, so as to act spontaneously and fluidly. She has trained for such stimuli and her triggered response, with all its flexible options, must now kick in as she accelerates her pace. All the rules that govern her day-to-day thinking have to be discarded. All those habits and routines must now be thrown away. Anyone who gets in her way may die now, as her new set of rules that thumbs its nose at the Law of Structured Morality attacks the new problem at hand.

The options are complex and she has to out-logic her adversaries. She has to think beyond her axiomatic inclinations and frame of habits. The Law of Routine is what the enemy is anticipating. They expect her to reason with coherence, but the difficulty of the task before her has reached critical mass and so she has now to challenge her exploratory drive, which is at this time saturated as all the obvious options have evaporated. Angela must be ready to pounce on chance and

150

hope that success favours the brave. She must rely on habit and the impulse to keep moving in the direction of District Six. At the pace she is keeping, the district is about four minutes away. She has just passed under the highway and the single-story buildings of that area are straight ahead of her. She hopes that she has a deeper strategy than her follower and that she can have enough randomness and improvisation in this pursuit to defy the tunnel vision thinking of her tracker, who she hopes is a mediocre thinker who would reject extraordinary moves for inadequate ones. She has to provide variety in her zigzagging through the maze of District Six, yet always be subtly heading towards F's house and her safe-haven shelter under the floorboards, beneath the mattress in my room, where her cousins, when they had lived there, had built a false ceiling in the room underneath. Between that false ceiling and my floorboards a person could hide, in the eventuality that something like this should happen. The space under the floorboards is the floor dimension of my room, but 4-feet high. There is a mattress there where an average person can sit up straight and lie down comfortably. The space has candles and matches, as well as nuts and raisins in well-sealed plastic bags. There are also an additional number of spare plastic bags for ablutions, five bottles of water and vitamin C pills.

Angela knows this awaits her if and when she gets there.

She organised the hideout while I was at work. My bedroom is never locked, because it is easy to break into anyway, for anyone who wants to do the dirty deed. Meanwhile, she hopes that her crisscrossing looks haphazard. With this plan of hers, she has the risk of taking longer, but the advantage of tiring out her opponents, as she intends to go over the rooftops on a cross-building, hurdle type of a course. She also knows that she is fitter and faster than any man she has ever known besides some professional runners and that her long jump is second to none.

She anticipated that there could come a time when she would

have to flee for her life into the district and she also anticipated that the pursuers might include police dogs. Her designated route includes many long jumps between the buildings. The final jump she plans will be from the adjoining building alongside F's property, which is 4 feet higher than the flat roof of my bathroom where she will land. It is a 15-foot jump over the alleyway onto that concrete roof. The fifteen-foot jump would be too much for the dogs, but well within her range even without a long run up. She would have to execute the landing well and tuck-roll after her feet hit the concrete roof to ensure no injury to her arms and legs.

Angela knows the rooftop route extremely well and can reconstruct it blindfolded in her head and so she can plan her moves rapidly and keep one step ahead at all times. Because of the nuances of the buildings, one from another and where to jump from and what to land on, they should never get any closer than 60 yards and from that sort of distance they would not be able to follow her exactly, so she would be able to pull away easily. This is her outline of a plan. Another advantage to her is that she has been in the habit of only straying from District Six when the deep fog comes in, which the sea has provided today, thereby taking helicopters out of the equation and even making it difficult for the police cars to manoeuvre, especially as the roads are either very potholed or under construction.

She knew that she needed a red herring to throw to the hounds in case there were any dogs involved in tracking her. So, yesterday, anticipating a possible chase, she, using tweezers, picked up a hairclip that had been mislaid on the couch in F's lounge, which belonged to one of the male porno actors, and placed it carefully into a small, sealed plastic purse. Using the same tweezers she interjected a sprinkling of hair that had been freshly cut and was lying on the floor, into the hairclip so that the dogs would follow someone else's scent. In another sealed, plastic bag she placed a fillet of kipper to use around my room and balcony, to throws the dogs off her scent. What Angela does not know, is that the hair from the floor of F's lounge is actually pubic hair and not head hair and that Jacque the director, otherwise known as The Doctor, had ordered it cut from around the male lead actor's penis, in order that the actor's member should appear larger and longer.

The plastic purse with the hairclip and pubic hair sealed inside it, as well as the sealed kipper fillet, is at this moment lying inside the pocket of Angela's running pants and is being jogged about with every step Angela takes in her stride towards F's house.

Life between the blinks goes oh so fast.

37

Blind runners in the night, race and run along; the end is out of sight!

Irreverent Reverend Tom Groans

As Angela's legs take her ever faster forward, her brain tunes out from having to think about the actions her limbs are going through and her mind starts wandering onto other matters of a psychological nature. Right now, she sees herself as a Coloured person in the process of being pursued. This thought is rushing at the pace of her flying feet as she continues to ruminate over what it means to be a half-breed, a mongrel, an outcast and a potential political enemy. It is simply a sign that they give her that she only sees and feels because of their pointing. When she is with her immediate family, who are all a darker shade of white than she is, then she sees herself as a relatively lucky young lady.

As she forges ahead, her shoes pounding the street, her diaphragm filling and deflating, she recaptures her thoughts. To most White South Africans, the word 'Coloured' means a little degenerate and something not positive, whilst to a Coloured person like herself, it means just a normal human being who is unlucky enough to be born in South Africa at this time. It suddenly amazes her that at such a critical time such as this, her mind can digress into the stratosphere of philosophical thought and yet, she knows that it is simply some kind of displacement that she has created to deal with the on-going assault.

Angela knows that in a Eurocentric way she is beautiful, which has given her an added advantage in terms of self-image, even amongst the Coloureds, who know that the whiter one is, the better off one is in South Africa. Angela has another thesis that she is working on that has to do with the Coloureds self-image. The Mulatto, of mixed ancestry, have another problem that they have to come to terms with, which is, not only are they the descendants of loser slaves, but they are also the descendants of loser rapists as well. These are the thoughts of Angela as she crosses into the district. These are the crosses her people have to bear, as the peoples of South Africa are at cross purposes, even regarding the simple word 'Coloured'. How will we ever all sit on the same page, to be able to meet mind to mind?

Right now, there are more pressing things Angela has to deal with as she climbs a wall on her way to the roof level of District Six.

A stitch in time can get one killed.

38

Fate slips into you, it takes you by surprise and how
you deal with it either demeans or satisfies.

Irreverent Reverend Tom Groans

Everything that Angela anticipated happened. The dogs were brought into the equation, culminating in her dropping the contents of her plastic purse into the alleyway without her fingerprints or odour being on them and smearing the kipper fillet around the rooftop and my front door. She then hid in a space under my floorboards until the danger had passed, which I had absolutely no idea existed.

I did help her, as I had not yet left for work. I heard her particular, bird-like whistle call for help and immediately implicated myself in the drama by telling the police, who eventually arrived at the adjoining building with their dogs, that I had seen someone fitting her description land on my roof and drop into the alleyway from my balcony.

After the hairclip with the male pubic hair had been found in the alleyway and the smoked herring had successfully disseminated the dog's minds, the pursuers were led asunder and away from Angela. The pubic hair was immediately sent to a bureau think tank to be puzzled over. The conclusion the group came to, with special dogs playing some part in the identification, was a shock that truly confounded the minds at the Bureau of State Security. They concluded that it was indeed a hairclip, but that the hair was definitely that of a male. How they came to this conclusion is anyone's guess. Maybe some residue of sperm had remained? In the words of the officer who was in the original pursuit of Angela, 'It has come as no surprise that she was a chick with a dick. I did not doubt it for a second, because no real woman could run that fast and kick my ass the way she did!'

You're always on the outside, when looking in.

39

It's only as an outcast that he can be seen, sorting through his disreputable and often obscene spats with the status quo and their preserves, while there's nothing tortured that ever unnerves him.

Irreverent Reverend Tom Groans

F's impenitence, with his lack of remorse and his iconoclastic attack on anything and everything at odds with Apartheid, is bafflingly strange in that his politics is at odds with his particular lifestyle. All these private submersions into the underbelly of his obsessions are anathema to the ruling party and are serious felonies. His apparent ease with these excrescences and the comfortable way he slips into this lifestyle makes his own philosophy sound like double-talk. If you watch him long enough, his high ground caves in.

Due to the volume of F's marijuana intake, his manner at home is never fierce and he is always very steady on his feet, precisely because he moves so slowly when stoned. He sometimes looks like a mountain, tall and shrouded in a cloud of smoke. The window of opportunity to have a meaningful conversation with him is narrow, as you have to get him just before he gets high.

By the time F is ready to go to work in the evening, an

amazing transformation takes place in both his demeanour and appearance. It is as if a chimney sweep has been into all the recesses of all the passages in his brain and cleaned them out. He always leaves home squeaky clean and as fresh as can be expected from a man who wears shapeless drab suits and looks like the reincarnation of Lincoln. This contrast in his demeanour is part of his idiosyncratic makeup. F might give the impression of being unobtrusive because, as he says, he does not make laws, but merely follows them. Naturally, when it suits him not to follow rules, he will change his principles. At best, he is complicit in the corruption around him.

Russell's relationship with F is a clandestine operation from Russell's perspective that is worthy of a movie script. Russell is the mole in the ointment and the instigator for all that is happening in F's house. Angela is his intermediary, or liaison officer, in the shenanigans. She organises the set, so to speak. What F does not know about Russell could kill F and give his friends a few laughs. To put it succinctly, F stands for almost everything Russell despises. Russell, besides being an archaeologist, is also a rabid anarchist who believes in violence not only against frontline soldiers, but also against those technicians and bureaucrats, the decision makers, who operate with impunity in the background and who keep the circle of atrocities circulating. F would fit into Russell's definition of someone who keeps the circle of fear alive, as he is the editor of a right-wing paper that keeps the government's propaganda wheels turning. F's complicity at best is a huge problem for Russell, because Russell believes that those who do not oppose the atrocities and just sit on the proverbial fence are guilty of complicity in the offences, because 'they also serve who only stand and wait'.

Being a weak individual is not an excuse for inaction in Russell's book. Russell believes that to use violence against a perpetrator of violence does not put you in the same immoral category. He feels that anything a corrupt government sanctions will be ineffectual.

As an archaeologist who works the land, Russell sees ownership of personal property as stealing from what should be everyone's right of use and access. He is an egalitarian and an anarchist who believes that the eradication of the hierarchy of government will allow people to be free, where voluntary cooperation between people will keep order intact and only through violence, he believes, will those that want to hold onto the reins of power be forced to let go of their intransigence and advantages. Rhetoric, with its reliance on persuasion, will never work. Russell believes that it is difficult to ask anyone to commit suicide.

Angela's disagreements with Russell are about his egalitarianism, because for egalitarianism to succeed, people would have to be persuaded to behave reasonably and she does not believe that most people are either reasonable, or fair, or have much ability to sympathise. Russell would be constantly at war with anyone who wants to accumulate more things for himself than what his neighbours have, which is our God-given right according to F. Therefore, F sees the left's insistence on taking from the successful as a form of totalitarianism. Ironically, on these points, Angela is adamantly on F's side of the argument, while Russell's socialistic outlook would place him at odds with Angela.

Is one of Angela's roles to sabotage Russell? With her Capitalistic bent being at odds with her anti-Apartheid leanings, is her role in all this to manoeuvre the Marxist-leaning ANC towards the West and away from the Soviet Union. The US needs South Africa's plutonium and Angela would be a huge string to their bow. Big business would even finance a West-leaning anti-Apartheid regime, even though the US had supported the Apartheid Government. Maybe the West was looking to a future beyond Apartheid and would bury someone like Angela into its midst like a mole.

Ironically, the one small area of agreement between F and Russell is not on a political theme. They both agreed with the notion that artists do not have to be over-sensitive neurotics who are born to suffer. Being miserable should not be the price tag of being talented.

F has never talked politics directly with either Russell or Angela, but both have heard F's views exposed in overheard conversations. Russell is the person who organised the pornographic movie as a ruse for filming an anti-Apartheid documentary, using his filmmaker friends from Paris who came via Oxford. F has fallen for this ruse: nook, line and penis. I think he believes that the visa given to the filmmakers by the government to film Cape Dutch architecture was a ruse by Russell and company to film pornography, because there is more money in sex than in stone. F, I believe, turned a blind eye to this because he wanted to experience Russell's blind eye. All puns intended.

F appears oblivious to most of the goings-on in his house and this morning he has not unwound himself from Russell as they lazily sleep upon their ruffled bedding, just as they had the morning of Angela's narrow escape from the law.

Angela, for her part, has not left the house in a week for fear of being detected. She is in my room this moment drinking a strong mug of Columbian coffee and is sitting naked in front of me in the lotus position, while I am lying naked on my back, my eyes squinting against the sunlight that is streaming through the windows. Angela seems translucent as the light in the room encases her, but I intuit some anxiousness and a slight tension in the flicker of her eyes. Under the circumstances, it would be abnormal if she felt otherwise, but of late she has been alert, approaching and retreating from every room silently. She seems to dissolve into and out of doors like a shadow. She has to be vigilant in staying sharp right now, because of the endless possibilities for making mistakes.

This quietness, this abnegation that I see in her behaviour, allows all five of her senses to become extravagantly magnified and tuned, which is proving much to my advantage, as she is diligently concentrating and allowing those senses to resonate in me as the high tide of her sexual urge surges in. The chaos of sensations that these hormonal surges has on Angela allows her to escape the order she has imposed on herself. Her powerful 'tsunami orgasms', as she has talked about, gives her the sweet sensation of 'drowning' in a deep physical release that lets her flee her anxiety overload.

Everything about Angela has contradictory characteristics, for instance the hair on her head is very fine and blond, in contrast to her tight-knit pubic hair. Angela takes a deep breath and with my eyes closed against the sunlight, I anticipate that she has something to say to me.

'Aaron, every day we non-Whites walk a tightrope; we have to be careful about what we do and what we say, who we can hang out with and where we hang out. We don't just have to work a full day, but we have to work a full day with a fist up our ass.'

'Yet nearly all of you underlings still believe in God?' I interject.

'Yes, because it gives people something to hold onto.'

'Even though It is letting you down?'

'Yes, because this is my theory. We embrace the White man's God because the White man has given us a break, particularly on Sundays, from breaking our backs. So, paradoxically, in a way, the White man's church, more than God, has saved us and given us a day off work. Saved, not through revelation, but through relaxation.'

'So you yo-yo between belief and not having any?'

'I have no faith! Anyway, I just focus on sensual feelings, simply because they feel good.'

Angela always returns to her theme of sex and love and yet there is very little bohemian about her. She is deadly serious.

'Aaron, you get the point. Meanwhile, to change the subject, it's becoming a little redundant, us always analysing F, as he's too far gone and beyond redemption.'

Like an ostrich, its head buried in the sand, I bury my nakedness within you.

40

It often seemed to her that only when on her back does she have any meaningful conversations.
Irreverent Reverend Tom Groans

My eyes follow Angela nostalgically, even though she has not yet left. She is waiting until after dark to depart via the roof route. At this moment she is peeling an apple, using a fruit knife with her pinkish-white, enamelled hands. Her joint purrs in the ashtray beside her on the floor, drifting off a wisp of light brown smoke that soon assimilates itself into the air.

A moment before the apple peeling, Angela had said that she would have to take leave soon, as she has something important to do elsewhere. How long? The less I know, the less I have to lie about, she informed me. Right now, I try to take in and remember as much about her as I can recall, so that she can live longer in my head than she otherwise would.

The apple peeling is almost over and she says in quite a matter of fact way, 'I knew a light-skinned Coloured girl who like myself also passed for White. She killed herself with a prescription-drug overdose last year because her White husband had, for quite a while, not been giving her enough attention. Barely a week after her funeral, her husband fell in love with another girl. Had my late friend known at the time how much less attention her husband had really wanted to give her, I think she would have killed herself earlier.'

It is the first time I have seen a deep sadness in her eyes, as they usually hold, like the edges of her large mouth, a subliminal impression of amusement.

'What are you saying?' I enquire, a little bewildered by the strange story and stranger afterthought that has cropped up in her head. Is she giving me some sort of message? Is she telling me that whatever I think I know about her is not quite the whole picture? Does she think my position is precarious? A small vein pulses on my temple.

She answers, 'Maybe one does need as much embellishment as one can digest in order to get the most out of a picture. My late friend was always confused about her husband's feelings towards her and she never sat down with him to really talk. She had a tendency to evade details. Intimacy is in the details.'

Angela is the opposite of laconic, as she has a whole dictionary of words at her mouth-tips and is irreverent in her usage of them.

'Intimacy comes with being able to relate to the person you are involved with,' she says and continues, 'I'm not sure about the relaxing part because when I relax I lose my edge and tend to only gain lethargy. I have to stay a spring chicken and not become an autumn hen. I have to remain sharp like I'm in the middle of guerrilla warfare. Naturally, I've my own ethical guide to live by, as I have no faith in anything but myself being the intelligent designer of my own life. Those who have faith in God behave no better than people of no faith, in fact, I think, on the contrary, those of faith behave worse.' She immediately changes the subject to one of a sexual nature. The energy is with us. 'Sex is my religion with its ritual cleanliness, sacred bed space, self-belief and pleasure.'

'What do you mean?'

'Sex, for me, is a vocation and the only missionary work

needed is the missionary position.' She licks a speck of apple from the corner of her mouth.

'Well, sexual appetite keeps one young,' I add.

'That is because orgasms release the lactic acid build-up in our muscles, while its pleasurable sensations distract us from becoming too solemn.'

'Yes,' I respond, 'one should always let an orgasm's success go to the head of one's –'

'Penis!' she shoots in and gives a dramatic sigh. It is call and response time. Her sighs are an aphorism embodying the general truth of her relaxation and at times such as this, she is indiscreetly erotic.

'Angela, what dedication you have!' I say, stroking her thigh.

'I've a pugnacious, monk-like dedication to sex!'

'What part, Angela, is monk-like?'

'The part where my ego is not involved is monk-like, as well as my dedication,' she retorts.

'True,' I agree.

'My sex is voracious, Aaron. I'm a sexual self-plagiarist, always copying some earlier successful move, but I'm also always aware that I do not become a parody of my sexual self, so I keep trying to be inventive.'

'Well, you've a highly developed imagination.'

'Yes,' she adds with a wicked twinkle and continues, 'I'm certainly more grounded because of the pressing issues here. You know, Aaron, the high moral talk here in South Africa, for the most part, is full of feigned sensibilities that are really veiled snobbery, stayed for the benefit of showing off to others a paternalistic superiority in regards to us unfortunates, whom one wishes to help in order to show something akin to benevolence.'

She has finished dressing and with a small backpack and wearing tennis shoes below her Levis, she moves towards me. We kiss and I feel her wet, warm tongue on mine, then she is suddenly gone into the night, over the rooftops like a cat. Many animals are forced out of their burrows, but Angela, for fear of retribution, is forced into burrows. She once said to me that she lived on 'burrowed' time.

A jigsaw is puzzling when a piece of it goes missing.

41

I request, that you tread gently on this chest.
Irreverent Reverend Tom Groans

'Hello, my name is Officer Arcane.'

The voice comes from the vicinity of the floor and belongs to a stocky, proportional dwarf whose big ears are useful for picking up fallaciously deceptive statements and whose equally large African-elephant-shaped, slightly hooked nose comes in handy for smelling the fear sweating out of his detainees.

Officer Arcane, who is standing in the middle of the opened front door, introduces himself to Russell and me and at the same time displays an official Secret Service silver badge that he has brought out from the inside pocket of his blue jacket.

'I notice the look of surprise on your faces,' he continues. 'To be forewarned is to be forearmed and I don't want you armed in any sense of the word. I detect that your surprise at me being here is twofold: one, me being here and two, my stature. One does not expect to find unusually small folks like ourselves in such an aggressive profession, "out in the field," or for someone so short to have worked his way "up" in the ranks. Do not underestimate the magical powers of us little people. When one does not have the size, one develops other things like intuition and strategy. I am also, as my name Arcane suggests, a person who understands secret things because of an intuitive gift I have acquired, which enables me to extract information out of thin air, if you know what I mean. I will get right to the point. Do you know, or have you seen anyone who resembles the woman in this photograph, if she is a woman?' The badge has disappeared and been replaced by a photograph between his stumpy little fingers. The switch has been so quick it is as if he has done it by sleight of hand.

Russell and I both take a step forward and stretch our necks around the photograph.

I speak. 'Just looks like a normal baby to me and the diapers are covering its sex, but it could be a boy. It's hard to tell.' I am trying to comply with the officer's request and at the same time, cannot for the life of me believe the officer is serious about the two of us trying to identify an infant who was only a foetus less than a year ago.

Officer Arcane quickly turns the photograph around so that he can re-examine the photo and realises that he has taken out a photograph of his one-year-old nephew by mistake. He quickly replaces it with the intended photo without showing any sign of embarrassment. This time I have to bite my lower lip while at the same time try to keep a poker face and not show any sign of distress.

The photo is of two people, taken at a distance of about 30 yards by a surveillance camera. The girl in the out-of-focus photograph is definitely Angela to my knowing eyes, but what is more shocking to me is the fact that the male in the picture talking to Angela is my deceased friend from the army, Jerry Jacobs.

'Well, officer,' says Russell. 'The male looks like a man and the woman looks like a woman. I do not know what you mean by saying, "If she is a woman"?'

Officer Arcane replies, 'The person in question is the person on the left in the photograph. There is a question about her sexual identity because her athletic skills are extraordinary and we found some hair samples that might suggest that this person might in fact be a man in drag.'

'I have never seen that face before, as far as I know,' I answer clearly.

'Well, sir, you are Aaron Aardwolf, are you not?' Officer Arcane comes back sternly.

'Yes. Why?'

'Was it not you a fortnight ago who mentioned to the police that the fugitive who was being chased by their dogs had dropped from your roof into the alleyway behind this house?' Officer Arcane levels back at me.

'Yes!' I answer, unshaken.

'Well, Mr Aardwolf, that fugitive was the person seen in the photograph, was she not?'

'To tell the truth, officer, I didn't get a good look at the face as she was moving very fast and I only saw her in profile, but I don't remember her being as attractive as the girl in your photograph and in fact, on that day, my first impression was that the person being chased was some kind of male hippie from the area, with long sun-bleached hair, as we have quite a few here.'

Officer Arcane brushes my comment aside, as one would an irritating fly, with a quick shake of his head. 'May I come in for a moment?' he asks, but it is not really a question, as he walks in before waiting for a response from the two of us. He walks down the hall ahead of us, turns into the lounge and seats himself on the sofa, his one short leg crossing over the other short leg, both legs a long way from the floor. Talking up to us as we are still standing, he says, 'Do you know why I have such a big nose? It is because I have huge olfactory nerves to smell out rats and I smell a rat!'

'Meaning what?' I enquire, frowning.

'Meaning that she or he was heading in this direction and

seemed to know the terrain too well for a first-timer. What's going on here is a hunt, a fox hunt. The elite, upper-class wolves, which are the lower-class fox's natural predator, are dying out and being rapidly replaced worldwide by plebiscite democracy. Natural selection is disappearing fast. It's a case of bad luck for the upper-class wolf and Christmas day for the serf fox. The lower-class fox, whom the upper-class wolf kept under its control, has now become king of the dunghill. Because of its natural lowbrow habits and appetite for taking what it never deserved to have in the first place, it's become a mass killer of culture, etiquette and societal obligations. My job as the hunter is to track down the weak and the lame of these foxes and put them out of our misery as quickly and efficiently as possible, lest the countryside slide into anarchy. Correction, I'm not the huntsman; I'm in fact the lead hound. The fox is never torn apart by the hounds on a hunt, but its dispatch is accomplished only by the lead hound like me, who is first on the scene and who snaps the fox's neck in a fraction of a second so there's no cruelty merely for pleasure's sake!'

To me, one thing is for certain and that is that political correctness is definitely not in charge here. Funnily enough, Angela also uses the analogy of a hunt in regards to this pursuit of her by the authorities. According to her, all hunters attempting to curb freedoms are fascists, no matter whether they are fascist leftists or fascist rightists.

The irony is that in the 1920s, Russian Jews abandoned promising careers in fascist Germany to come home and serve the ideals of the fascist, anti-Semitic Revolution, where they would in turn be murdered. Only Stalin's death in 1953 prevented the total extinction of Jewish life in the USSR.

'My God!' Angela once said. 'This Apartheid government has just banned the classic book, *Black Beauty*, not because of content – the story is about a horse – but because of its title!'

After this brief sojourn into the realm of reflection, I am back to the present with wee Arcane before me. It is Russell's voice that jars me out of my contemplation.

'What is the person's name?' Russell asks.

'Leah is the name we think she goes by. She is just an organism to me, to be squashed like one would a poisonous spider. For anyone to get caught in her web would be a deadly mistake. She has the guile to rope people into her schemes and leave them in the lurch while she makes off. I cannot tell you specifically what her crimes are, but if you should see anyone matching this description, call me on the number I am leaving on your table. She is armed and dangerous, but the more serious problem we have is that this person, this organism, for want of a better description, has the cerebral equipment to work with.'

'What equipment?' I ask, but I am being facetious as I know what he means.

Officer Arcane likes talking in riddles. 'Grey matter! Brains!' he answers in his obsessively meticulous way.

I am thinking, thank goodness that F is not here at this time, because if he was then Angela would be done for and therefore, possibly Russell and the whole gang, as in South Africa at this time you can be found guilty by association.

F is tied into the Nationalist Party hierarchy, so he would just plead ignorance, which would be true in regards to Angela is what I think. To F, it might be a possibility that Angela is just another gorgeous chick and his main connection with the Europeans boys. On the other hand, he might well be in on it all and might be the spider responsible for setting the trap. Who in the hell knows what is going on in this house? One thing is for certain and that is I had better not be too inquisitive.

I look at Officer Arcane and try to understand what I see in the features of the man sitting on F's couch. Firstly, Officer Arcane looks like a three-dimensional collage made up of different slabs of meat, something akin to the smudged-faced, seated men in Francis Bacon's oil paintings. He is always in a state of perpetual motion. The facial texture is uneven and seems to have been pitted by the elements, as if he has spent much time in harsh winds out at sea. Russell, at the same time, thinks that Officer Arcane must be a composite created in a movie studio.

The present situation, if seen by a fly on the wall, would look hilarious. It must look like the psychologist is sitting on the patient's couch, while the two patients stand. Officer Arcane suspects everyone indiscriminately, not because one person looks particularly more suspicious than anyone else, but because he sees the criminal in everyone, as all he can see is criminality. You are guilty until proven otherwise and then you are still lucky to get off, is the officer's reasoning. As an aside, Officer Arcane thinks everyone is homosexual until proved bisexual, himself and a few others being the heterosexual exception.

Officer Arcane thinks that he has an eye for sorting out irreverent pretentiousness from phoniness, sorting out bullshit from bullshit, because everything is some sort of bullshit. He has no time for any sort of dilatory, wasteful action; he has to have all his facts in place and is relentless in his pursuit of information, but once he has it, he is like a rabbit on a rabbit. His motto is, 'Information, then Irritation.'

Officer Arcane's baritone voice breaks the hiatus. 'I am the environment that this organism has a relationship with. I must give a steady drying effect on the amount of water available for this organism's needs. Anyone collaborating with her feeds her this and will be held accountable. Good day, as they say in the US of A!'

Before Russell and I can blink, Officer Arcane is off the couch and placing his card on the table. Without shaking hands, he strides with fast little steps, like a mechanical toy, down the corridor on his way to the front door.

Officer Arcane knew about me being in the house, so surely he must know that this house belongs to F and yet he never mentioned him. Where does F fit into the equation?

Make sure you save your lies.

42

Everyone repeats the mantra, mantra, mantra . . .
Irreverent Reverend Tom Groans

An explosive storm has erupted outside of F's house, generating high velocity winds with biting rain coming down off the precipitous edge of Table Mountain's expansive vertical drop. Darkness has fallen and F has departed, having left for work right before the storm came on about an hour ago. The documentary on the plight of the Coloureds of District Six can continue by stealth, without his knowledge.

With few exceptions, most of the Coloureds interviewed in this documentary are articulate and educated because the producers want an emotionally and intellectually detailed picture and besides, most of those interviewed started off their lives in dire straits and can thus empathise with the plight of their less fortunate brethren.

Inside, overhead lights are glaring at the family seated on the two couches facing the camera. The Coloured family consists of a mother, father and their two sons, both in their twenties.

The father is fifty-eight; Douglas is his name. He is a successful merchant and well-read autodidact who has had no formal education beyond the age of ten. The mother's name is Peggy and she is forty-eight years old. Robert is their eldest son and

Keith the younger. They are both philanthropic, abstract-thinking intellectuals who have returned from England having taken a hiatus from their studies abroad. The camera is rolling and this is the sequence of their interview:

Robert: 'Obviously there is a lot of negativity amongst us who have been ripped out of our moorings.'

Keith: 'The hopelessness here gives others the impression that we are calm to the point of complaisance and I suppose that is true, because we either have patience or we go insane.'

Douglas: 'I want to talk about what this move away from here means to us. I heard your interview the other day with that poor alcoholic older chap, where all he could say was that he misses the place. He was just as inarticulate as those guys the Americans sent to the moon, whose comments told us absolutely nothing emotionally or even aesthetically about what they felt or saw when looking back to Earth from that deserted rock. I will tell you what this loss here means to us. Where do I start? For many years I had cherished the hope to live here as an equal with all the peoples of this country, but this longing faded with time, leaving only tenderness for the view. This view! It is human nature with its perfidious behaviour that is frightening. Now these views have been wretched away as well.'

Robert: 'In real estate there is a saying that says, "location, location, location," and there is no better location in Cape Town than here in District Six!'

Keith: 'My brother is being a little facetious, but he is also correct. Getting back to the bigger picture, I liken the White ruling class to a comatose person in that he is comatose in his capacity to empathise with those people he regards as non-persons.'

Robert: 'I had to get out of South Africa and only because I was fortunate to be academic could I get scholarships, just like my brother, in order to go to an English university and become educated and thereby return and be on some kind of par with White South Africans.'

Robert: 'Our education has been our motivator.'

Keith: 'Our Coloured stereotype here in South Africa is of being superficial, jovial drunks and half-breed, petty criminals or worse: in-breeds! What has happened here is what happens to the under-class when the ruling-class stereotypes them. The self-hating Coloureds perpetuate and reproduce that caricature that the ruling party paints and the regular Coloureds like us have to live with the consequences.'

Douglas: 'It all comes down to image. Trafficking on the credulity of people to believe anything well marketed, such as the superiority of Europeans under divine command, for they appear to have the right of way, to promulgate laws against the inferior half-breeds has been reinforced by self-serving superstitions. Security is a superstition anyway and White security is an absolute superstition. You will see what I mean in another twenty years.'

Keith: 'Do you know what the similarity is between having faith in a leader in our society and faith in any major religious icon? Both are established on the reliance of someone superior for your decision making!'

Robert: 'I want to speak about something no one will talk about in South Africa and which should be the crux of this documentary of yours, something that should not just be touched on, but which should be highlighted. If what I have to say to you gets to the authorities and it would, if this documentary you are filming should get into the wrong hands, then both you guys and I will be in very serious trouble. What I'm going to give you is the whole speech verbatim that SS Reichsführer Heinrich Himmler gave in Posen on October the fourth 1943 to a meeting of his SS Nazi generals. I'll link that talk of Himmler's to what's happening here in District Six. I know the whole speech by heart, because it touches on everything the Apartheid regime has bought into: namely the twisted morality and the sentimentality of the toughened hero who has a dirty job to do, but "someone has to do it"! Here's SS Himmler's speech:

'I want to speak very frankly about an extremely important subject. Amongst ourselves we will discuss it openly; in public, however, we must never mention it! I mean the evacuation of the Jews, the extermination of the Jewish people. This is something that is easy to talk about. "The Jewish people will be exterminated," says every member of the party, "this is clear, this is in our program: the elimination, the extermination of the Jews: we will do this." And then they come to you; eighty million good Germans and each one has his "decent" Jew. Naturally, all the rest are pigs, but this particular Jew is first rate. Not one of those who talk this way has seen the bodies, not one has been on the spot. Most of you here today know what it is to see a pile of one hundred, or five hundred, or one thousand bodies. To have stuck it out and at the same time, barring exceptions caused by human weakness, to have remained decent: this is what has made us tough!' Robert takes a deep breath, and continues. 'Take this speech and eliminate the word "exterminate", because we have not been exterminated, nor is it their intention, even if it might be their desire. And replace the word "Jew" with the word "Coloured". And instead of seeing thousands of bodies, replace that with seeing tens of thousands of people being displaced from their homes here in District Six and you'll get the same sentiment, about how tough it is for the Whites to have to do this necessary thing of forced removal, because they are suffering in their White bleeding hearts, each and every one of them, for that rare "good and decent" Coloured that they have to do this terrible thing to, because of the majority of us Coloureds who are pigs! Oh, how the authorities suffer with this emotional conundrum for our sins. It's the cross they just have to bear, doing a bad thing, but for a good cause. Every church has its decent Jew hanging on its walls, having to suffer for the naughty Jews that are responsible, and the Christians suffer every day for having to watch their image of Jesus suffering on the cross, so that every now and again the majority of pig Jews in one community or another get rounded up and exterminated so that Jesus doesn't suffer alone. This vicarious redemption of throwing your sins onto another person can be twisted to endorse scapegoating.'

Keith: 'What my brother says is absolutely correct. The Apartheid Government has done to us a very similar thing to what they did to the Jews initially, when forcing them into ghettos. They dispersed an identifiable group of people from their homes and assembled them in a remote place separated from family and long-time neighbours and friends. As long as people remain isolated within their class, the authorities have every opportunity to exploit and control them. The real reason for the break-up of District Six, aside from the fact that it was situated in the best location, in the heart of Cape Town, under Table Mountain, was because for over a hundred years, people of different races lived together, alongside each other harmoniously. Jews, Christians and Muslims, Coloureds and Blacks, Whites and Asians, all coexisted and would have made a good blueprint for a democratic South Africa that the government just could not allow.'

Robert: 'The term "Coloured" means people of mixed blood, so the vast majority of people born in South Africa are Coloured, White Afrikaners included, who have an average of five per cent Black blood running through their veins, from interaction with the slaves and Khoisan peoples. Now, to change the focus and show a little reverse racism, we have another conundrum. Walter Sisulu of the Black ANC anti-Apartheid group had a White father. Winnie Mandela's mother was light-skinned with blue eyes and flowing hair, whilst her husband, Nelson Mandela, who refers to himself as a Xhosa, has maternally inherited DNA of the Khoisan tribe carousing through him, as his facial features clearly show and yet, when Mandela's ANC and other blacks refer to Africans, they exclude these other peoples whose blood they share. This is ridiculous, that the first peoples of Southern Africa are excluded from the term African. The Khoisan lived in Southern Africa thousands of years before the first 'Colonial' Blacks arrived from Central Africa. I just want to articulate that District Six was a perfect melting pot that worked and should have been nurtured. Will Mandela, if he ever gets out of prison, stand up and announce that he's proud to be Coloured? I doubt it! Nearly everyone has the racist concept of pure blood carousing about their heads and they don't want to accept any tainting of that blood. We're all tainted! We're all like diamonds.'

Keith: 'I want to go back to our point earlier about false martyr-hood; the stoic hero who grits his teeth, the person who suffers for what he has to do and proclaims that this doing on his part is what enables you to live a better life. I think that the Jesus myth has been very dangerous, not only because it gets everyone really antagonistic about the group Jesus belonged to, because our emotions are stirred even more so, because someone is suffering in silence, while the group responsible takes no heat whatsoever in his punishment. This story is vehemently and virulently racist because it fosters our basest feelings of revenge.

Robert: 'So the message is clear, that it is okay to let some innocents, like Jesus, suffer for the greater good of the mankind. It is the opposite of "Let ten guilty men go free so that one innocent person should not suffer". It's a precarious philosophical slope that we can all potentially slip down, rather than one that needs to be predicated on an initial grand delusion such as the desire to exterminate another race. It's the lumping of people into this group marked X and that group marked Y, etcetera, that will be this country's undoing and is this country's sin.'

Keith: '"The meek shall inherit the earth" is another false myth to keep those *not* meek in powerful positions. What bullshit!'

Robert: '"The meek shall inherit his girth." Ask any choirboy.'

Peggy: 'Okay, you guys. Enough!'
There is a pause then Doctor Jacque calls, 'Cut!'
The day's shooting ends.

Life is in the past lane.

43

*Like a savage salvaging for your stray words, he
lingers.*

Irreverent Reverend Tom Groans

Officer Arcane is at his destination: our front door. His perpetual
pedalling in search of a culprit gives him the 'right of return'
into our lives. We are in the same war, but on different sides.
Officer Arcane is the visible enemy in a conflict of attrition.
Everyone is looking for check-mate.

This time, Officer Arcane has his superior, Officer Stratagem,
in tow. In a nutshell, Officer Stratagem is a hard nut to crack.
He is a former international rugby front-row forward, who is
backward in every way, except where his beer-belly protrudes.
He talks with a lisp, which makes him doubly difficult to
understand, because Afrikaans is his mother tongue.

'Thtep off-thied!'

'Yes, step aside!' Officer Arcane repeats.

The two men advance past me, down the entrance hall and
into F's study. It is early evening and again F is at work.

Officer Arcane announces, 'We are here to capture our target.
This is our concern. Her name is Leah. Our sources tell us that
she is headed to this house and that she will be here within
the hour.'

'I do not know who Leah is,' I say.

'We will thsee,' Stratagem says sceptically.

'We will wait here and see. Make yourself at home!' Arcane re-joins.

'It is my home!' I joke feebly.

'Just stay in the house and do whatever you were doing before,' Arcane orders.

'I was just leaving,' I blurt out honestly.

'Eth-thep that!'

'Except that. You must not leave!' Arcane paraphrases for Stratagem.

'I phweel a twickle on the back of my head thath thumbthing ith up.'

Officer Arcane interprets again, 'When Officer Stratagem gets a gut feeling about something, he gets this tingling sensation that makes the hairs on the back of his head stand up. He senses that something is coming down!'

Both officers smile.

Officer Arcane emphasises, 'You had better take our presence here very seriously indeed. We are closing in on our prey!'

'Leth uth Pway!'

Officer Arcane parrots again, 'Yes, let us pray! I can feel the dilatation of the skin vessels on my arms, just as Officer Stratagem feels it on the back of his neck. It is exciting bringing something one has worked on for so long to fruition. The question is who is she coming here to liaise with?'

Officer Arcane's walkie-talkie starts to buzz and an Afrikaans voice mentions that the 'subject' is on her way.

Officer Arcane talking into the walkie-talkie barks, 'Do not intercept her; let her come to the house and we will take it from here.'

There is a knock at the door. Both officers have their pistols drawn as they proceed down the corridor to the front door.

Officer Arcane opens the door with his pistol down at his side. Standing tall, square and blonde, and looking very similar to Angela, is an Angela look-alike. It is not Angela. This girl has slightly smaller breasts and her beautiful full mouth is slightly fuller than Angela's and turns up at the ends. She is also slightly less muscular, but only by a bit. I realise from my late friend Jerry's description of her that this must be Angela's cousin, Monique, the other girl involved in the South West African intrigue. I also now know with certainty that this is the girl who was involved in the fight in that café, my first evening in District Six. It is also obvious to me that the authorities do not have a clear image of what the other girl working with Angela, alias Leah, looks like. The two girls, to anyone not familiar with either of them, look like identical twins. Maybe the authorities have seen both of the girls separately in the past, but thought that they were viewing the same person. They could never have suspected that twins were involved. Even when Jerry was arrested in South West Africa, in that bar, the action happened so fast that neither of their features would have been easily identifiable or distinguishable in the chaos that followed.

Monique appears surprised. 'What the Fuck?'

'Leah?' Officer Arcane questions.

'Who?'

'You are Leah, right?'

'Fuck no! Who the hell are you and why do you have guns?'

Officer Stratagem steps into the conversation. 'You caweeing ID?'

'No, I am not Karine Idee either; she's in India.'

Officer Arcane says sarcastically, 'You're fuckin' funny. Do you have identification on you?'

'Oh, ID? Yes I do, but who are you?'

'Don't be so goddamn stupid. Who do you think we are dressed in police uniforms?'

'You could be going to a fancy-dress party.'

Officer Stratagem adds, 'You phink thith ith a joke?'

184

Monique takes the offensive, 'Let's see some ID of yours!'

Officer Stratagem is now aggressive. 'Fuck you, lady. Here ith my ID!'

He sticks the gun in her stomach. Monique quickly produces a South African passport out of her handbag and hands it to Officer Arcane, whom she thinks is in charge. He looks at the name in the passport, then at the picture. The name reads *Monique de Villiers.*

'And I'm six years old!' Monique adds.

'Fuck you!' Stratagem curses.

Officer Arcane shrugs, 'No, she is telling the truth, sir; she was born on the twenty-ninth of February in a leap year. She is six years old.'

The pursuers shout. The hunted tell jokes. Both attend their schemes.

44

As long as someone else is being dumped, you can be impartial to that beating!

Irreverent Reverend Tom Groans

There is now less bravado in the demeanour of both officers, as if they have been deflated, the belligerence in both of them subdued and extinguished. The tide has gone out, so to speak, in Officer Stratagem's blue eyes, swinging the keel of his pupils, the hulk of his disappointment, to and fro, like a boat caught in seaweed. The strained intent sits heavily on Officer Stratagem's broad, muscular shoulders. Officer Arcane's eyes blink over Monique and he compresses his lips tightly, having been unnerved by the disappointment of not having Leah in his custody.

Monique, for her part, sits unself-consciously, her ankles drawn up onto the couch beneath her in the lotus position. She sits in exactly the same position as Angela would normally sit on this couch. She says, 'So you obviously want to know what I am doing here in this house. You were expecting this other person, Leah, whoever she is. I came here to visit my friend, Russell, who I know from university at Oxford, England, who should be here shortly. I also came here to the house in order to meet Aaron, whose poetry I've read, but whom I've never had the pleasure of meeting before now. I also wanted to talk about the possibility of him editing a book that I'm writing, but now is obviously not the right time to have visited.'

'I also went to Oxford, way before your time. What kind of book are you writing?'

'You went to Oxford?' Monique is surprised and so am I. She continues, 'Well, Officer, if you really want to know, it's a book correlating the shape of a person's buttocks to that person's personality. The book is to be called 'Tongue in Cheek', as it is a subjective hypothesis. People read faces, people read palms, while I read buttocks!' This, Monique has spoken without mischievousness and without suggesting anything immodest. She, like her cousin, has a husky, low, strident voice and humorous, dancing eyes. Both girls have none of the tedious complexes of someone their age and they both are by nature, positive, with the natural poise of someone who strives for adventure and happiness.

This is a girl without pride, I think. I like it that she has no modesty. I am also looking forward to the sequel of Monique's 'buttock' conversation.

Officer Arcane produces a photograph and says to Monique, 'Have a look at this photo. Does the girl in the photo not look like you?'

'A bit.'

'It looks like you for sure!' Arcane asserts.

'Maybe it does look like me.'

'I wonder why Russell didn't say the image looks like you when we asked him?'

'You'd have to ask Russell that question, but the obvious answer is that the photo is not of me, so Russell was correct; he doesn't know this person. I have a look-alike. So what? We all have doubles somewhere. Anyway, besides visiting Russell and Aaron, my family lives here in the area and I have a three-week break from university. I arrived in the country two months ago and prior to arriving in South Africa I had not left

187

England in six months. You can see from my passport where I have been the past five years.'

Officer Stratagem comes to life suddenly with, 'Bworders are pworewiss!'

'What?' Monique cannot understand his lisp.

Officer Arcane repeats, 'Borders are porous. Criminals can get in and out of a country without having their passports stamped and besides, passports can be counterfeit is what Officer Stratagem means, which is why in about fifteen minutes a female member of our finger-printing staff, Officer Flaccid, no joke, will give you a quick physical examination and take your thumb print. By the way, how long have your family lived here in the area?'

'For a hundred and twenty years, from the time when we were classified Coloured and long before we were reclassified White, as both my parents, when they were alive, by all appearances appeared to be lily white.'

Both Officers glance quickly at each other. They both know that in South Africa people are classified and reclassified all the time.

Officer Arcane interrogates, 'What are you studying at Oxford?'

'Wet-nursing.'

'Don't be a smart-arse!'

'I'm studying philosophy and politics.'

'So you must think the politics suck here? You do know the saying, that a conservative is a liberal who's been mugged?'

'So what? A slut is a virgin who's been seduced!'

'What's your point?' Arcane is getting annoyed.

'Not every liberal who's been mugged goes on to take a conservative stance, just as not every virgin after sex ends up a slut!'

'Wait until you get mugged then we'll see your politics change direction.'

'I never discuss sex, politics or religion with strangers!'

Monique jests.

Officer Arcane turns ironic. 'Don't think of us as strangers!'

Monique jousts back, also ironically, 'I love the politics here.'

'That's bullshit!'

'Why ask the questions if you already know the answers?'

'Because I want to get it from the horse's mouth.'

'Then you have the wrong animal. I'm all filly!'

'I don't trust you, not one bit!'

'That's not the bit in your horse's mouth is it?'

Officer Stratagem is confused, 'Whath the fuck are you twu twalking abouth?'

Officer Arcane explains, 'She's just being facetious.'

Monique questions, 'You don't trust me just because I look similar to a girl you suspect of being a criminal?'

Officer Arcane shoots back, 'No, because you are professionally cool in your responses and you have such pat answers. You seem to have all your bases covered. In other words, you are too good to be true. You're too cute!'

Monique lashes out with her fast tongue, 'Don't discriminate against me just because I'm good looking!'

'There you go again with a smooth answer! Do you have a family member who goes by the name Leah?'

'Not as far as I know, but I have a very large extended family, many of whom I have never met and my late father fucked around, so I might have many half-siblings somewhere or other that might look like me.' She says this with an implicit undertone of steadfastness and assurance. She looks the two officers in the face and asks, 'What did you say this person, Leah, whom you were expecting, did exactly?'

Officer Arcane is fuming inside, but holds it in, 'We did not say. Do you know anything about diamonds?'

'Diamonds are forever?'

'Anything else?' The officer is getting used to Monique's sarcasm.

'They're a girl's best friend supposedly, but I hate jewellery!'

Officer Arcane ignores the comment and says, 'I'm going to ask you a question and don't be cute with your answer. What's a carat?'

'Something you obviously want to check, to see if I have it in my panties, or God-for-bid underpants, otherwise why else would I need a physical examination by an attending female officer, with the name of Flaccid. Of course, you could also be looking for diamonds up one of my apertures, or is a carrot something fillies eat?'

Both officers look at each other again. Monique is really playing cool and playing it confidently.

Monique asks, 'Is this Leah person a guy, otherwise why would I need a physical examination? I'm no transvestite; every part of me is a woman.'

At this moment Russell walks into the room and announces, 'I can vouch for that!'

He has come into the conversation at the end of Monique's comment. The film crew, with Doctor Jacque in tow, meander into the room and are surprised to see the two cops in uniform. Jacque and his film crew leave the room. Russell embraces Monique by kissing her on both cheeks and says, 'Mono, what's up?'

Officer Arcane answers before Monique can answer, 'We are just continuing our investigation, but I have a big question to ask you, Russell. Why did you not even for a moment hesitate in saying that the girl in the photograph was not Monique, when to anyone slightly perceptive the blonde girl in the photograph that I showed you earlier looks almost identical to her?'

'Because it's not her. I know Monique very well. Do you know how many people here in District Six look like Monique? I've seen two just today!'

'You didn't even make a comment about the similarity of their looks.'

Russell is nonplussed. 'I'm very observant and detail-orientated and I knew it was definitely not Monique. Why should I give more information than I'm asked? Why should I waste your time?'

Russell excuses himself, saying he will return with coffee for everyone if they wish. They answer in the affirmative as all their mouths are parched.

Monique continues, 'By the way, to answer your earlier question, all I know about a carat is that it is the ancient weight of a diamond that has been standardised. What that weight is, I have no idea.'

At this moment, a flat-breasted, short, redheaded police officer enters the room, a member of the film crew having let her into the house. Officer Flaccid, as her name suggests, is the silently, gloomy type. After a brief introduction, she and Monique disappear into the bathroom for the examination and fingerprinting.

Russell, who has been making coffee during this time, returns with four mugs and everyone around sits down in silence, waiting eagerly for the results of Officer Flaccid's examination of Monique.

My instincts tell me that the two male officers are lost. The inflections in their voices have become less assured and their half-smiles have become inauthentic. Both officers have taken to some nervous fidgeting and are unconvincing in their attempts to appear at ease with the situation. Their guesswork is in ruins. I imagine that the worn timbers in their heads are creaking right now. I also imagine that the knots in their stomachs are so hard and cold that even a hot coffee would not be able to warm them up.

Braille-way station needed for the blind.

45

A circle is a line encamped araound itself.
Irreverent Reverend Tom Groans

Monique's genitalia were in accord with her female identity. All this was much to the chagrin of the two male officers.

On Monique's return from her examination with Officer Flaccid, she again explained that they had taken so great a latitude in regards to the female's height, weight, colouring and that abstract term, 'beauty,' that they were almost sure to find such an expectation easily fulfilled anywhere in Cape Town with such an assiduous approach.

With Monique's skill at delving through the murkiness of futurity, her psychic edge suddenly shook her out of her lack of being taciturn and prodded her, that she ought to remain silent, lest the officers get smart and bring the person who had informed on her face-to-face with her.

Monique knew who the informer was from the moment she arrived at the house to find the two officers there to greet her. The informer is a first cousin of Monique's called Felicity and it was she who attacked Monique in the café that day. Felicity's side of the family has not been designated White. This cousin is short, dark and has a swarthy complexion and by most standards would be regarded as plain, with narrow cat eyes, a downward-turning mouth and an anorexia habit of body. She also has an understandably large chip on her shoulder.

Felicity had an auspicious beginning as a brilliant cellist as a child, but has descended into drugs and alcohol abuse since then. Felicity van Welkom is her full name and even though the word 'felicity' means cheerfulness, Felicity has no capacity for grace or happiness. Felicity van Welkom cannot tell the difference between Angela and Monique visually, Monique surmised incorrectly, because earlier that day in the Way's butcher shop, when Felicity had greeted Monique, she had greeted her as if she were Angela, but Felicity knew the Bureau of State Security was watching and listening and therefore, she threw them a red herring.

Felicity was one of the few people who knew that Angela's middle name was Leah, because Angela, as a young kid, used her middle name until she was about seven years old, when she reverted back to the name Angela, as she had matured into liking the idea of being a devil disguised as an angel.

Felicity's lack of exact visual recognition of Monique, Monique again incorrectly surmised, was because she had not seen much of the two first cousins, as the two girls had been living abroad and even before that they had drifted apart, especially with the 'Whitening' of District Six, when the van Welkom's had been not welcome and had been forced to move with the other forty-thousand Coloureds, Malays, Indians and some Blacks to the windy Cape Flats.

Felicity, in reality, was protecting Angela and her parents. If the officers had known that Angela's family were hiding Angela, alias Leah, the whole family would have been arrested.

There was one thing Monique had to do now and she would have to do it fast. She had to get out of the house as quickly as possible, find Felicity van Welkom before the officers do and put her out of her misery.

Monique would have to kill her relative.

The owl and the cat both chase mouse, at the same time, at a little past house.

46

I place people in their various over-simplified boxes, such as the human-owls, human-monkeys and human-foxes.

Irreverent Reverend Tom Groans

Monique knows that Angela, in disguise, returned under darkened skies, over the rooftops and is at this very moment upstairs in the safe space under my floorboards in my bedroom. Even I at this specific time am unaware of Angela's presence there. Monique now has to get upstairs and have Angela return in her stead. In that way, Angela can get out of the house safely to pass on information she has on tape on her person. The whole area is teeming with uniformed and plain-clothed police and Angela must be soon on her way, or better yet, get a safe ride out of District Six with the two officers in their jeep because, at present, there is a tight cordon around the area.

Monique's plan is that with Angela safely out of the district and with the latest valuable documentary film smuggled out on her person, she can then, unencumbered, hunt down Felicity van Welkom.

At this moment Monique catches my attention by thrusting her head forward and raising her eyebrows in the direction of

F's downstairs bathroom, while at the same time she says to me, 'No one's in the toilet?'

This is my cue. I am quick to get the hint. 'Thanks!' I respond to her obvious request that I use the downstairs toilet so that she may then take leave to use the upstairs toilet in my quarter, as a ruse to having Angela return downstairs in her place.

Thirty seconds after I disappear into F's bathroom, Monique says that she has to use the toilet as well. She says that she will use the upstairs bathroom, as I am in the downstairs one and will be back in two jiffies. Before she leaves, she asks if the officers are going anywhere near the docks, as it is where she is headed. Officer Arcane replies that she is welcome to have a ride with them.

Officer Flaccid now takes her leave as Monique walks towards the outside courtyard on her way towards the stairway and my two rooms. In my room the swap is done quickly and professionally. Angela, dressed in Monique's clothing, returns downstairs in her cousin's place and Monique, dressed in black sweatpants and black T-shirt, heads out over the rooftops in search of Felicity van Welkom.

The subterfuge is successful. The two officers are hoodwinked.

Maybe it is successful precisely because all tall, blonde, blue-eyed girls mesmerise guys, so that the guy's awareness of other details becomes compromised.

Passing the baton is always a delicate balancing act.

47

A pendulum has conspired with time.
Irreverent Reverend Tom Groans

Felicity van Welkom, though a Coloured girl, at age seven, was regarded as a prodigy in terms of her cello playing amongst the White fraternity in Cape Town. At age eighteen, she was a high school dropout and heroin addict. When Felicity was twenty-four, Gregory, aka Pound Current, the jazz pianist and also Angela's father, was brought in by Felicity's mother to try and sort Felicity out, but that did not help because Gregory was the source of the problem. Music was the glue that brought Felicity and Gregory together, while the sex between them was to be the bomb that rendered them apart. Only the three half-sisters know that Felicity, like them, is also Gregory's biological daughter, the result of an affair her mother had had with Gregory all those years ago. In her diary, Felicity had written that in our society the victim has to play the part of the victim so that people can apply labels associated with that stigma. She had also written that Gregory has not violated her in terms of the sex – certainly not as far as she was concerned – but there was incest, although the stigma of victim could not be applied to her. She had been violated, but not as one would think, in the traditional sense. Her trauma was that he had left

197

her! She was rejected by him and put aside. It was *not* the sex that scarred her, but the withdrawal of it! Felicity had also written that her life was unbearable because life is either too cryptic or too shallow and that she was going mad yo-yoing in-between. She felt either overloaded or sucked dry.

Felicity, in her pathological state, never stopped missing or caring for Gregory, who is as mentioned, her, Monique's and Angela's biological father, which is the reason she pointed out Monique instead of Angela in a plea bargain with the Bureau Of State Security. Felicity knew what she was doing by informing on Monique, because only a handful of Coloureds know that Gregory is Monique's biological father. Everyone else considers Gregory Angela's father, so nothing could lead the police to Gregory by her fingering Monique who looks like Angela. Gregory is still where Felicity's heart languishes, while her depressed body has become dejected and sad.

Felicity's plea bargain was that in exchange for being an informer she would not get jail time for a previous drug offence.

Felicity knows that her two half-siblings look identical, so her disinformation in exchange for the plea bargain would never look intentional. At worst it would look like a case of mistaken identity. In her intoxicated state, however, she did not inform either Angela or Monique about the intentional lie she told to the police. It irked Felicity that she was too inebriated or stoned to inform her cousins about the reason behind her intentional perversity. Felicity did ponder whether this misinformation would cost her dearly in the future not only with the Bureau, but also in her relationships with her extended family.

Felicity would protect Gregory by any means.

Gregory, unlike the Saints, not only interprets his holy blues and jazz, but he also is the sound of God himself, as he appears mesmerising through his own virtuosity. Gregory makes a sacrament of the piano, because when life is bad and you are feeling down and out, as one can feel in South Africa, then, to quote him, 'The piano can save your life.' This is a saying often heard around the Ways' household. Another direct quote often heard about the Ways' dining room table, a saying penned by Gregory's first cousin's son, the indomitable Irreverent Reverend Tom Groans, who also happens to controversially be Gregory's biological child, through wayward intercourse, is, 'Curb your God!'

Gregory Ways, when younger, had also indulged in some frolicking hanky-panky with his first cousin, Slyler, which produced the erstwhile poet and ragamuffin, Tom Groans.

There is a saying, that beauty usually skips a generation and in flamboyantly handsome Gregory's case, it is certainly a case in point because Groans is an ugly chip off the splendid old block, but luckily for him, Gregory's intellectual smarts have been passed on.

Sensuality dominates the intellect; objects of pleasure can conquer all.

48

You are the accumulated character of all that you've read.

Irreverent Reverend Tom Groans

I sit on the balcony handrail outside my room, listening to my breathing and the sound of my own voice in my head. My brain has been chattering and tickling itself for quite some time now about what has been going on in F's house, with all sorts of possibilities or leads jangling like carrots in front of me to be followed or rejected. In my mind's eye I replay all the rushes over and over again. There are many questions, but few answers.

I look at Table Mountain's parapet as it squints out of the tablecloth of cloud streaming down off it, like locks of hair fallen from a forehead, that partially cover the eyes. 'Parapet' is a good description, a good choice of a word, I think, for the elevated, protective barrier that runs the long, straight, horizontal length at the edge of the balcony that is Table Mountain's pinnacle.

The word 'parapet' plays in my head. I break it down into its two parts, 'para' and 'pet'. A 'pet' as I know, is a domesticated animal kept as a companion, or a 'pet' can be someone or something cherished or preferred, like a 'pet' theory, or the word 'pet' can be used as in 'to pet', as in 'to engage in amorous caressing'. In F's house, who is the pet? Who is whose companion? Who is being cherished? Who is being preferred? Only one thing is for sure, that there is much petting going on in the house.

The other word within the word 'parapet' is 'para' and it is a three-pronged prefix, which could mean 'besides', as in 'paradigm', or it could mean 'beyond', as in 'parapsychology', or it could just be an auxiliary thing, as in 'paralegal'. I wonder if F is the puppeteer who keeps the enemy 'besides' him as a pet companion, using them, the enemy, or are the pets in charge and beyond his grasp and are they in fact controlling him? Could both sides possibly be 'auxiliaries', using each other for their own selfish ends? Is everything really just a bunch of 'para-lies'? I feel paralysed in my analysis, as if I am sitting on a perforated parapet. These are the other fundamental questions I ask:

Has F worked out what The Bureau of State Security has not?

If F knows who Angela really is, then he knows that his lover, Russell, by being Angela's friend, is implicated.

Are F and the Secret Police working together, the one corralling the prey for the other to scoop up?

Why is F never at home when the investigators show up?

Why is it that F is never mentioned in the questioning by the investigators, even though he is the prime renter of the house?

Do the investigators know that F lives in the house?

Is F completely oblivious to what is going on?

I cannot even think of discussing Angela with F, just in case she is his Venus flytrap to catch whatever falls into her. Guilt by association is a fact of life in South Africa.

My final thought and one that I think is quite valid, is that it is possible that F knows exactly what is going on and does not wish to put an end to his physical fun or intellectual banter, with either Russell, Angela or the film crew at this particular juncture.

F is full of contradictions and emotions are nearly always contradictory. Is he playing both sides of this double-edged sword?

Vanity and boredom are great motivators.

49

I'm not my brother's metre so I need to keep a beat that's mine.

Irreverent Reverend Tom Groans

After spending an hour drinking coffee and pondering the situation, Officers Stratagem and Arcane drive Angela, who they think is Monique, to the docks where she is to meet a friend. They have now arrived at dockland in their military jeep. Angela is sitting on the passenger side, in the front, alongside Officer Arcane who has been driving. Officer Arcane instinctively senses that Monique, who he thinks he has in the car right now, is somehow involved in the intrigue, because, for a start, Monique was coming to the same house that Angela was heading for during her escape over the rooftops some weeks prior to today and although she did not enter the house, her projected route was in the house's direction. Officer Arcane thinks that this is more than a coincidence.

The young woman in the jeep alongside him will have to be watched closely!

Angela is now ready to leave the vehicle and Officer Arcane extends his hand to shake hers. A strong, firm-gripped handshake is what Officer Arcane wants to extend, as a coded message that she is within his grasp. He wants to bring her down a notch, not in so many words, but by implication. The solid handshake will be his implication. His compulsion is to crush, but he has to curb the impulse to crush the living daylights out of his passenger, by implying it with as grinding a grip as he can grasp in his little, juvenile palm. He extends his hand sanctimoniously towards Angela, but Angela does not return the gesture, as there has been no deal done and they are not friends. She leaves his hand flapping in the void between them. Her avoidance of his hand is oblique enough to not offend him too much and with possible largesse, she gives the two officers a thumbs-up. She is not going to be their victim. She puts aside her truculence, as she is going to be the perpetrator of these miscreants' frustrations and with an enigmatic smile, she descends from the jeep. She has defeated them yet again, while abiding to the rules of mutual civility.

Angela is cramping their style. She thinks that inhibiting their behaviour could produce childhood frustrations in the two men. The first signs of it, Angela had noticed, are that both officers look dishevelled, like two kids barred from eating their sweets.

Even though Angela has left the jeep, Officer Stratagem still sits deferentially in the back seat, having been quietly intimidated by Officer Arcane and Angela's intellectual verbosity during this truth game, as each side brandished their shields.

Never mock a killing bird.

50

We're sadists and assassins, too, we advocate this mindless zoo; I get to kill, as Life kills me, we're lunatics in lunacy.

Irreverent Reverend Tom Groans

How does one obtain redress for wrongs done and injuries received and more than that, how does one prevent such wrongdoings from happening in the future? This was the question swirling around in Monique's brain. Monique had learnt to never let the same dog bite you three times!

Monique's allegation that Felicity was the informer who ratted on her was correct, but she surmised incorrectly that Felicity thought that she, Monique, was Angela. Felicity van Welkom knew full well that Monique was Monique, but was merely protecting Gregory from serious trouble by association.

When eventually confronted by Monique, Felicity van Welkom could not rebut Monique's allegation of her complicity in fingering Monique as Angela, because she was deliriously trashed on marijuana, out of her head, dead drunk and totally incoherent at the time. Timing had conspired against Felicity van Welkom and this time it was quite literally a matter of life and death.

*

Monique knew where Felicity could be found every late afternoon or early evening and that was in the illegal brew house. Within its cool darkness and lying below the heat of the day, beyond prying eyes, beneath the surface of a life barely possessed and in the realm of forgetfulness, Monique clung onto her toxic brew as if there was nothing else in the world. There, Felicity would drink the strong homemade 'shimyyan' and smoke the pungently sweet, 'Durban-poison' marijuana with other members of her self-medicating, rambling entourage.

Monique waited outside, dallying with her own thoughts in the sombre, foreboding dusk, envisioning the ambush of Felicity that would soon occur. As the stiflingly humid summer's day passed into evening, the timelessness of this Cape sunset was set against an orange-pink firmament, while against this backdrop a moving sky of swallows heralded an approaching storm. As Felicity exited the shebeen and made her staggering way across the street towards an awaiting, hidden Monique, the tumultuous, blackened clouds straight off Table Mountain opened up and all heaven guttered down in a torrential, icy downpour. A melancholy and sudden chill rushed at Felicity as she turned the corner, moving her into a gale-force headwind, while instantaneously as she rounded that bend, two powerful hands seemed to have reached out to her from nowhere, grabbed her two shoulders and forced her brutally sideways into the alley and out of the storm.

When Monique held the razor-sharp butchers' carving knife to Van Welkom's neck and ever so slightly drew a sliver of blood from it with a quick flick of her wrist, Felicity sluggishly admitted that it was she who had informed Officer Arcane about her whereabouts, but she omitted to explain why she had done the informing because she could hardly string two words together, never mind a simple sentence. Monique ascertained by correct conjecture that Felicity had agreed to inform Officer Arcane of Angela, alias Leah's whereabouts, in a plea bargain with Officer Arcane and this was because of his promise to have some drug trafficking charges against her dropped.

That was how Felicity van Welkom became a spy for the State.

This was not a case of Monique having to tame an unruly passion of barbarism for revenge, but a valiant encounter by her to eliminate treachery once and for all, lest it happen again, because Van Welkom, Monique incorrectly assumed, could never, ever be trusted. If Angela were to go down in the future, so would the whole family and many others besides.

This killing seemed like the jurisprudence of brute over brain, but there was no alternative to the hardheartedness of this decision as far as Monique could see. With a deep forceful slice of her butchers' razor-sharp boning knife across Felicity van Welkom's throat, she was dispatched. The throat had been cut deeply, with the professionalism of a butcher, as Monique, like Felicity and Angela, come from a family of butchers. Her aorta was pierced. It caused a jet of bright red blood to squirt like an erupting volcano over Monique's shoulder. There, its redness splattered against the narrow alleyway's white wall, running down it, leaving the image of the tentacles of a large octopus, as if on an artist's large, concrete canvas.

Felicity fell into the gutter where she had been standing, jerked four times, sat up involuntarily and died.

Monique did feel deep remorse for what she felt she had to do. Had she known of Felicity's intentional misinformation, her remorseful disquiet would have been even greater. As it was, Monique, throughout this episode, felt like she was enthralled, whilst in an altered state of consciousness, for this was the first time she had killed anyone she had known and she had known Felicity well, as well as the whole sorry story of Felicity's history. It made Monique question more clearly the fundamental question of death: who was that person and where had she gone and why did this person's life, out of the billions on this planet, suddenly merge with hers? It was as if a large, grey wave had washed over Monique and made her sluggish.

There was another reason for Monique's angst and that was the genetic fact that they were half-sisters. Angela's piano-tinkering dad had really tinkered around.

Like Angela, Monique is also a published poet and that night she wrote:

Let some blood out of me, my tears are spent,
With eyes parched and dry, like cracked cement.

Grit happens.

51

The fisherman tending the shark nets, on noting the
dolphins snared in the netting, said that that is just
the price they pay, to keep the eager surfers jetting.
Irreverent Reverend Tom Groans

Angela feels curiously lightheaded as she strides away from the
two officers. She feels somewhat extravagant, having spent the
past half hour in close proximity with the enemy without them
knowing who she is. She is 3 yards away from the jeep when
the radio intercom in the jeep crackles to life. A voice speaking
Afrikaans says with a desperate edge that a Coloured woman,
who looks like the informer, has been found killed, with her
throat cut in District Six and that the murder appears to have
happened sometime within the past half hour.

Angela has now walked a further 20 yards from the jeep
and is entering a building that borders the docks. She hears a
voice behind her mention the name Felicity van Welkom. The
voice is coming through the intercom speaker behind her, from
inside the jeep. The sound of the name, 'Felicity van Welkom,'
almost stops Angela in her tracks, but the momentum of her
movement urges her onward and forward. Angela hears Officer
Arcane's voice behind her call out after her, what he thinks is
her name, 'Monique, hold it! Stop! Halt!'

Angela pretends not to hear Officer Arcane's command as she enters the building quickly, turning a corner out of sight.

As far as the officers are concerned, Monique, who is Angela, has been with them the past two hours, so this girl is not a suspect in the killing.

Monique, meanwhile, having done a switch with Angela in my room at F's house, had gone on to kill Felicity van Welkom and is at present out of District Six, heading to Clifton Fourth Beach on a moped that she had earlier hidden in a cluster of bushes just outside of the District, in case of such an emergency as this.

Now, Angela must separate herself quickly from the two officers. She thinks that at moments like this, as in moments of utter catastrophe, one does not think too much. The head goes blank. One's mind is plagued with getting out of the way. The urge is to run out of a picture that is askew and it is to find one's equilibrium that propels one onwards. You have got to keep moving for your life depends on it. You have got to keep pricking yourself so that you do not go numb, so that your vision does not get hazy by your proximity to the danger. She is now running, drawing away, swept up in a current of survival, heading for the quay and her contact's little fishing boat. Way back out, behind her in the distance and out of sight because of the gathering thick evening fog, Angela hears the calling of her name, or rather the calling of Monique's name, and feels it settle around her neck like a boomerang trying to take her back to them.

She eventually finds the boat with skipper, her contact, standing on the bow waving and climbs on board with her backpack and its precious cargo of secret film within it. She quickly lies down on her stomach on the deck, peering out into the fog in search of her two predators and finds nothing. Beneath her she can feel and hear the shoving of the ocean against the hull and the droning and hammering of the turbines under her belly.

Skipper pours a flagon of petrol into the carburettor and starts the vessel out to sea, out and away across the bay. He hands Angela binoculars and she peers back towards the docks where she can now see the two officers darting frantically left and right, looking everywhere except in the direction of their fast-disappearing little boat.

The boat is high in the water as it is empty of fish. It slides past the last jetty. The only sound now is the distant, deep staccato thudding of the engine beneath them as the boat pitches back on its own steeply angled bow wave and the smell is acrid coming from the engine. What is in view now is the blinding, bitter cold, silent fog, which absorbs the thudding sound of that engine and ricochets it back like a close echo all around, encasing everything within its cocoon.

The way to steer is by compass and instinct, as the boat revolves around the last point of land like a spoke about a hub. The forlorn din of a distant foghorn seems muffled in cloth, like a trombone with a fist in it. The whiteness of the fog seduces and sucks the boat into its dense vortex of alien silence, where perspective space disappears, reducing everything, including the embodied politics of the different races to a levelled nothingness. The canvas is blank. There is no peopled landscape. It is a case of 'Fog the Leveller', which ruptures the consciousness of separatism.

Angela feels the aged, salt-worn timbers of the old ship's railing beneath her fingers. It is not age solely that enhances and refines the fibres of the timber of this aged vessel, but the wrenching of the boat at sea, as well as the hydrocarbon actions of the bilge water and flimflam. The activity of the many cargoes the trawler has carried has burnished its decks with a patina of polished smoothness. The timber and beams made from oak and mahogany have splendidly adorned the grains, while the many years of traffic have tightened the pores and ebonised the hue of these timbers in rainbow, kaleidoscopic acuteness as an antique. Angela thinks that the qualities of people, who like this vessel have carried their responsibilities through the waters of life, are also imbued with distinction. The wrenching and straining of a life lived virtuously and even the sweetness of the trials seen through, get into the pores and fabric of character.

The three crewmen are organising the fishing nets on the front deck as the moisture settles on everyone's faces and Angela hands Skipper the package with the film in it.

This is the first time Angela has met Skipper face-to-face. She had never seen him except through other people's descriptions and had only known his thoughts through other people's lips. Before today, he was only a vague hulk of a man representing steadfastness and resilience.

Skipper is a bronzed, Coloured man of medium height who is a referent of physical power, vitality and endurance. His thick musculature is the regalia he wears in regards to these qualities he has. He has been able to bench-press with one arm every women he has ever dated and though he prefers slim, small, muscular girls, he has dated some mammoths in the past, hence his current preference for the petite type, for he needs to conserve his strength for work. His thin lips he keeps firmly set, giving the impression that he is a man of few words, which is true, as he always gives short instructions or clipped answers. He does, however, have a philosophical bent and his two pet peeves are that depression is just masked boredom and that he feels that White people who complain of psychological ills are servile self-seekers needing attention, as they should have nothing to complain about. Skipper is proud to be a Coloured person, mentioning that mongrels, are a more hardy variety than 'pure'-bred dogs. Skipper says that his genetic makeup is an aggregate of all the races of South Africa and that within him flows an encyclopaedic rearrangement of other people's beliefs, proverbs and stories picked up by his Coloured ancestors and passed on to him. Skipper points out that his English and his Afrikaans are a

Coloured mimicry, a re-enactment of those languages. The Coloureds have transposed their own texture in the regurgitation of what comes out of their mouths, which does away with much of those original languages' formal features.

Right now, Skipper stands amid-ship, peers to his right into the ever-so-slowly clearing fog and says to Angela, 'I can't see the tugboat yet, but we should be rendezvousing with it at any minute! Oh, yes, there she is! That's her!'

About 30 yards away, a red tugboat can be seen low in the water heading towards the little fishing vessel. It now bears across the fishing vessel's bows and approaches alongside Angela and Skipper. Its navigation lights hover as if disembodied high above the steering cabin. Both boats engines cut off. They are two solid blocks seen against the mist. The two vessels roll and rub against each other's shoulders above the swells they share. The sibilant sound of the water between them emits a liquid cry with the frequent splashes that spray upwards as the two boats toll and sway together.

A tall man standing on the edge of the tugboat, his long hair ruffled by the wind and his coat opened, recognises Skipper and waves. Skipper takes the package Angela has given him and hands it up to the tugboat captain who takes it with both hands carefully, as if he has just received a special gift. The captain turns on his heels and disappears into the cabin of the tugboat. For Angela, it is mission accomplished. The two boats separate. The secret film is on its way to a freighter that will take it out of South African territorial waters and onwards to London.

The evening will now be spent fishing off the coastline. In the morning, before Skipper and his fishing boat return to Table Bay laden with their fresh catch, Angela will be dropped off on a rocky outcrop of large boulders beyond the breakers on Clifton Fourth Beach. There she will meet with Monique at Dick Hymen's beautifully picturesque beach house, where the plan is for her to help him edit his latest novel, the soon to be, controversial and aptly named, *Supine Nipple*.

We're waiting in this vestibule, before we test the fool, to see if she is free or mule.

52

I am also a monster, for what I do not do, for I only serve myself, ignoring you!

Irreverent Reverend Tom Groans

I think that normalcy, like the humdrum ticking of any day, can be separated from abnormality by a strict boundary, a sudden unexpected occurrence, like the breaking of silence itself with a sound or the sudden, immediate cessation of breath with death. There is sometimes no discretion that warns one of what is coming next. One might not know that anything is happening at all below the surface, until it actually happens and then one is surprised, just like a car accident.

My intuition tells me that there is something below the surface, unseen and unheard, some sub-atomic, energetic quality about the house that I live in, that is building to a crescendo. I feel that something that is masquerading in normalcy and silence is about to rear its ugly little head and that Angela and Monique are about to get the short end of the stick. I think this is because F, for the past twenty-four hours, has had a sudden, added bounce to his step, his posture has improved and he seems much more focused energetically. He is less scattered in his demeanour and his mouth has been more firmly set, as if he is about to take a big bite out of something. Yes, I feel that something kinetic in the atmosphere is occurring alongside the silence.

Early last evening, immediately after F had left for work, Monique and Angela showed up at the house. Angela entered by the front door and Monique via the roof. It was already quite dark. In my room, Angela produced a bottle of Cape white wine, while Monique withdrew some aged parmesan cheese and black olives from her backpack.

'Aaron,' Angela said, uncorking the wine, 'as a gesture of our loving feelings towards you, we, Monique and I, would like to present you with an olive branch each, as a symbol of understanding, as well as an olive. Before giving you the two olives, Monique and I each bite off and eat half of our own. These two half-eaten olives we present for you to nibble. It bonds us!'

'I've never heard of this ritual,' I said.

'Of course you haven't heard of the olive branch and the olive ritual; it's our invention,' Angela admitted with a smile.

'Sentimentality is a luxury that is usually ill-afforded. It's an indulgence, just like crying, for those who have nothing more important to do. Let's each make a silent wish,' Monique suggested.

That was last night.

I ruminate over the fact that there are many types of silences, like the one underlying the present quietness in the house, which is like the quietness before a storm, like the one I am sure of that will soon permeate and penetrate the calm around me, accumulating as it gathers its unseen force towards its build-up. Right now, the emotion I sense is anticipation and its accompanying tension.

Patience is a virgin.

53

He who laughs last might just be slow.
Irreverent Reverend Tom Groans

White public opinion is the law of the land in South Africa. Even divine laws are either trampled on or manipulated to support White public opinion. In a nutshell, 'White has right of way and dark can't bark.'

To be labelled a non-White is total disqualification from high government office and with that labelling comes the deprivation of all of one's full rights of citizenship, including the right to have equal voting privileges. These laws are vigorously supported and their support strongly expressed with a vengeance. Therefore, when a measured, professionally researched documentary, like the one Doctor Jacque has made, has determined without a figure of a doubt that a certain high-ranking government official, an elder of the Dutch Reform Church and a potential future prime minister, has non-White blood cruising through his lily-white veins, then the very foundation and the White bonds of reason are challenged and rendered open to ridicule. The official's extended family are in fact Coloureds, living right at this moment on the Cape Flats, having originally been shunted there from District Six some five years previously,

This was not just a bit of spit to be wiped away with the

217

help of a handkerchief, but a scar that was skin deep. The emperor might have had new clothes, but the blood flowing through his veins was tainted.

The challenge of this documentary, with its many hours of interviews determining the truth of its supposition that this particular White political leader was in fact a Coloured person, was tantamount to mortal combat, as the accused would have to fight for his political and private life.

There is a truism that if you want to keep a secret you must never open your mouth about that secret to anyone. The authorities, with the help of an informer, found out about the 'race card' being emphasised in this documentary and under the orders of 'the powers that be', who were obviously deeply concerned what sort of embarrassment could come from such a disclosure, closed ranks. Having exhausted their search for the missing film, which unbeknown to them was on its way to London, hidden on a freighter, they decided that the best way to solve this particular problem was damage control. The politician involved was offered refuge from the accusation that could be easily proven and he was pressured to resign all his posts, which he duly did.

The media elite created a black hole that sucked the public and private life out of this political man and made him a *persona non-grata*. Two weeks later he was killed in a mysterious private plane crash.

Had the documentary clip been found, it is very likely that all eight members of the accused politician's extended Coloured family would have been somehow murdered and the film destroyed. With the demise of the politician, all that was left was the rounding up of the culprits involved in the making of the documentary and their treasonous cohorts.

The attempt to comprehend the lightning speed with which the 'forces that be' can act upon individuals walking out of goose-step with the government can leave one dizzy. The scenery can shift with meteorological velocity without any early warning signal. Monique's arrest is a case in point, as it has come without any tangible build-up. A knockout punch comes without forewarning. This hard, sombre, sobering ground of reality has surprised me, as if I have jumped off a trampoline and hit solid earth.

Dick Hymen's picturesque beach house had been staked-out by the Bureau of State Security. It was there that Monique was apprehended during foreplay, as she was about to mount Dick Hymen in his hot tub, while the two of them were awaiting Angela's arrival from her fishing experience.

The Bureau's men had been told that Angela was the South African connection to the French film people. They had been tipped off that Angela, whom they still did not know was also Leah, visited Dick Hymen's place on Clifton Fourth Beach on a regular basis and that she was the inspiration behind the main protagonist in Dick Hymen's new book. This was the reason the Bureau was at the beach house, waiting to catch their fish.

Officers Arcane and Stratagem were at Dick Hymen's beach house as well, as they were told that the girl matching the description of the person in their picture was Angela, but they were under the illusion now that Angela, Leah, and Monique were all one and the same person. This girl, whoever she was, was their bone of contention. Also obvious to the two officers was the fact that someone else within the terrorist ANC network had killed Felicity, as Monique was in their company at the time of Felicity's demise. What they did not know was that they were about to catch two birds with one boner, at big Dick Hymen's place.

Two minutes after they had captured Monique in a compromising position, onto the property completely unawares, sauntered Angela. She had come onto shore from the boulders at the land's end after alighting from the fishing vessel where she was promptly surrounded and handcuffed. With the two look-alike girls in their custody, everyone was doing double-takes.

There was no evidence provided for a search warrant, never mind two arrests, but in South Africa, merely being under suspicion is enough and one can be held indefinitely like Mandela. These two psychedelic flies hitting the ointment certainly did make his summer, Officer Arcane had thought gleefully to himself. His head was buzzing in a masculine, one-upmanship tradition. This capture had made his low threshold of a life, very high at that moment. The sun will sink again, Arcane surmised, so he might as well take an enormous gulp of frugal sunshine while it lasts because it may be some time before the next hit comes along.

Amazing how hormones can pre-empt the rational brain. Angela had been blighted by Dick Hymen's libidinal prowess. She had taught herself to look and then to relook at every situation. Even this, she discarded. Her testosterone just ignored that well-engraved piece of advice. Yes, it had not only been a tight rope she had been balancing on, it had been a precarious 'white rope' that hangs. How many of the mighty have gone out, not with a bang, but with a whimper?

Monique had gone out with a bang, but they should both be whimpering now, Officer Arcane philosophised. He sneered at the two girls' flower-power-paisley cuteness. They were the *enfant terrible* of his career. They had the bad manners and gall to go on living in their anti-war, sexual freedom, civil rights, bohemian way.

'For the two of you, chaos now reigns!' he announced, pleased with himself at his play on words.

Meanwhile the two girls, Angela and Monique, knew that there was nothing more pitiable than to be caught with not only their pants, but also their guards down. They had been quite prepared to die on cue, but like this? This was truly pathetic. They did not think it was an attribute to be a divinely inspired, doomed artist, struck down by fate! No! No sentimentalised life for them. Not them ever! They would get out of this fatal web. They had blackmail tapes of dignitaries in undignified positions that could extricate them from this mess.

It was F who had introduced Angela to Dick Hymen and Angela had subsequently introduced Monique to Dick as her backup in matters of the flesh and intellect.

'Fuck F!' was all Angela could think of saying out loud as she was handcuffed, but it was she and her cousin who had been truly screwed, is what the arresting officers thought.

With a curious half-smile and a barely discernible wink, Angela whispered to Monique, 'Never read your reviews until after your funeral. It ain't over till this dark lady sings!'

Oh, to work so hard, only to be taken down over nothing.

54

Everything's fallible, including your parable!
Irreverent Reverend Tom Groans

A tall, lean, handsome penis with rosy cheeks is how I would describe Dick Hymen, the writer and part-time lover of both Angela and Monique. It was at Dick's beachside home that the two girls were arrested for obstruction of justice and aiding and abetting the enemy under the Suppression of Communism Act, even though at this stage of the proceedings there was no evidence against either of them.

Dick Hymen has extravagant, dressed-to-the-nines taste that mirrors his success as a writer and full-time connoisseur of beautiful, intelligent and highly sexual women. Dick is a lubricious, pleasantly lecherous old roué, with an easy magnetic charm and an inexhaustible and intriguing, manipulative understanding of the young feminine psyche, on whom he likes to indulge his caprices with his bestial phallic restlessness. He is always confident in the depth and immutability of his relationships with these youthful gazelles, so to have not read the two girls well has lowered his self-esteem somewhat.

In another life, if he were a lower-grade type of dramatic personality, he would be the dabbler of all trades, half-master of none. But, in this life, everything he touches turns to gold and this success radiates itself onto everyone around him, which is why the arrests of his two lovers, the openly seductive nymphs, were a shock to him. The girls' positive exuberance and vulnerability, their attachment to the sexual, arrested in them any malignancy of sorrow and loneliness and drew him closer to them, even more than if this magnetism were only based on their magnificent beauty.

He is not used to being in the vicinity of failure. Dick Hymen had no idea that the two girls were involved in politics at all, as they had kept their political beliefs to themselves in regards to Dick because he was a friend of conservative, pro-government F. Dick had seen the girls as beautiful, artsy intellectuals with sex on their brains and curiosity in their riveting blue eyes, with both their bodies dominated by the most spectacularly large and shapely breasts he had ever seen. He saw their breasts as being even bigger than they really were because he spent so much time under them, looking up as they hung down, torpedo-like and voluptuous.

Dick Hymen arrived at F's house in District Six ten minutes ago. His English sports car is parked across the street. He is sitting in F's lounge in a state of shocked bewilderment. His imprudence for not checking on the two girls' backgrounds has been exposed. He feels violated by the State's flagrant breach of privacy and their lack of hospitality. The authorities had interrupted the coitus going on in his hot tub and adding insult to intercourse, forced him to emerge from the bubbles before his erection had subsided.

Explaining away the Bureau of State Security's behaviour to the fanaticism of the age, with its barbarous excesses, did not console him. Being unable to protect the girls had made him feel less than chivalrous and even more than that, it had made him feel as impotent as a monk. It was madness on a grand scale and there is no incantation or spell now that can make him feel any better. Dick hopes that the goings-on have reached their climax and that some Apartheid goon, with horns, a long forked tail and cloven hooves, won't suddenly emerge to rope him into what could be an on-going nightmare, or worse.

I had let Dick into the house. F is showering and the place is completely deserted, as the whole film crew, including Jacque and Russell, were arrested in the early hours of this morning. Their equipment and films were seized and confiscated as well. Everyone was packed off in two large police trucks. I did not see any of the arrests as F came up to my room and told me to stay put and make myself invisible until everything was over.

'Do not get involved!' is what F had said to me.

I had come down to F's section to let Dick in. Dick had been insistently knocking for one minute and because of its intensity, I had thought that it was the police at the door.

Dick and I are drinking coffee out of elephant-shaped mugs, whose ears we are holding. F is singing in the shower, which seems quite incongruous with the situation being what it is and under the circumstances, especially as all his friends and/or lovers have been arrested.

These are the lyrics that F is singing:
Don't judge me because this cocks on top
Cause pecking order is a chicken's lot
I like a good fuck
Better than being fucked up
Better than being fucked around
Better than being fucked off
Don't judge me because this cocks on top!

He emerges from his bathroom naked and walks over to Dick, indicating that he need not get up off the couch. F now attempts to shake Dick's hand, but Dick ignores him.

'What's going on, F?' Dick asks.

It is also my question, but Dick has asked it first.

F shrugs and shakes his head.

'That's the best that you can do? You introduced me to the girls knowing they are a political liability?' Dick asks.

'They've all been involved in activity to undermine the government, is what I've been told. Exactly what, I do not know.'

I can tell that F is lying about what he knows and what he does not know. He also knew of Monique and therefore he must have known, or at least he would have heard from Dick, that the two girls were almost identical in appearance. He keeps touching his nose, as if looking for something to hold on to.

'They're all a bunch of anarchists. They throw the word democracy around like they know what they are talking about!' he spits out with venom and continues, 'Don't talk to me about democracy. India is democratic and the people there are starving to death, yet they've three hundred million heads of inedible, sacred cows! Don't talk to me of majority rule. Hitler was democratically elected!'

'And White!' I add.

F ignores my comment and continues, 'Don't talk about what the majority of people want. I'm a snob. I've no time to listen to people who have a sub-hundred IQ. Bottom line is that whoever is in power controls and has the favoured position. Before the White man arrived, the Africans were already unsound primitives destroying the land. Their primitive mentality was and still is shuffling in a mind-set where only the dominant tribe gets any power and there's no trickle down to the underlings. The rest of the civilised world, meanwhile, have moved on towards your numbing-down-to-average democracy. When the Blacks take over here in twenty or thirty years, they will not give a flying fuck for anyone, black or white, and God help the Indians who they hate and the Coloureds whom they think of as a bastard race! White Apartheid will become Black Apartheid, unless the West intervenes for its own economic self-interest. These Blacks don't have the foresight. I don't know whether it is genetic or cultural.

They don't seem to have the ability to step back and scrutinise, to see the big picture.'

'Do you have any more stereotypical caricatures to offer? You are all heart!' Dick says with irony.

'All these qualities are scientific facts?' I ask.

'Like one and one is two!' F answers with conviction.

'Hitler said the Jews were inferior as well,' Dick attacks.

'He didn't say they were inferior intellectually, only morally!' F is quick to point out.

'And you believe that shit?' I question accusingly.

'No, as a matter of fact I don't believe that shit. But we are talking intellectual prowess here. Hitler used some correct facts, mingling them with nonsense to suit his ends.'

'And you are not, I suppose? Also, tell me, where does love fit in?' Dick is being ironic.

F, in a lecturing mood, says, 'Listen, while we're on the subject of Jews, let's talk about the heavy Apartheid against the Jews in Hafez al-Assad's Syria right at this moment and the fucked-up world is silent. The world is only worried about us here in South Africa and they ignore the fact that Jews in Syria are required to live in ghettos and are not permitted to travel more than four kilometres from their homes, while anyone attempting to flee the country can be jailed and tortured. Jews in Syria today are required to carry identity cards with the word 'Mussawi' or follower of Moses on it in red ink. Jewish homes and businesses have to have a red sign, a colour indicating un-cleanliness. No government official or member of the armed forces can trade in a Jewish establishment either. Jews cannot go to high school or university. I could go on and on, but no one is saying boo, and Western countries still continue to do business and play sport with Syria! Hypocrisy everywhere, you mother fuckers! We are White and we are on top right now. Here in South Africa it's a war of attrition and the numbers are on their side.'

Dick gets up to go and with the flick of the back of his

hand, dismisses what F has had to say and says, 'You love throwing in such well-worn clichés. Where does empathy fit into your equation? Where does understanding and hope come into your view of the world? Where is your solution that will not end in violence?'

F just shakes his head, like he has been talking to children who just do not understand and says, 'You two are just a bunch of ignoramuses! You want to know about love? Wake up! Will love feed you? Will Empathy put a roof over your head? By the way, when the White man met the Zulus for the first time, the Zulus didn't even have the wheel! The original inhabitants of Southern Africa were not the Bantu either, or the Whites, but the Bushmen, Hottentots, *et al*, whom the White man and the Black man hunted down, because these indigenous people were hunters and the Whites and Blacks were herdsmen who found their cattle with spears in them or worse, gone! Survival of the fittest is the name of the game. I do not give a hoot about Mr Bloody Average, but I will keep him fed and housed so that he doesn't take what's mine away from me by stealth. Watch, when they are free to do as they please, they will be free to starve and they will pray for the good old Apartheid days. Mark my words! When faith wins over facts, concepts formulated with passion come to the fore with no attention paid to evidence.' F is shouting.

Dick stands to shake my hand and says, 'Come and visit, Aaron, but don't bring this arsehole with you. It's ironic that he calls me an ignoramus. In fact, it's downright funny that he should call me that, using the word ignoramus, because he should have taken his own advice and ignored Amus, instead of emulating him. Amus was his father's name. Now he's just a chip off the old block!'

'Ha ha! Very funny! Ignoramus! That was very funny, but my father's name was Amos, not Amus. Your puns are juvenile,' F cuts in.

Dick continues, closing his eyes to F's retort, 'I know what happened here. I get the whole picture. You can throw around every great virtue you wish, such as fortitude, intelligence, patriotism, fidelity to agreements and contracts, the temperance of a people, etcetera, etcetera, but empathetic charity and generosity of spirit are unknown to you, you sick bastard!'

I add my pennies worth. 'F, valuing principles over people is wrong.'

F interrupts, ignoring my comment and says, 'Dick, you're abounding with moral clichés. It's your lack of perspective that paints everything with the same moral brush. "Thou shall not kill," or "Honour your father and your mother," which you mix in every situation in just proportions. These thrown-about thoughts are just another form of despotism, of not giving to every separate situation its own particular merit.'

Dick interrupts F this time, saying, 'Governments should have the best interests of the governed at heart!'

'Exactly!' says F. 'The majority of sub-hundred IQs don't know what's in their best interests! Even constitutional governments, where all the adult people participate, have undemocratic additives, such as secrecy in matters of intelligence, where transparency has to be treated differently. Secret intelligence is information our enemies don't wish us to have and it allows the democratic state to understand the threats facing it. We need these valuable advantages to stay solvent. Most people need protection from themselves!'

Dick is irritated and ignoring the last comment, retaliates with, 'That secrecy, *vis-à-vis* "intelligence" collecting, has to be moderated by accountability and so the people heading those departments must be public figures who can be checked out by everyone. Meanwhile, the few in power here, who are undemocratically elected, live a protracted, defensive, stunted life that is bereft of humanity.'

F jumps in. 'I'm liberal in matters of art and music and sex, but conservative in matters of politics.'

Dick interrupts F again and says, 'No, you're a hypocrite. You're what you hate. Your newspaper hounds out homosexuals, yet you're one yourself! You hate those that don't see the big picture, yet you only see the small picture. I could go on and on. You are such an arsehole! You don't give others the same rights to be different!'

F waves Dick's comment aside. 'I'm self-indulgent because I don't give much consideration to your self-indulgence? "It's not if you win or lose, but how you play the game," is your motto, but it's not a game of bloody cricket! We're at war, and war is only about winning! You bloody idiot liberals are such admirers of all perceived underdogs, as if it's a blessing to be subservient. You bloody English liberals hold to the supremacy and eminence of the underling and it comes from your envy of the upper crust. In Britain, you English have been conquered by the Danes, Saxons and French. You've a victim mentality, even acquiescing to the Roman religion after Constantine, Christianity. No one's to be panegyrised just because they are the underdog. The situation here in South Africa should be looked at with impartiality. The underdog is not necessarily the more respectable character.'

'Are you quite finished?' says Dick. 'It's you who are making war!'

'No!' screams F. 'Just look at the rest of Africa! Do you want to live in a Third World country?'

'Well,' says Dick, 'eighty per cent of the rest of this country lives in the Third World and you ride on their backs!'

'Then all I can say is that I'd rather it be their backs than mine. Meanwhile, they're not starving. If the situation were reversed, we'd be battling to put food in our mouths!'

Dick walks straight past F and leaves the house.

F goes to the kitchen for another cup of coffee, which gives me time to think about the similarity and differences between F and Angela and the way in which they state their arguments and impose their logic. The difference in my mind at least is that F is a dramatist who relates to past events and appears as a thrusting, but jaded man who surveys that past, quietening his listeners and moving them backwards and forwards at his will. If F talked with a pillow draped over his head so that his personality could be rapt away from distracting his listeners, it would be preferred, so that the content of what he is espousing is king, rather than he himself being the focal point. Angela is the opposite. Where F is a dramatist, Angela is a mime who puts herself forward so that we take exclusive interest in her and her immediacy, so that we slow down and share in the plights and the delights of her soul and forget ourselves in the vivid effects of her sensuousness. With F, one is a listener. With Angela, one is a passionate watcher, always on the alert with slightly less reflection than when in the presence of F. Angela infuses everything she does with her confidence and they are both charlatans of sorts, each of them vaulting the high hurdles of a decaying social system. Both their ends justify this charlatanism and people are more impressed by nature's sleight of features, such as Angela's magnificence and F's majestic stature, which like a sleight of hand, tricks and indelibly impresses, thus startling the crowd into listening. Both their radicalisms are a vague mixture that are even more emotional than, if I may dare say so, political. They wantonly tread all over popular morality and established modesty. 'Two wrongs do make a right' is both their credos, if their wrong is the lesser of the two evils in the conflict. They both feel that they should play as dirty as the opposition, so that there is a level playing field. Their corrosive invectives are dipped in acidic irony and are against intellectual, aerial aloofness and reflection devoid of action and deeds done. They are both nihilistic, bonded to a cult of egoistic freedom, but their caprice and arbitrariness is never promoted at the expense of their personal reasoning. Investigating alternatives and researching the particular history leading to whatever particular situation they find themselves in is their stock and trade. They abide by eternal truths, but both F and Angela require that those truths be seen and questioned, particularly in the light of survival. For example, both foster the idea of a multicultural society, one in which they are the king-pins, but they do take umbrage when a group emitted under that multicultural banner do not believe in the concept of multiculturalism themselves. Radical Islam is anathema to them both. If the radicals in Islam were only 10% of Muslims, their number would be around 100 million. They were also both horrified at the lack of protest following the recent slaughter of Israeli athletes at the Munich Olympic Games by Islamic terrorists.

Early Christianity is also problematic to F and Angela. They are acutely sensitive to their immediate surroundings, as well as the emotional and physical conundrums of the moment, where choices that are not perfect, but are in their opinion the lesser of two evils, have to be made. They are both fluid in how they regard themselves, alternatively engaging in virtually every aspect of European culture: left, right and centre, at one time or other, absorbing whatever aspect into their behaviours when it suits the social and political milieu they find themselves in. How they see themselves, depends on the historical circumstance in which they find themselves.

Unlike Jesus, they both feel it is better to survive once they have chosen a stance than to die, no matter the moral compromise, which they as modernists will rework to serve themselves. Winning is everything, but they have their own moral standards to which they must adhere, based on kindness, unless that kindness is ignored and not returned by their adversaries. Angela would on occasion assert that 'Thou shalt not kill' and 'Honour thy mother and thy father' are both 'truths' that are meaningless in themselves, especially if your life is in danger or if there was abuse in the home. Universal truths are merely a guide because everything has to be seen in the context of a personal agreement based on logic that you negotiate with yourself.

'To fondle life' is the name of F and Angela's game. Hedonism and paganism is their milieu and their flexibility is that they are also both corruptible. They are both against the schism between flesh and spirit and desire that the beast kicking in all our breasts be vindicated, but within reason and reasonableness.

'I live where the road forks,' Angela once said to F.

F now returns and takes Dick's seat on the couch. I say to him, 'Us Europeans have screwed up every culture whose throats we have put our hands around, from both North and South America, to Africa, to Australia, to Asia, vampirising the local natives of their vital mineral resources.' I take a breather and continue. 'F, I couldn't disagree with you more.'

'Aaron, you have been hanging around Angela too long. If I were you, I'd keep these dangerous ideas of yours to yourself.'

I say, 'You're aware that I'm leaving to go back to Durban at the end of this month?'

'Sure and don't let the door hit your behind when you leave. Stay out of trouble!' F says nonchalantly.

'By the way, what's your role been in all that's gone on in this house? Where do you fit in exactly?'

'You ask too many questions, Aaron. You'd have been in a lot of trouble had I not been vigilant and paid attention to you. You're so naïve. Didn't I tell you to stay in your room when the police arrived?'

'Yes, but what about your relationships with everyone else, especially with Angela and Russell? They were your friends were they not?' I enquire adamantly.

'Aaron, you know they took advantage of my courtesy and used me.' He looks at me closely, checking me out for my reaction, and says in a matter of fact way, 'To answer your first question about my intimacies with that group of interlopers, well, let's just say that I fucked for my country!'

I let that sentence resonate.

F then asks, 'By the way, that daily diary you mentioned that you kept, when you first came here, have you kept it updated?'

'Yes.'

'It's also an account of your daily activities, right?'

'Yes it is.' Shit, I should have said no! He would not want a record of all the goings-on in the house now that the proverbial shit has hit the fan.

'You're still going to write that book about life in this place that you said you might write when you first arrived?'

'I'll say it's a fictional story based on life in a house in District Six, not necessarily this house. I might use some of the characters I've met here, but I'll change their names and locations.'

'Don't write about anything here!' It is an order from F.

'Well, as I said, I would only use some of the characters I've met here and anyway, that would be a long way down the road, if at all.'

'You have all my talks written down?' he quizzes.

'Just a few.'

'And what name would you give the fictitious me?'

'I'd call you F, for Fuck It, and I'd call Angela, Angela, because she's angelic!'

'Angelic she might be, like the angel of death! I don't like the idea at all of my intimate conversations being displayed in the public domain, even if it's written as fiction!'

'Forget about it. I won't write a thing. Don't worry!'

'Throw the diary away, or tear out the passages with any of my conversations in it!'

'I will.'

'Do you have the diary upstairs? I'll just feel more assured if I saw you extract my stuff from it! Let's go upstairs. I will shred it!'

Now I have to lie to F. 'I've sent all my papers ahead of me to Durban, including the diary. Don't worry about it. I'll take everything about you out. All the pertinent, amusing points you've made in conversation, I've kept in my head anyway.'

For the second time in less than a minute, I have said the wrong thing.

'Well then, I'll just have to shred you!'

I feel uneasy.

He continues. 'When did you send it?'

'Yesterday morning,' I lie again.

'Aaron, just forget about me in your book, in terms of what I do privately between these sheets! What you can say in some future writings is what I've always said about the good that White colonialism did in Africa. You can say the Whites did disconnect many Africans from their culture, but that there was no bigger disconnect, than what the Black Swahili slave traders did. The Swahilis were displacing or murdering over half a million Black people a year. Doctor Livingstone considered White colonialism as a humanitarian effort amidst inter-tribal warfare. In fact, Livingstone pointedly stated that the Arab slave trade was, and I quote, "...a small evil by comparison with the perpetual capturing and killing of children by Africans themselves." White colonialism brought skills and medicine. Just make sure you don't get roped into all this liberal propaganda that slants the truth!'

'F, if we don't like your principles, you'll always find new principles we might like. Even if it's true that Blacks treated each other just as badly as the Whites treated them, two wrongs don't make a right and just because someone has become used to being a victim, doesn't compel anybody to step into the shoes as his new attacker. The left are idealists. They want a perfect world,' I say.

'They're a bunch of naïve idiots. Remember when those ten Frenchmen sat around my bed, trying to induce one of their implausible meditative states? They were trying to function as a giant superconductor, because they believed that when a certain critical mass of psychic energy is achieved they could levitate my exhausted penis after a day spent in bed with Angela. Remember, they failed to even move my member!'

'They said you got an erection!'

'Nothing at all happened to my body with the ten Frenchmen meditating until the eleventh Frenchman who had nowhere else to meditate, because there was no more space, sat on me!'

'I guess then, that the eleventh Frenchman was the critical mass needed?' I joke.

'My point is that wishful thinking, or their collective meditations, couldn't do anything to my nether-regions, so sitting around meditating on love, love, love will not bring their mantra of peace, because power is what everything's about!'

'And absolute power disrupts absolutely!' I interject.

'Anyway, forget about writing about me or this house. Okay? That is my advice for your own good. Goodbye. I must be off. Remember that power never prevented anybody from being happy.'

'You always have an answer.'

'Without a shadow of doubt.'

'No doubt!'

One is either not immaculate or polished like a coffin.

55

Every hedge has a route and every bush a hole, while every rough you get into, you can escape just like a mole.

Irreverent Reverend Tom Groans

Someone once said to me that a restructuring of a situation is necessary to a joke. Yet, the ground beneath my feet had suddenly shifted and I did not feel like laughing. Maybe I am still too close to the situation, in proximity and time, to feel the release of tension of being safe again when what was unsafe, having reached its critical crescendo, has passed on.

The front door to F's house is open. I can hear from the Zulu song being sung outside in the street that the singer, even before I can see her, abounds with metrical romance. I picture her in my mind's eye as a gliding bird. Her voice is perfection.

'Hello!' I hear from the front door.

I turn into the corridor on my way to the front entrance. A chocolate-bronzed, female swims in front of me. Before my eyes her beauty stands fresh and she seems in a state of graceful relaxation, with an attitude of command and power. She is certainly the loveliest Bantu that I have ever seen. Standing at 5 foot 7 inches and trim with perfect proportion, she is in the prime of her female-hood. Her short, dark, tightly knit hair shines. Her large hands are placed on either side of her broad, muscular hips. She is in a posture of relaxed languor. This broad-shouldered countenance of hers is matched by her relaxed facial features and her fully curved lips curl away from each other like two waves breaking in opposite directions.

I meditate on her and on her full smile that seems to purr above her large breasts, that her sweater barely contains. I give the obligatory shrug and smile of someone who knows that he has spent a little too long taking in her appearance.

'I'm Nundi and you're obviously Aaron. I'm Angela's university friend from near your hometown, Durban. I know that F is out because I've been watching the house for the past hour and I saw him leave. Naturally, Angela said I could trust you. I've come to pick up a tape that is in the space under your mattress in your bedroom. This tape, just like the other tapes, is important because, if push comes to shove, we might have to use a little blackmail, if you know what I mean. A number of prominent people in government are on this tape, in compromising positions of a sexual nature, including our wretched friend, F. This tape will turn them all into desperados.'

I ask, 'Won't you be an easy target walking around here with this tape on you after you leave the house? There aren't many Zulus or Xhosas around the area.'

'Aaron, in this country my Black skin is my camouflage fatigue, as we are constantly underestimated by the fools who think that their little bitty noses and slit-mouthed lips are a mark of superiority. What a sham! We are so dark in their minds that they have shadowed us out!'

Nundi and I both stroll lazily up to my room with me leading the way. On the balcony at the top of the stairway, she says, 'Angela says that you are quite the massage person and I could really do with a massage before my long trip home to Zululand. What do you think?'

We are now in my upstairs bedroom. The mattress is bare of bed linen. I have already packed for my thousand-mile trip back to Durban as well. My suitcase stands by the door.

'Are you ready for your rub-down?'

'Wow!' Nundi thrills back, 'It's one thing to sleep with a light-skinned Coloured person in this country and quite another thing to fuck a Black kaffir like myself. You must be very brave.'

'Or maybe I'm just a stupid White man.'

'You are just a stupid White man!' Nundi jokes while closing the door behind her, kicking off her white tennis shoes and unzipping her jeans.

Her sweater is now tantalisingly off and her large, coco-coloured, bra-less breasts hold their positions. I can smell the natural oil aroma of her hair. The texture of her copper-toned skin has a gleam to it. With her jeans and panties removed, the subtle muskiness of her genitals wafts in the humid air. I gaze over her quivering flesh.

'What a spread!' I say.

'With matching cups and a full bounty,' she adds as she helps me to pull off my T-shirt.

'What about the tape?' I ask.

'Later, Aaron, it's not going anywhere with us on top of it. Besides, we'll be done in an hour then we will both be on our separate ways to Durban.'

'An hour? I'm glad to see you have confidence in me.'

Nundi dressed without washing, retrieved the tape from the safe area under my bed and quietly left the house. Her wry contribution to my making sense of Angela's character, against an ever-defective memory on my part, is when she quite unselfconsciously announced as we lay entangled, 'Except for Angela, everyone I mingled with at university was subversively flippant. Only she recognised the sobering ironies that retrospection and time bring to the equation.'

I rhymed with tower, as I washed in the shower.

56

*We're co-dependant, that's where we're at, in fact the
dog's tail, can wag the cat.*

Irreverent Reverend Tom Groans

Watch, as I shower at F's place, having said goodbye to Nundi.

Watch, as I leave F's house for the last time, having dropped
the front door keys through the mailbox.

The car is packed and ready to go, having been serviced the
previous day.

I start to cross the road in the direction of my parked vehicle
and look up over my left shoulder at magnificent Table
Mountain. I feel unusually emotional. I did not get to say my
goodbyes to either Angela or Monique and God knows what
is in store for the two of them. I also did not get to discuss
with Angela that it is not only the Coloured people who are
descendants of slaves and rapists. I would like to have added
that we are also all descendants of lovers.

I stand on the broken line in the middle of the road and
wait for a moment to gather my thoughts, trying to recreate
the reality of what has gone on in my life this past year. Sketch
marks dot my consciousness, eliciting powerful emotions from
the impeccable geometry of the mountains and old Cape Dutch

buildings, to the action-oriented aspects of the people, characterised by enthusiasms and orgasms.

I remember how both girls would talk of the importance of words, how they could both suggest so much with so little, yet the bottom line for both of them was not if you could talk the talk, but could you walk the fork in the road least travelled?

I reach into my left trouser pocket for my car keys, but find instead a Photostat copy of a poem Monique wrote called, 'Colour Politic'. I unfold the sheet of paper and start reading it to myself while still standing in the middle of the deserted road:

I don't understand the serenity of White,
How it holds its silence
In the midst of the violence of all its Colours.
White sits astride the fence,
And, is against us, at our own expense,
For it chooses no path,
Remaining just as calm in our aftermath.

I don't understand the serenity of Black,
It's ignorance of all the Colours
Under attack.
Black sits astride the fence,
Oblivious, at our own expense,
For it chooses no path,
Remaining dark-glasses calm, in the aftermath.

I remember the abilities of both girls to reveal the moral vulgarity behind the bourgeois behind. The main practice decried by Angela was 'conscience-interruptus', of not getting involved and not doing the right thing.

Angela's masculine aggression was combined with an intellectual assertiveness. She also combined a confidence in whatever milieu she was in, with the critical edginess of an outsider. Her Oxford tutorials honed her felicitousness to ask the right questions – 'Why do you do this?' and 'What does it mean?' She always said that she had a CPA, which was to Communicate, Perform and to Assert.

I remember both girls' frenetic quality of being able to rapidly bridge the two worlds of non-White and White, breaking the solid line that keeps one in place and how they actually perforated through that line, allowing them to see both sides of whatever coin they looked at. Even though I would consider these memories crudely rendered and installed in my head, they are affixed forever there and will colour everything I will ever see in my future.

I stroll towards my car. Under my windscreen wiper is a piece of folded paper. I remove and open it. Written in barely legible handwriting is a poem, which reads:

> *I'm a hitchhiker with a bad thumb, caught between the desire to not move and the desire to groove up someone else's bumper sticker, someone else who's ticker is quicker, someone to take me somewhere fast, somewhere to camouflage my past, somewhere to veil the fact that I'm a somewhat common act, for I'm proof of the survival of the least fit. I'm the criminal that didn't get my Mommy's tit.*
>
> Irreverent Reverend Tom Groans

Now, having seated myself in my blue Morris, I peer into the rear-view mirror and scan the back of the vehicle. I catch you returning my stare from the back seat. You have gleaned some kind of insight into who I am. One thing I take away from this whole experience is that one must sacrifice one's own suffering and confidently keep moving forward. Suffering is something that will prove harder than you think to give up as we are hypnotised to sacrifice ourselves.

Once alerted, forever lucid.

57

In a sun-splash, by a roadside, there's a sad case with life-stroke; he can't do breaststroke in a desert.
Irreverent Reverend Tom Groans

When I left Cape Town I had a 1,000-mile journey to transverse in order to reach my destination, Durban, and during this time I allowed my thoughts to coalesce and amalgamate in a sensible way as to what had happened in the house and to me this past year. It is known that under extreme conditions, the vast majority of people yield to group pressure. This majority, who tend to conform, give evidence of an inability to cope well under stress. Non-conformists, on the other hand, do not panic under conflicting pressures. Conformists have feelings of inadequacy and are usually emotionally closed down, lack insight into their own selves and are not spontaneous, while non-conformists feel more competent and autonomously expressive in their choices. A person who has a sense of their own freedom is not nearly as likely to be controlled by the dominant group.

In this house in District Six, I was caught betwixt two expressively dominant groups of people: the extreme left and the extreme right of the political spectrum. This allowed me to constantly adjust and readjust myself, until I could see the important significance of having my own inner autonomy and commitment to myself first, irrespective of the environmental jostling going on all about me.

Midway on that long drive homeward, I decided to commit a vocal summary of the year to the tape-recorder that I had placed between my open thighs and under the steering wheel as I was motoring along. After five hundred miles, which is about midway to Durban and moments after turning off the tape-recorder and placing it in the cubbyhole, the incident occurred.

Along a monotonously straight, two-lane highway, travelling at 70 miles an hour, there was an abrupt and loud metallic thud under my driving seat. Just as suddenly, the car dipped down to the right, hitting the tarmac at high speed. Out of my peripheral vision I saw the front, right wheel of my car rolling away from the vehicle, faster than we were now travelling because we were now dragging on the road. The wheel sped past me and off in the direction of an oncoming car then disappeared into bushes on the other side of the road. The oncoming car appeared to be about 100 yards away and was the first car I had seen in over two hours.

At first, I thought I was in a dream and kept shaking my head in order to wake myself from this nightmare, but I soon realised that even if this were a dream, I was to be in it for the long haul. The only thing to do was to remain in seated inertia, subservient to the imprudent, ballistic motion of nature's shocking dexterity, as the car pitched down and forward-right. Then time and motion slowed as the back of the car lifted after the forward pitch and started to flip up and come on over my head from behind. Meanwhile, I, at the same time, was bumped forward in my seat and thrust face-downwards, my chest pressed into the steering wheel, as gravity and the G-force took over. I was not wearing my seatbelt but was held incarcerated in my metal womb, tumbling helter-skelter in irregular rotation in what appeared to me to be ferocious silence. I heard nothing of the turmoil. I was held captive and there was nothing for me to speculate about, as I was locked in the absurdity of no choices, which is the reverse of my compulsion to take the reins.

My helplessness helped me to resign from my desperation within seconds. Time was concertinaed into fractions of a second, even before one could stutter a cry for help. There was no forewarning and there were no precautions that could have been taken as I was being swept out of existence and hurried into bewilderment. I was at a point where I had bypassed any emotion of being ashamed at the impotence of the scenario that was unfolding. In fact, impotence was accepted. There was no attention to spare for anything except accepting the tumbling, while everything else was forgotten in the personal isolation that ensured. I did not cover or cower. Everything in my life seemed lost and that was fine. There were no thoughts to be collected, as the machine I was slave to had also lost its own mechanisation. My vision was hazy and the taste in my mouth was that of dust.

I was fully conscious throughout, but time was lost between my blinks, until everything came back together in real time, effortlessly and in an instant, as if daily reality had been lying in wait for me to arrive. At once, everything felt as if what had happened had happened a long time ago. All of a sudden appeared two heads, who regarded me with curiosity as I was still alive.

Sounds re-emerged.

All four wheels of the car were strewn randomly, hundreds of yards away from the vehicle and in all directions, as were the contents of all my luggage and all the doors had been ripped off like disregarded children's toys undone by a giant. The entire roof was crushed onto the seats in the front and back of the car, except for where I was sitting. My head held the roof up directly over me but the lower discs of my spine were crushed. I felt little pain while my whole system was in shock.

The body of the car in which I was pinned had settled upright and was bobbing on top of a barbed-wire fence alongside a field, 100 yards from the roadside and sixty feet below the highway. My car, according to the passengers of the oncoming car that I narrowly missed, had somersaulted six times over the 60-foot cliff then luckily landed, bouncing like an irregularly shaped ball, on an angled decline, which is what saved my life, before settling onto the barbed fence.

I was 500 miles from home and in the middle of nowhere and it took an ambulance an hour to get to me after another passing car went to get help from the nearest town, 30 miles away.

Who would want me silenced?

Bitter dreams are made of these.

Postscript

Anything that gets in their way, the people with power will snuff out! Once they understand that you have much on them for them to be afraid of, they will run you over like a bulldozer! Truth is threatening.

I was a troubadour-fly on their wall, rambling around the rooms of that house, connecting to the inspirations while jotting down all that was happening.

I was the lone writer who, with pencil and notepad, appeared on the same stage as the big men and women. In a plaintive voice I wrote about what I saw and heard. I needed to make some sense of it all.

I think of myself as the solitary harmonica player who could one day put my lips to instrument and hopefully blow the whole world away. The revolutionary singer Sixto Rodrigues does it with his sexual songs and probing lyrics. He is a witchdoctor. I want to be on that same trajectory, coming from sober reality. With my pen I have been given another instrument to tell it like it is from deep undercover.

I need to escape the media cliché of pop culture sentiment. To quote the otherwise despicable F, 'You cannot call pop-peace-icon Mandela a hero, if by his means he encourages murder of "soft targets"; ordinary men, women and children, no matter his end game!'

So here I am reflecting back. I did bite the bullet; it just missed me, while the somewhat relatively calm environment I have been in has changed suddenly and dramatically.

A punctured tyre is one thing, but the total dismantling of the wheel so that it actually disengaged itself from my vehicle a day later on route? The technical ability and know-how required to have pulled this off could only have been done at Gregory's Garage and Car Wash, where I had had a full service the day before leaving Cape Town for Durban.

The garage was used by most of the characters I knew during my year in District Six, so all of my suspects could have had access to my car. Gregory owns the garage and could have had his own motives for having me silenced. Virile Gregory would almost certainly go out on a limb to protect his daughter, Angela, from anything negative that I may conceivably know about her. Connected to the garage is Gregory's illegitimate son, Tom Groans, who worked there as an assistant mechanic. Groans would do all in his power not only to protect his biological dad, but also his half-sister, Angela. The list of the garage's alumni furthermore includes F, Angela and Monique, all of whom had cars regularly serviced there.

Now what was really dramatic was that I found out that supposedly a gun had been placed somewhere inside my car prior to my trip! An indiscreet, chummy detective had told me the day after my accident, in the hospital, that the authorities had received an anonymous phone call a day and a half after I had left Cape Town and a few hours before my accident, suggesting that there might be a weapon in my vehicle, so they had been looking for my car along that thousand-mile stretch for quite a while. Subsequently, no gun was found in or around the wreckage.

In retrospect, a number of people could have been responsible for my misadventure and perhaps the actual act of placing a gun in the vehicle and the tampering of the wheel was left to someone who had slipped under my radar? Even though a gun was not found, it could have evaded the police's detection by being camouflaged in the dense foliage surrounding the accident.

Nundi, Angela's friend, who was not involved in the house and was not even in my mind's eye a suspect, might have been brought in as a 'sweeper' to clean up after the fact. Nundi was the last person I saw before I left and she had said that she had been watching the house for an hour before approaching it, to make sure that F had left. She had also certainly lulled me into complacency by her overt sexuality and casual, easy nonchalance, even insinuating having sex ahead of her mission to retrieve the tape from under my mattress.

Sometimes, that which is right under your nose is ignored.

So, who is the enemy? Who is my enemy? There might be a clue to that answer in something Angela had said early in our friendship. She had stated that the enemy is not black or white, left or right. 'No,' she had said, 'the enemy is black and white, the enemy is the extreme left and the extreme right, the enemy is the tyranny of Trust; the tyranny of your trust in other people's truth, with all those authoritative technocrats able to manoeuvre you towards their standardised point of view. And all of us who are too lazy to question, who are so easily manipulated into following orders, are also the enemy!'

The accident had crushed and dislodged vertebrae in my lower back and injured discs in my neck. The broken vertebrae in my lumbar area also severely impeded normal nerve function to the leg and genital area. The orthopaedic surgeon decided at the time not to operate once the swelling had subsided, as the spinal cord was not damaged. An operation would have been too risky because of all the bits of bone floating about.

It took about three months for the inflammation to dissipate and roughly ten years of painful rehabilitation on the lower back and legs to get my gait and dexterity back to the point of normalcy. My dislodged vertebrae, void of discs, fused naturally over time.

Forty years on, the occasional painful episode is now

tolerable, although I am always at risk of paralysis if my back should be jarred for any reason.

I am eternally grateful and buoyant about the fact that I do not have any worse sensory impairment today other than surface muscle spasms and the occasional pins and needle numbness below the waist. Burning sensations in my lower extremities occur, but usually subside over a few weeks.

If Angela was in cahoots with the 'powers that be' then why was she arrested? Was the arrest merely a staged accident, a march through, a show parade for those frontline soldiers, technicians and bureaucrats, second-level decision makers who operate with impunity in the foreground and background and who keep the circle of atrocities circulating, as Russell used to say? Maybe the arrests were to assure Russell's masters in Europe that Angela and Monique were still 'good and kosher' as far as their allegiances to the ANC were concerned.

The big question swirling in my head was whether Angela had acted treasonously with myself as well as her own party, the ANC? Why would anyone act treasonously and foul their own nest? Blackmail, revenge and contempt. Angela certainly had contempt for the way the ANC related to the Coloured community as second-class citizens. The ANC as well, has a certain Communist bent that Angela and most certainly the West would like to see nipped in the bud.

Did the government later veto the arrests? There was no trial nor was there any mention in the newspapers of their arrests. But that was not so strange in South Africa, where much of what transpires is kept under wraps. 'Ask me no questions and I'll give you no information that can get you into trouble' could well be the mantra in South Africa.

Had Angela, or even more likely, Monique, choosing to protect Angela and wanting to deflect the focus off her by implicating me in the shooting of Officer Blank in Cape Town, instructed Nundi to stow a gun in my car, knowing there was to be an accident? Or had Angela done the instructing? Even if no gun was ever placed in the car, but the phone call about it was made in conjunction with a possible reference to the assassinated Blank, the authorities would have eventually realised that there was a connection between Officer Blank and myself. In my first conversation with Angela at the hotel bar after our initial meeting, she had said that she hired people for specialised jobs. Had she hired Nundi to set me up?

I certainly had a motive for killing Blank, who was my despicable disciplinary officer in Pretoria while I was in the military. If the gun was found in my car, with South African justice being what it is, the odds would have been stacked against me, what with my prior history.

The biggest question pertaining to me was, were Russell and I under surveillance the whole time, suspected of being involved in Communist activities? I certainly fitted the bill: educated at an exclusive, left-leaning high school; a problematic military service, during which time I had spent considerable time in the presence of Max Goldman, the renowned Communist, who was under surveillance by the government. It was Jerry's misstep of not reporting my meeting with Goldman that tripped him up so badly. I was clearly anti-establishment. I had in addition spent three months volunteering as a teenager on a communal kibbutz farm in Israel, picking bananas and becoming familiar with an egalitarian way of life that worked and therefore, in their way of thinking, I was clearly liberal and left-leaning. In other words, I would make a perfect suspect for being a Communist spy.

Communism was the enemy and even my virulent posture against Communism might have been seen as a case of 'he who protests too much'. I was so naïve and innocent in my demeanour and appearance that they might have suspected me for being a polished professional at these sorts of shenanigans.

Had Angela been monitoring me the whole time, or was I merely the side order to Russell's main course? As far as F was concerned, I knew too much about his idiosyncrasies, his drug-taking and homosexuality, and I had a written record of his philosophical conflicts with the status quo. F and Angela could well be unlikely tag-team mates. While they stood in opposite camps, their rules of engagement and dedication to the cause were extremely similar, much like rival sports fans fighting viciously, despite the fact that their mind-sets and personalities are almost identical. Both were prepared to trample anyone and anything in pursuit of their cause; F betrayed all his lovers and Angela, it seems, was willing to remove me from the scene once my usefulness was spent. F and Angela both believed in natural selection's 'survival of the fittest' – to live and let die.

Ten years later, I decided to take a shot in the dark, hoping for some response, some clue as to my misfortune, by sending a short, coded note to Angela via her dad, Gregory, on the off-chance that he would be able somehow to get the note to her, wherever she was.

The note bore reference to Angela and Monique's last meal with me, where we broke bread together with cheese and wine and where they each presented me with an olive branch, succeeded by the sharing of two olives in a bonding ritual of sorts. The coded note I wrote read:

Angela Brutus asked Aaron Caesar how many olives he had eaten today and Aaron Caesar answered questioningly, 'Et tu, Brute?'

Even you, Angela?

Epilogue

Nearly forty years on now, in London, I was coming out of acupuncture treatment for my painful lower back when I saw a beautiful, forty-something-year-old Coloured women with a South African accent paying her bill. After she had stepped away from the counter, I approached her, asking if she was from the Cape. She answered that she was in fact from Cape Town. She was born in District Six and as a pre-teen, she and her family were moved out of the district to the windy Cape Flats. I asked her if she remembered the Ways family, particularly their beautiful daughter who went on to Oxford. The lady remembered her well, even though Angela Ways was twenty years her senior. She was a heroic figure in the struggle against Apartheid in the Cape and Miss Way's father, Pound Current (with the legendary pianist, Dollar Brand), was a seminal figure on the jazz landscape at the time. The lady said that Miss Ways was arrested by the government and disappeared without a trace, but that many years later there were rumours that reached her ears that Angela Ways had married a wealthy Indian and was living on the spice island of Zanzibar, incognito.

A year after that meeting with the South African in the acupuncturist's office in London, I received an anonymous postcard in the mail at my home in Cornwall, England. My address on the web is easy enough for anyone to find. The card had come from Tanzania, the coincidence being that Zanzibar, where it is rumoured that Angela is now living incognito, is a semi-autonomous part of the United Republic of Tanzania, East Africa.

Written on the card were four words and it was left unsigned. The laconic message read:

I am so sorry.

Angela used to say that she had an infallible ear for vocal tone and that she only trusted what was spoken after taking into account the facial signals of the speaker mouthing those sentiments. She always focused on cadence, modulation and physical hints to find the speaker's authenticity and meaning. She was also always dubious about what was written, so if this message was from her then it was with a touch of irony that it was sent, using the uncertain printed word unaccompanied by nuance as a peace offering.

THE END